W9-BUE-566

THE CAVALIER IN THE
YELLOW DOUBLET

THE CAVALIER IN THE
YELLOW DOUBLET

Arturo Pérez-Reverte

TRANSLATED FROM THE SPANISH BY
Margaret Jull Costa

G. P. PUTNAM'S SONS
NEW YORK

PUTNAM

G. P. PUTNAM'S SONS
Publishers Since 1838
Published by the Penguin Group
Penguin Group (USA) Inc., 375 Hudson Street, New York, New York 10014, USA •
Penguin Group (Canada), 90 Eglinton Avenue East, Suite 700, Toronto, Ontario
M4P 2Y3, Canada (a division of Pearson Canada Inc.) • Penguin Books Ltd,
80 Strand, London WC2R 0RL, England • Penguin Ireland, 25 St Stephen's Green,
Dublin 2, Ireland (a division of Penguin Books Ltd) • Penguin Group (Australia),
250 Camberwell Road, Camberwell, Victoria 3124, Australia (a division of
Pearson Australia Group Pty Ltd) • Penguin Books India Pvt Ltd, 11 Community
Centre, Panchsheel Park, New Delhi–110 017, India • Penguin Group (NZ),
67 Apollo Drive, Rosedale, North Shore 0632, New Zealand (a division of
Pearson New Zealand Ltd) • Penguin Books (South Africa) (Pty) Ltd,
24 Sturdee Avenue, Rosebank, Johannesburg 2196, South Africa

Penguin Books Ltd, Registered Offices: 80 Strand, London WC2R 0RL, England

Copyright © 2003 by Arturo Pérez-Reverte
English translation copyright © 2003 by Margaret Jull Costa
First published in Spain by Alfaguara in 2003 as *El caballero del jubón amarillo*

Library of Congress Cataloging-in-Publication Data

Pérez-Reverte, Arturo.
[Caballero del jubón amarillo. English]
The cavalier in the yellow doublet/Arturo Pérez-Reverte; translated from the Spanish by
Margaret Jull Costa.
p.   cm.
ISBN 978-0-399-15603-8
1. Alatriste, Diego (Fictitious character)—Fiction.   2. Swordsmen—Spain—Fiction.   3. Spain—
History—Philip IV, 1621–1665—Fiction.   I. Costa, Margaret Jull.   II. Title.
PQ6666.E765C3313   2003   2009023056
863'.64—dc22

Printed in the United States of America
1   3   5   7   9   10   8   6   4   2

Book design by Marysarah Quinn

Germán Dehesa,
for all the small honorable acts

Hated and envied,
Vilely slandered,
More soldier valiant
Than captain prudent.

Though bold and capricious,
And at times vicious,
This was not his sin,
But the times he lived in.

THE CAVALIER IN THE
YELLOW DOUBLET

1. THE CORRAL DE LA CRUZ

Diego Alatriste was in a devil of a hurry. A new play was about to be performed at the Corral de la Cruz, and there he was on the Cuesta de la Vega, dueling with some fellow whose name he didn't even know. The play was by Tirso de Molina, and any first performance of a play by Tirso was a great occasion in Madrid. The whole city, it seemed, was either crammed into the theater or else forming a queue outside in the street, and no one in that queue would have thought it unreasonable to knife his neighbor if it meant getting a seat or even standing room. There was, however, neither rhyme nor reason to what he was doing now, namely, getting involved in a minor skirmish following a chance collision on a street corner. Such conflicts were, of course, a regular enough occurrence in the Madrid of the day, where it was as common to unsheathe one's sword as to cross oneself. "Why don't you look where you're going, sir!" "Why don't *you*, my man—are you blind?" "God's teeth." "God's and anyone else's." And it was that disrespectful "my man"—for the other fellow was young and quick to anger—which had made a fight inevitable. "You, sir," Alatriste had said, stroking his mustache, "can call me 'my man' or even 'boy' all you like, but only with sword and dagger in hand on the Cuesta de la Vega, which is, after all, just a step away—always assuming, of course, that you're gentleman enough to spare me the time." The other man did apparently have time to spare, or was, at the least, unprepared to modify his language. And so there they were, overlooking the Manzanares River, on the top of a hill to which they had walked, side by side, like two comrades, without saying a word, and without unsheathing the swords or daggers that were now clashing loudly— *cling, clang*—and glinting in the afternoon sun.

After an initial cautious circling of blades, Alatriste was startled into full attention by the first serious thrust, which he parried with some difficulty. He was more irritated with himself than with his opponent, irritated with his own irritation. This was not a good state of mind to be in; any sword fight, when life and health are at stake, requires both a cool head and a steady hand. If you lack either, there is a risk that your irritation—or whatever other emotion you happen to be feeling—might slip from your body, along with your soul, through some previously unnoticed buttonhole in your doublet. But what could he do? He had left the Inn of the Turk in that same black mood, following an argument with Caridad la Lebrijana. The argument had erupted as soon as she returned home from mass and had involved smashed crockery, slammed doors, and a consequent delay in setting off for the theater. The chance encounter on the corner of Calle del Arcabuz and Calle de Toledo—which would ordinarily have been resolved with common sense and reasonable words—had instead channeled all his ill humor into this duel. Anyway, it was too late to turn back now. The other man was in deadly earnest and, all honor to him, very good with a blade and agile as a deer. He seemed to Alatriste, from his manner of fighting, to have a soldier's technique: a wide stance, a quick hand, and many a riposte and counter-riposte. He would unleash fierce attacks, intent on wounding, give stabbing thrusts, then withdraw as if to cut and reverse, always watching for the moment when he might lunge forward on his left foot and hook the hilt of his enemy's blade with his dagger. It was an old trick, but effective if the person performing it had a good eye and an even better hand. Alatriste, however, was an older and more battle-hardened fighter, and so he kept moving in a semicircle in the direction of his opponent's left hand, thus thwarting his intentions and wearing him out. He also took the opportunity to study his opponent, who was a good-looking young man in his twenties. Despite his city clothes—short suede boots, an over-doublet of fine cloth, and the brown cape which he had placed on the ground along with his hat so as to be able to move more freely—he had, at least to the eye of an expert, a soldierly air about him: confident, brave, tight-lipped, and certainly no braggart, but concentrating on the job at hand. He was perhaps from a good family. The captain ignored a feint and made a circling movement to the right so that the sun was in his adversary's eyes. He silently cursed himself. By now, the first act of *The Garden of Juan Fernández* would be in full swing.

He decided to finish the business, although not so hastily that it might work against him. Besides, there was no point in complicating his life further by killing a man in broad daylight, and on a Sunday. His opponent made a lunge, which Alatriste parried, making as if to deliver a straightforward blow, but instead shifting to the right, lowering his sword to protect his own chest and, in passing, dealing the other man an ugly cut to the head with his dagger. A bystander might have described this as both unorthodox and somewhat underhand, but there were no bystanders. Besides, María de Castro would already be on stage, and it was still a fair walk to the Corral de la Cruz.

This was no time for niceties. More important, the strategy had worked. The young man turned pale and fell to his knees, bright red blood gushing from his temple. He had dropped his dagger and was resting all his weight on his sword, which buckled slightly beneath him. Alatriste sheathed his own sword, then went over and disarmed the wounded man by gently kicking the blade from under him. Then he held him up so that he wouldn't fall, took a clean handkerchief from the sleeve of his doublet and bandaged the gash in the man's head as best he could.

"Will you be all right on your own?" he asked.

The young man looked at him, confused, but did not reply. Alatriste snorted impatiently.

"I have things to do," he said.

The man nodded weakly. He made as if to get up, and Alatriste helped him to his feet, letting him lean on his shoulder. The blood was still flowing beneath the improvised bandage, but the man was young and strong. The bleeding would soon stop.

"I'll send help," added Alatriste.

He couldn't wait to be gone. He looked at the tower of the Alcázar Real that rose up above the walls, then back toward the long Segovia bridge. No constables—that was one good thing—and no bluebottles either. No one. The whole of Madrid was watching Tirso's play, and there he was, wasting time. One way to solve the problem, he thought impatiently, would be to slip a *real* to some errand boy or footboy, of the sort usually to be be found loitering near the city gate, waiting for travelers. They could then take the stranger back to his inn—or indeed to hell or wherever else he might choose to go. He helped the wounded man sit down on a large boulder that had once formed part of the city wall. Then he restored to him hat, cape, sword, and dagger.

"Can I do anything more for you?"

The other man's breathing was somewhat labored, and his face was still drained of color. He looked at Alatriste for a long while, as if he found it hard to make out his features.

"Tell me your name," he murmured at last in a hoarse voice.

Alatriste was brushing dust from his boots with his hat.

"My name is my affair," he replied coldly, putting his hat back on. "And I don't give a damn about yours."

Don Francisco de Quevedo and I saw him enter just as the guitars were signaling the end of the interlude. Hat in hand, short cape folded over one arm, sword pressed to his side, and head lowered so as not to bother anyone as—with many a "Forgive me, sir," "Excuse me," "May I come past?"—he pushed his way through the people crowding the yard. He arrived at the front of the lower gallery, greeted the constable of the theater, paid sixteen *mar-avedís* to the man selling tickets for the tiered seats on the right, then came up the steps and joined us where we were sitting on a bench in the front row, next to the balustrade and near the stage. I was surprised they had let him in, given how packed the theater was, with people still standing out in the street, protesting because there was no more room; later, however, I learned that he had managed to slip in, not through the main door, but through the carriage gate, which was normally used by the ladies to reach the section reserved for them. The porter there—wearing a buffcoat to protect him from the knife-thrusts of those trying to sidle in without paying—was apprenticed to the apothecary in Puerta Cerrada owned by Tuerto Fadrique, an old friend of the captain's. Nevertheless, once the captain had greased the porter's palm, paid for the entrance fee and for his seat, and made the usual charitable donation to Madrid's hospitals, the cost came to two *reales*: no small drain on the captain's purse, when you think that, for the same price, you could usually get a seat in the upper gallery. Then again, this *was* a new play by Tirso. At the time—along with the venerable Lope de Vega and that other young poet treading hard on his heels, Pedro Calderón—this Mercedarian friar, whose real name was Gabriel Téllez, was both filling the purses of theater-owners and actors and delighting his adoring public, although he never reached the heights of glory and popularity enjoyed by the great Lope. The Madrid garden near Prado Alto from which the play took its name was a splendid, peaceful place, much frequented by the court and known as a fashionable spot, perfect for a romantic rendezvous, and, as I had seen during the first act, it was being used to good effect. The moment Petronila appeared, dressed as a man, in boots and spurs, alongside Tomasa disguised as a young lackey, and before the beautiful María de Castro had even opened her mouth, the audience had begun applauding wildly, even the *mosqueteros*—the musketeers, or groundlings—who were, as usual, crammed into an area at the back of the yard. Their name derived from their habit of always standing together, wearing cape, sword, and dagger, like soldiers ready to be inspected or to go into action—well, that and their tendency to make rowdy comments and to boo. This time, however—urged on by their leader, the shoemaker Tabarca, the musketeers had greeted Tomasa's words, "Maid and court are two ideas in mutual contradiction," with warm applause and the grave approving nods of real connoisseurs. It was always important to gain the musketeers' approval. This was a time when bullfights and plays were attended by both the common people and the nobility, a time when there was a real passion for the theater, and much depended on the success or failure of a first night, so much so that even famous playwrights, hoping to win the musketeers' favor, would often address a prologue full of praise to that noisy, hard-to-please audience:

Those who have it in their power
To make a play seem good or dire . . .

For in that picturesque Spain of ours—so extreme in its good qualities, and in its bad—no doctor was ever punished for killing a patient through bloodletting and incompetence, no lawyer was ever banned from practicing because he was conniving, corrupt, or useless, no royal functionary was ever stripped of his privileges, having been caught with his hand in the money box; but there was no such forgiveness for a poet whose lines did not scan or who failed to hit the mark. Indeed, it seemed sometimes that the audience got more pleasure from seeing a bad play than a good one; they enjoyed and applauded the latter, of course, but a bad play gave them license to whistle, talk, shout, and hurl insults—"A pox on't," "I'faith," "Od's blood," "Why, not even Turks and Lutherans would put on such a shambles," et cetera. The most hopeless of blockheads made themselves out to be experts, and duennas and clumsy serving wenches assumed the role of learned and discerning critics and rattled their keys to show their disapproval. They thus found an outlet for that most Spanish of pleasures, namely, venting all the spleen they felt for their rulers by kicking up a row in the safety of the crowd. For, as everyone knows, Cain was an hidalgo, a pure-blooded Christian, and a Spaniard.

Anyway, as I was saying, Captain Alatriste finally joined us, where we had been saving him a seat until another member of the audience demanded to take it. Wanting to avoid a quarrel—not out of cowardice but out of respect for the place and the circumstances—don Francisco de Quevedo had let the importunate fellow do as he wished, warning him, however, that the seat was already taken and that as soon as its rightful occupant arrived, he would have to relinquish it. The disdainful "Hmm, we'll see about that" with which the man responded as he made himself comfortable was immediately transformed into a look of wary respect when the captain appeared. Don Francisco shrugged and indicated to the captain his now occupied place on the bench, and my master fixed the intruder with his cold green eyes. The man was a wealthy artisan (as I found out later, he held the lease on the ice wells in Calle de Fuencarral), and the sword hanging from his leather belt looked about as much in keeping with him as a har-quebus would on a Christ. He took in at one glance the captain's ice-cold eyes, his veteran's bushy mustache, the guard on his sword all dented and scuffed, and the long, narrow dagger, the hilt of which was just visible at his hip.

Without saying a word, as silent as a clam, he gulped hard and, on the pretext of leaning over to buy a glass of mead from a passing vendor, shuffled farther up the bench, robbing his neighbor on the other side of some of his space, but freeing up my master's place entirely.

"I thought you weren't coming," commented don Francisco.

"I met with a slight setback," replied the captain, shifting his sword slightly to one side so that he could sit more comfortably.

He smelled of sweat and metal, as in times of war. Don Francisco noticed the stain on the sleeve of his doublet.

"Is that your blood?" he asked, concerned, arching his eyebrows behind his spectacles.

"No."

The poet nodded gravely, looked away, and made no further comment. As he himself once said: Friendship is composed of shared rounds of wine, a few sword fights fought shoulder to shoulder, and many timely silences. I, too, was looking at my master with some concern, but he shot me a reassuring look and a faint distracted smile.

"Everything in order, Íñigo?"

"Yes, Captain."

"How was the farce before the interlude?"

"Oh, excellent. It was called *The Coachman Cometh*, by Quiñones de Benavente. We laughed so much we cried."

Then all talk stopped, for at that point the guitars ceased playing. The musketeers at the back of the yard hissed furiously and cursed impatiently, demanding silence in their usual ill-mannered way. There was a furious fluttering of fans in the ladies' sections up above and below; women ceased signaling to men and vice versa; the sellers of limes and mead withdrew with their baskets and demijohns; and, behind the shutters on the balconies, the people of quality returned to their places. On one such balcony, I spotted the Count of Guadalmedina—who paid the vast sum of two thousand *reales* a year to ensure a good seat at all the new plays—along with a few gentlemen friends and some ladies. At another window sat don Gaspar de Guzmán, Count-Duke of Olivares, accompanied by his family. Our king was not, alas, there, even though this fourth Philip of ours was very fond of the theater and often attended, either openly or incognito. On this occasion, however, he was still tired from his recent exhausting journey to Aragon and Catalonia, during which don Francisco de Quevedo—whose star was still in the ascendant at court— had formed part of the entourage, as he had in Andalusia. The poet could doubtless have had a seat as a guest on one of those upper balconies, but he was a man who liked to mingle with the populace, preferring the lively atmosphere in the lower sections of the Corral, and, besides, there he could enjoy the company of his good friend Diego

Alatriste. For while Alatriste may have been a soldier, swordsman, and a man of few words, he was also reasonably well educated, having read good books and seen a great deal of theater; and although he never gave himself airs and mostly kept his opinions to himself, he nevertheless had a sharp eye for a good play and was never taken in by the easy effects with which some playwrights larded their work in order to win the favor of the ordinary people. This was not the case with such great writers as Lope, Tirso, or Calderón; and even when they did resort to the tricks of the trade, their inventive skill marked the difference between their noble stratagems and the ignoble impostures of lesser writers. Lope himself described this better than anyone:

Whenever the time comes to write a play
I put Aristotle under lock and key
And stow Terence and Plautus out of the way
So that I'm deaf to their shouts and pleas,
For even mute books have something to say.

This should not be taken as an apology by that Phoenix of Inventiveness for employing stratagems lacking in taste, but, rather, as an explanation of why he refused to conform to the tastes of those learned neo-Aristotelian scholars, who, as one man, censured his wildly successful plays, yet would have given their right arm to put their name to them or, better still, to take the money. The play that afternoon was not, of course, by Lope but by Tirso, although the result was similar, for the work, a so-called cloak-and-sword drama, contained much wonderful poetry and turned, inevitably, on love and intrigue, but touched also on more somber themes: for example, Madrid as a place of deception and delusion, a place of falsehood where the valiant soldier comes to be rewarded for his valor and finds only disillusion; it also criticized the Spaniards' scorn for work and their hunger for a life of luxury beyond that appropriate to their station. For this, too, was a very Spanish tendency, one that had already dragged us into the abyss several times before and one that would persist for years to come, exacerbating the moral infirmity that destroyed the Spanish empire, that empire of two worlds—the legacy of hard, arrogant, brave men who had emerged out of eight centuries spent cutting Moorish throats, with nothing to lose and everything to gain. In the year one thousand six hundred and twenty-six—when the events I am relating took place—the sun had not yet set upon Spain, although it very soon would. Seventeen years later, as a lieutenant at Rocroi, I would hold on high our tattered flag, despite the battering from the French cannon, and would myself bear witness to the sad fading of our former glory as I stood in the midst of the last squadron formed by our poor, faithful infantry. When an enemy officer asked me how many men there had been in the old, now decimated regiment, I said simply: "Count the dead." And it was there that I closed Captain Alatriste's eyes for the last time.

But I will speak of these things when the moment arrives. Let us return to the Corral de la Cruz and that afternoon's performance of a new play. The resumption of the play aroused the same state of expectancy that I described earlier. From our bench, the captain, don Francisco, and I were now gazing across at the stage, where the second act was just beginning. Petronila and Tomasa came on again, leaving to the spectators' imagination the beauty of the garden, which was only hinted at by an ivy-clad shutter placed at one of the stage entrances. Out of the corner of my eye, I saw the captain lean forward and rest his arms on the balustrade. His aquiline profile was lit by a bright ray of sunlight that found its way through a tear in the awning erected to shade the audience from the glare, for the Corral faced west and was on a hill. Both female players looked very striking in their male costumes; this was a fashion which neither pressure from the Inquisition nor royal edict had managed to expunge from the theater, for the simple reason that people liked it too much. Similarly, when some of Castile's more Pharisaic councilors—egged on by certain fanatical clerics—tried to ban plays in Spain altogether, this was again thwarted by the ordinary people, who refused to have this pleasure taken away from them, arguing moreover, and quite rightly, too, that part of the price of every ticket went to support good works and hospitals.

However, to go back to the play, the two women disguised as men stepped out onto the stage and were warmly applauded by the audience—packing yard, tiered seats, galleries, and balconies—and when María de Castro, in her role as Petronila, spoke these lines:

Count me, Bargas, as good as dead,
My mind is gone, I am not myself . . .

the musketeers, who, as I mentioned before, were very hard to please indeed, showed clear signs of approval, standing on tiptoe in order to get a better view; and, in the upper gallery, the women stopped munching on hazelnuts, limes, and cherries. María de Castro was the most beautiful and most famous actress of her day; she embodied, as no other actress, the strange, magnificent human reality that was our theater, a theater that always hovered between, on the one hand, holding up a mirror to everyday life—at times a satirical, distorting mirror—and, on the other, presenting us with the most beautiful and thrilling of fantasies. La Castro was a spirited woman, with a lovely figure and an even lovelier face: dark, almond eyes, white teeth, pale skin, and a beautiful, well-proportioned mouth. Other women envied her beauty, her clothes, and her way of speaking the verse.

Men admired her as an actress and lusted after her as a woman, and this latter fact met with no opposition from her husband, Rafael de Cózar, who was equally celebrated as an actor and as one of the glories of the Spanish stage. I will have more to tell of him later, but for now I will just say this: Cózar specialized in playing fathers, witty knaves, saucy servants, and rustic mayors, roles which—to the delight of adoring audiences—he performed with great style and swagger. Theatrical talents aside, however, Cózar had no qualms about allowing discreet access to the charms of the four or five women in his company, on receipt, naturally, of an agreed fee. The women were, of course, all married, or at least passed as such in order to meet the requirements of edicts that had been in effect since the days of the great Philip II. As Cózar said, with pleasing effrontery, it would be both selfish and lacking in charity—that theological virtue—not to share great art with those who can afford to pay for it. His own wife, María de Castro (years later it was learned that their marriage was, in fact, a sham), proved to be a mine more profitable even than those of Peru, although he always held in reserve—as the most exquisite of delicacies—that Aragonese beauty with chestnut hair and the sweetest of voices. In short, the clear-headed Cózar fitted, as few men else, this dictum by Lope:

> *The honor of the married man is a castle*
> *In which the enemy is the castle's keeper.*

Let us, though, be as fair as the present story demands. The truth is that La Castro did sometimes have less venal ideas and tastes, and it was not always jewelry that made her lovely eyes shine. Men, as the saying goes, are there to be kissed, cozened, or cuckolded. As far as kissing goes, I will just say, dear reader, that María de Castro and Diego Alatriste were rather more than just friends—the captain's ill humor and the quarrel with Caridad la Lebrijana were not unrelated to this fact—and that afternoon at the Corral de la Cruz, during the second act, the captain kept his eyes fixed on the actress, while I kept looking from him to her. I felt concerned for my master and sad for La Lebrijana, of whom I was very fond. Then again, I was also thrilled to the core to be there, reliving the impression La Castro had made on me three or four years earlier, on my first visit to the theater to see *El Arenal de Sevilla*, in the Corral del Príncipe, on that memorable day when everyone, including Charles, Prince of Wales and the then Duke of Buckingham, was embroiled in a fight in the presence of Philip IV himself. I may not have thought the lovely actress the most beautiful creature on earth—that title belonged to another woman known to you, dear reader, a woman with devilish blue eyes—but I was as stirred by her looks as every other man present. I could not have imagined then how María de Castro would complicate my master's life, and mine, placing both of us in the gravest of dangers, us and the king, whose life, during that period, was quite literally on a knife-edge. All of this I propose to recount in this new adventure and thus prove that whenever a beautiful woman is involved, there is no madness into which a man will not fall, no abyss into which he will not peer, and no situation of which the devil will not take full advantage.

Between the second and third acts, the musketeers called for and were given a *jácara* entitled *Doña Isabel the Thief*. This was a famous ballad written in thieves' slang and was, on this occasion, sung with great gusto by a mature, but still attractive, actress called Jacinta Rueda. I, however, could not give it my full attention, because the moment she started singing, a stagehand came up the steps, bearing a message for Señor Diego Alatriste, saying that he was expected in the dressing rooms. The captain and don Francisco de Quevedo exchanged looks, and when my master got to his feet, the poet shook his head disapprovingly and said:

Happy the man who dies on leaving 'em
Or succeeds in living without their love,
Or, better yet, gets to dig their grave.

The captain shrugged, picked up hat and cape, muttered a brusque "Stay out of my business, don Francisco," donned his hat, and pushed his way past the other spectators on the bench. Quevedo gave me an eloquent look which I took to mean what it usually did, and so I left my seat to follow my master. "Let me know if there's any trouble," his eyes had said from behind his spectacles, "two swords are better than one." Conscious of my responsibilities, I checked that the dagger I wore at my belt was in place and, discreet as a mouse, went after the captain, hoping that this time we might be able to watch the end of the play in peace. It would, after all, have been both a shame and an insult to spoil this first performance of Tirso's play.

Diego Alatriste had been here before and knew the way. He walked down the steps from the benches, turned left opposite the passageway that housed the stall selling mead, and followed the corridor that led underneath the boxes to the stage and the actors' dressing rooms. At the far end, his old comrade from Flanders, the lieutenant of constables, Martín Saldaña, was standing on the steps, chatting with the owner of the Corral and a couple of acquaintances, who were also theater people. Alatriste stopped for a moment to greet them and immediately noticed the worried look on Saldaña's face. He was just taking his leave when Saldaña called him back and, casually, as if suddenly recollecting some minor matter, placed his hand on his arm and whispered gravely:

"Gonzalo Moscatel is in there."

"So?"

"Best let sleeping dogs lie."

Alatriste's expression remained entirely inscrutable, then he said:

"*You* can keep your nose out of my business too."

And he stalked off, leaving his friend scratching his beard and doubtless wondering who else had poked his nose in where it wasn't wanted. A little farther on, Alatriste drew aside a curtain and found himself in a windowless chamber used as a storeroom for the wood and the painted backcloths needed for the stage machinery and any scene changes. On the other side were various curtained cubicles that served as the actresses' dressing rooms, the men's being on the floor below. The room itself, which, beyond yet another curtain, gave onto the stage, was used by members of the company waiting to go on, but also served as an area to receive admirers. At that moment, it was occupied by half a dozen men, amongst them actors costumed and ready to take the stage as soon as the ballad was over—Jacinta Rueda could be heard on the other side of the curtain, singing the famous line "Pursued by the law, by bailiffs beset"—as well as a few gentlemen who, by virtue of their social status or their wealth, had been given permission to meet the actresses. One of these men was don Gonzalo Moscatel.

I followed the captain into the room and politely greeted Martín Saldaña as soon as I felt his eyes fix on me. The face of one of his companions on the landing seemed familiar, but I could not place it. In the corridor, where I stood, leaning against the wall, I saw my master and the gentlemen waiting inside exchange curt nods, but none of them doffed their hats. The only man not to respond to his greeting at all was don Gonzalo Moscatel, a picturesque character to whom I should perhaps introduce you. Señor Moscatel looked as if he had stepped straight out of a cloak-and-sword drama: he was big and burly, sported a ferocious mustache with extraordinarily long, upright tips, and was dressed with a mixture of elegance and bravado that managed to be simultaneously comic and alarming. He was got up like a fop, with a lace Walloon collar over his purple doublet, old-fashioned baggy breeches, a short French cape, silk stockings, black felt boots, and a leather belt studded with old silver *reales* and from which hung an extremely long sword; for he also fancied himself a bit of a ruffian, the kind who struts about uttering oaths—"Od's blood," "A pox on't"—twirling his mustaches and clanking his sword. He claimed, furthermore, to be a poet, and made a great show of his friendship with Góngora, for which there was not the slightest basis in fact; he also perpetrated some infamous, verbose poems which, being a man of ample means, he was able to have printed at his own expense. Only one loathsome, fawning fellow poetaster had bothered to pay him court and extol the virtues of his verse.

This same wretch, one Garciposadas, who penned stiff, dictionary-bound poetry—*a pyre he builds her and constructs for her a wall*, you know the kind of thing—wrote with a quill from the wing of the angel who visited Sodom and prospered by licking boots at court. He was, alas, burned in one of the very last autos-da-fé, condemned as a softling, that is, as one who had committed the nefarious sin. Don Gonzalo Moscatel had thus been left with no one to praise his muse to the skies until the softling's place was taken by a slimy, pettifogging lawyer named Saturnino Apolo, an inveterate flatterer and emptier of other people's purses, who shamelessly wheedled money out of Moscatel, and to whom we will also return later on. Otherwise, Moscatel had reached his position in society thanks to his role as chief supplier of meat, pork included, to the city's butchers, and thanks also—a few personal bribes aside—to the dowry of his late wife, whose father had been a judge of the kind whose justice was not so much blind as one-eyed, and who preferred the scales of justice to be weighted down with a few doubloons. The widower Moscatel had no children of his own, only a young orphaned niece over whom he stood guard in his house in Calle de la Madera like Cerberus, the hound of Hades. He was also keen to become a member of some military order and was sure, sooner or later, to end up with a red cross emblazoned on his doublet. In this Spain full of crooked, rapacious functionaries, you could get anything you liked, so long as you had stolen enough money to pay for it.

Out of the corner of his eye, Captain Alatriste could see that Gonzalo Moscatel was giving him a fierce look and that his hand was resting in readiness on the hilt of his sword. Alas, they knew each other all too well, and each time their paths crossed, the butcher's rancorous gaze spoke volumes about the nature of their relationship. This dated from an incident two months earlier, one night in the small hours, when the captain, swathed up to his eyes in his cloak, was walking along the dim, moonlit streets to the Inn of the Turk. The sound of an argument was coming from Calle de las Huertas. He heard a woman's voice and, as he drew nearer, saw two figures framed in a doorway. He did not care to get involved in lovers' quarrels or to interfere in other people's affairs; however, his path led him precisely in that direction, and he found no reason to take another. He eventually came across a man and woman standing outside the door of a house. Although they appeared to know each other, the lady, or whatever she was, seemed angry, and the man kept insisting that she let him in, at least so far as the hallway. She had a very fine voice, the voice of a beautiful woman, or at least of a young one. And, out of curiosity, the captain stopped for a moment to see what was going on. When the other man noticed him, he turned and said: "Be on your way, this is none of your business," a command Alatriste took to be reasonable enough; and he was just about to do as asked, when the woman, in a serene and worldly tone, said to the other man: "Unless, of course, this gentleman can persuade you to leave me alone and take you with him." Her remark placed the matter on a more uncertain footing, and so, after a moment's thought, Alatriste asked the lady if this was her house. It was, she said; she was a married woman and the gentleman bothering her had no evil intentions but was an acquaintance of both her and her husband. He had escorted her home after an evening at the home of some friends, and it was now high time, as she put it, for every owl to return to his olive tree. The captain was pondering the mystery of why her husband was not there at the door to resolve the matter, when the other man interrupted his thoughts with a few surly oaths, insisting that he clear off at once. In the darkness, the captain heard the sound of a span of steel being removed from its scabbard. The die was cast, and the cold night looked set to grow warmer. The captain stepped to one side in order to place himself in the shadow and the other man in the light from the moon that was slowly creeping up over the rooftops; he unfastened his cloak, wrapped it around his left arm, and unsheathed his sword. The other man did likewise, and both made a few rather halfhearted thrusts, always keeping a safe distance, with Alatriste saying nothing and his opponent cursing nineteen to the dozen. Eventually, the racket they were making brought a servant bearing a candle running out of the house, followed by the lady's husband. The latter—in nightshirt, slippers, and tasseled nightcap—was wielding a stubby sword in his right hand and saying, "What's going on here? Who dares cast a slur on my house and my honor?" and other similar remarks, spoken in what Alatriste suspected to be a distinctly mocking tone. The husband, it turned out, was a very pleasant, courteous man, short in stature and with a thick, German-style mustache that met with his side-whiskers. With appearances and husbandly honor duly saved, peace was restored in the nicest possible way. The night owl's name was don Gonzalo Moscatel, and the husband—once he had handed his own sword over to his servant for safekeeping—spoke of him as a friend of the family, adding, in conciliatory fashion, that he was sure it had all been a most unfortunate misunderstanding. This was all starting to look like a scene from a play, and Alatriste nearly laughed out loud when he learned that the gentleman in the tasseled nightcap was none other than the famous actor Rafael de Cózar—a man of great wit and theatrical skill, and an Andalusian to boot—and that his wife was the celebrated actress María de Castro. He had seen them both on stage, but that night, by the light of the large candle held on high by the servant, was the first time he had seen La Castro at such close quarters. With her cloak barely covering her lovely figure, she looked extraordinarily beautiful and clearly found the whole situation most amusing. She had doubtless experienced other such occasions, for actresses were not, as a rule, women of cast-iron virtue; indeed, it was rumored that her husband, once he had huffed and puffed and brandished his famous sword—which was known throughout Spain— was usually very tolerant of such admirers, whether it was his wife they were interested in or one of the other women in his company, especially if, as was the case with that supplier of meat to Madrid, the admirer had the wherewithal. His evident genius as actor aside, it was accepted as a universal truth that no man's purse was safe with him. This perhaps explained the length of time it had taken him to come downstairs to defend his honor. As people used to say:

> *Take twelve cuckolds or, rather, players—*
> *For they hardly differ as one may gauge—*
> *Add half a dozen ladies of the stage,*
> *And you'll have the six half-wives of the*
> *aforesaid players.*

The captain, fairly embarrassed by the whole affair, was about to make his excuses and continue on his way, when the wife very sweetly thanked him for his intervention, although it was impossible to know whether she did so in order to provoke her pursuer or simply because she enjoyed that subtle and dangerous game in which women so often engage. Then she looked him up and down and invited him to visit her at the Corral de la Cruz, where they were giving the final performances of a play by Rojas Zorrilla. She was smiling broadly as she said this, showing off the perfect oval of her face and her equally perfect white teeth, which Luis de Góngora—don Francisco de Quevedo's mortal enemy—would doubtless have compared to mother-of-pearl or tiny seed pearls. Alatriste, an old hand in these and other such situations, saw in that look some kind of promise.

And two months later, there he was in the dressing rooms of the Corral de la Cruz, having enjoyed the fruits of that promise several times—Cózar's sword not having reappeared—and more than ready to continue doing so. Meanwhile, don Gonzalo Moscatel, whom he had met on subsequent occasions with no further consequences, continued to shoot him fierce, jealous looks. María de Castro was not a woman to keep just one iron in the fire, and she continued worming money out of Moscatel, flirting shamelessly with him, but never allowing things to go any further than that—every meeting at the Gate of Guadalajara cost the butcher a fortune in jewels and fine cloths—and she used Alatriste, whom the other man knew all too well by reputation, to keep him at bay. Thus, ever hopeful, and ever starved, the butcher obstinately persisted, refusing to give up his chance of bliss. He was encouraged in this, too, by La Castro's husband, who, as well as being a great actor was also an out-and-out scoundrel, and, as he had with other such admirers, continued to use vague promises to squeeze Moscatel's purse dry. Alatriste knew, of course, that—Moscatel apart—he was not the only man to enjoy the actress's favors. Other men visited her, and it was said that even the Count of Guadalmedina and the Duke of Sessa had exchanged more than words with her; as don Francisco de Quevedo put it, she was a woman who charged a thousand ducats a stumble. The captain could not compete with either man in rank or money; he was simply a veteran soldier who earned a living as a paid swordsman. Yet, for some reason that escaped him—women's souls had always seemed to him unfathomable—María de Castro granted him gratis what she denied outright to others or for which she charged her weight in gold:

An important point, pray listen to me:
With moneyed Moors she asks a lot,
With Christians she does it for free.

Diego Alatriste drew aside the curtain. He was not in love with that woman, nor with any other, but María de

Castro was the most beautiful actress of her day, and he enjoyed the rare privilege of occasionally having her all to himself. No one was going to offer him a kiss like the one she was now placing on his lips, when, later, a span of steel, a bullet, disease, or time itself would set him sleeping forever in his grave.

2. THE HOUSE IN
CALLE FRANCOS

The following morning, we, or, rather, Captain Alatriste, came under a hail of harquebus fire from Caridad la Lebrijana, upstairs in the Inn of the Turk, while we, downstairs, heard only their voices. Or, rather, her voice, because she was the one who spent the most powder. The matter under discussion was, naturally enough, my master's fondness for the theater, and the name of María de Castro was uttered several times, attached on each occasion to a different epithet—"strumpet," "trollop," and "trull" being some of the milder ones—which was quite something coming, as it did, from La Lebrijana. After all, although she was, by then, almost forty years of age and still preserved the dark charms of her youth, she herself had worked unashamedly as a prostitute for several years before setting herself up with the money earned through her labors as the honest owner of that tavern situated between Calle de Toledo and Calle del Arcabuz. The captain had made her no promises or proposals of any kind, but on our return from Flanders and Seville, he had once again installed himself and me, as before, in the rooms above the inn; that winter, moreover, she had warmed his feet and other parts in her own bed. This was hardly surprising, for, as everyone knew, she was still madly in love with the captain, and had even waited for him chastely while he was in Flanders; for there is no more virtuous and faithful woman than one who leaves the profession in good time—be it via the nunnery or the cooking pot—before she ends up covered in buboes and left to die in Atocha Hospital. Unlike many married women who are honest because they have to be, but who dream of being otherwise, women who have walked the streets know what they are leaving behind, and how much they gain by that loss. La Lebrijana, as well as being exemplary, loving, still alluring, and voluptuous, was also, alas, a woman of spirit, and my master's dalliance with the actress was more than she could bear.

I have no idea what my master said on that occasion, if, of course, he said anything. Knowing my master, I feel sure that he simply stood firm under fire, without breaking ranks or opening his mouth, very much in the manner of an old soldier waiting for the rain to clear up. By God, though, it took a long time; indeed, the battle at Ruyter

Mill and at Terheyden put together were small beer compared to that quarrel, during which I heard turns of phrase one wouldn't even use against the Turks. When La Lebrijana resorted to throwing things—the sound of shattering crockery reached us down below—the captain picked up sword, hat, and cape and went out to take the air. I was sitting at the table next to the door, where I sat every morning, making the most of the good light there to study don Antonio Gil's Latin grammar, an invaluable book loaned to me by my teacher Pérez—an old friend of the captain's and mine—in order to further my education, which had been much neglected in Flanders. At sixteen, I was determined to pursue the profession of soldier, but both Captain Alatriste and don Francisco de Quevedo were most insistent that having a little Latin and Greek, a neat hand, and a knowledge of good literature would take any reasonably intelligent man to places that the sword never would, especially in a Spain where judges, functionaries, scribes, and countless other rapacious crows were always bombarding the poor and the uneducated—which was almost everyone—with mountains of paperwork, the more easily to strip and plunder them. Anyway, as I was saying, there I was, copying out *Miles, quem dux laudat, Hispanus est,* while Damiana, the serving wench at the inn, was scrubbing the floor, and the usual customers at that time of day, the Licentiate Calzas, fresh from the Plaza de la

Provincia, and the former sergeant of horse, Juan Vicuña, maimed in Nieuwpoort, were playing ombre with the apothecary Fadrique, the spoils being a few rashers of bacon and a large pitcher of Arganda wine. It had just struck a quarter past eleven on the clock of the Jesuit church opposite when a door slammed up above; we heard the captain's footsteps on the stairs, and the old comrades exchanged glances and shook their heads disapprovingly before returning to their cards. Juan Vicuña declared the suit, the apothecary put down the ace of spades, and Calzas trumped it. At this point, I got to my feet, covered up my inkwell, and closed my book; then, picking up my cap, dagger, and cape, I gingerly tiptoed out so as not to dirty the newly scrubbed floor, and set off after my master through the door that gave onto the Calle del Arcabuz.

We walked past the fountain at Relatores to Plaza de Antón Martín, and, as if to prove La Lebrijana right—for I was following the captain with a heavy heart—we then walked up to the *mentidero*, a place where people gathered to meet and talk. This was one of the three most famous *mentideros* in Madrid; the other two were to be found on the steps of San Felipe and in the courtyard outside the palace. The one that concerns us, however, was in the quarter inhabited by writers and actors, in a cobbled square where the streets of León, Cantarranas, and Francos meet. Nearby was a reasonable boardinghouse, a baker's, a cake shop, as well as a few good inns and eating houses. Each morning, the little world of the theater congregated there—writers, poets, actors, and owners, as well as the usual idlers and others who came merely to catch a glimpse of a famous face: one of the handsome young men from the stage perhaps, or an actress out for a stroll with a basket over her arm and accompanied by her maid or indulging herself at the cake shop once she had heard mass at San Sebastián and given alms at Nuestra Señora de la Novena. The actors' *mentidero* was justly famous, for in the great theater of the world that was Madrid, the capital of all the Spains, the place was like a gazette full of tittle-tattle. People stood around in groups discussing a play that had already been performed or was about to written; jokes did the rounds, either spoken or scribbled on scraps of paper; people's honor and reputations were destroyed in less time that it takes to say *credo*; the more famous poets strolled up and down with their friends and admirers; and starving young men longed to be able to emulate those who occupied that glorious Parnassus and who defended it as fiercely as if it were a bulwark besieged by heretics. The truth is that never in the world was there such a concentration of talent and fame. I need mention only a few of the illustrious names who lived within two hundred paces: Lope de Vega in Calle de

Francos and don Francisco de Quevedo in Calle del Niño, the same street in which don Luis de Góngora had also lived until his sworn enemy Quevedo bought the house from under him and put the swan of Córdoba out in the street. Tirso de Molina lived there, too, as did the brilliant Mexican Ruiz de Alarcón. "The little hunchback," as Quevedo dubbed the last-named, was removed from the stage by his own cantankerousness and by other people's loathing when his enemies wrecked his play *The Antichrist* by breaking a flask of some foul-smelling liquid right in the middle of the performance. Good don Miguel de Cervantes had lived and died near Lope's house, in Calle del León, on the corner of Calle de Francos, just opposite the Castillo bakery; and between Huertas and Atocha stood the printer's where Juan de la Cuesta had produced the first edition of *Don Quixote*. And then there was the church, Las Trinitarias, in which lay Cervantes's remains, and where Lope de Vega used to say mass, and amongst whose community of nuns lived a daughter of Lope's and a daughter of Cervantes's. And since "Spaniard" and "ingratitude" are two concepts that always go hand in hand, I should also point out that nearby was the hospital where the great Valencian poet and captain Guillén de Castro, author of *The Youth of El Cid*, would die five years later, so poor that he was buried in a pauper's grave. And speaking of poverty, I will just remind you that that most honest of men, unhappy don Miguel de Cervantes—whose modest wish to be sent to the Indies, citing the fact that he had lost an arm in the Battle of Lepanto and been a slave in Algeria, was refused—had died ten years before the events I am now relating, in the sixteenth year of the century, penniless and abandoned by almost everyone he knew. Alone and without ceremony, he was borne to his grave in Las Trinitarias along those same streets—with no public report of his exequies—and then promptly forgotten by his contemporaries. Only much later, when other countries were already eagerly devouring and reprinting translations of his novel *Don Quixote*, did we wretched Spaniards begin to lay claim to him, a fate which, with very few exceptions, we have always meted out to our finest sons.

We found don Francisco de Quevedo polishing off a pasty as he sat outside a cheap restaurant called El León, which was next to the tobacconist's, where Calle Cantarranas and the *mentidero* meet. He called for another pitcher of Valdeiglesias, two mugs, and two more pasties, while we drew up a couple of stools and joined him at his table. He was, as usual, dressed entirely in black, apart from the red cross of Santiago embroidered on his tunic; his neatly folded cloak lay on the bench beside him, along with his sword. He had come from an early appointment at the palace, where he was trying to resolve the seemingly interminable wrangle over who owned the fiefdom of Torre de Juan Abad, and was taking the edge off his appetite before returning home to correct the new edition of his book, *God's Politics, Christ's Government,* on which he was engaged at the time in an effort to stave off criticism from the Inquisition. Our presence, he said, suited him perfectly, as a way of keeping away undesirables; for now that his star was on the rise at court—he had, as I mentioned earlier, formed part of the royal entourage on the recent journey to Aragon and Catalonia—he was constantly being pestered by people hoping for some kind of favor.

"What's more," he said, "I've been asked to write a play to be performed at El Escorial at the end of the month. His Catholic Majesty will be there on a hunting trip and requires some form of entertainment."

"Plays are not exactly your specialty," remarked Alatriste.

"Hell's teeth, if even poor old Cervantes could have a go at playwrighting, I reckon I can, too. Besides, it was the count-duke himself who asked me. So from now on, you may consider plays to be my specialty."

"And is he actually going to pay you, or will he, as usual, set it against future favors?"

Quevedo gave a wry laugh.

"As to the future, I have no idea," he said with a

stoical sigh. "Yesterday is gone, the morrow has not yet come . . . But for the present, it's six hundred *reales*, or will be. At least that's what Olivares has promised me. As the poet says:

> *Ah, see what I have stooped to,*
> *Obliged by his high station,*
> *I to my painful duty,*
> *While he cries inflation.*

"We'll see," he went on. "The count-duke wants a play full of intrigue, which, as you know, is the kind of play the king likes best. And so, I'll lock up Aristotle and Horace, Seneca and even Terence, and then, as Lope says, I'll write a few hundred lines in the vulgar tongue, just foolish enough to please him."

"Have you thought of a plot yet?"

"Of course. Love affairs, secret meetings, misunderstandings, sword fights . . . the usual thing. I'll call it *The Sword and the Dagger*." Quevedo gave the captain a seemingly casual glance over his mug of wine. "And they want Cózar to put it on."

At that moment, there was a scuffle on the corner of Calle Francos. People rushed over to see what was happening, and we, too, looked in that direction. Afterward, various people walked past us, commenting on the incident: a lackey of the Marquis de las Navas had apparently knifed a coachman because he had declined to give way to him. The murderer had taken refuge in the church of San Sebastián, and the coachman, on the point of death, had been carried into a nearby house.

"As for the coachman," declared Quevedo, "he deserved to die for belonging to such a wretched profession."

Then he looked again at my master and returned to the matter in hand.

"Yes, Cózar," he said.

The captain sat impassively, watching the ebb and flow of people on the *mentidero*. He said nothing. The sun accentuated the greenish light in his eyes.

"They say," added Quevedo after a pause, "that our ardent monarch is laying siege to La Castro. Would you know anything about that?"

"Why would I?" asked Alatriste, chewing on a piece of pasty.

Don Francisco drank down his wine and said nothing more. The friendship they professed for each other excluded both giving advice and interfering in each other's affairs. A long silence ensued. The captain was still turned toward the street, his face expressionless; and I, after exchanging a worried look with the poet, did the same. Idlers stood around in groups, chatting or else strolling about and ogling the women as if trying to divine what delights their cloaks might conceal. At the entrance to his shop, the cobbler Taburca, still wearing his leather apron and holding a hammer, was holding forth to his stalwarts on the merits, or otherwise, of the previous day's play. A woman selling lemons passed by, her basket over her arm ("Fresh and tart as you like," was her cry), and became the object of lewd compliments from two students in cap and gown who were munching lupine seeds as they walked along, bundles of verses stuffed in their pockets, both clearly on the lookout for someone with whom they could exchange some banter. Then I noticed a dark, scrawny individual, with the bearded face of a Turk; he was standing in a nearby doorway, watching us as he cleaned the dirt from under his fingernails with a knife. He had no cloak on, but he carried a dagger, a long sword in a baldric, and wore a much-darned, tow-stuffed doublet, the floppy, broad-brimmed hat of a ruffian, and a large gold earring dangling from one earlobe. I was about to study him more carefully when someone came up behind me, casting a shadow over the table. Greetings were exchanged, and don Francisco rose to his feet.

"I don't know if you two have met before. Diego Alatriste, this is Pedro Calderón de la Barca."

The captain and I both stood up to greet the new arrival, whom I had seen occasionally at the Corral de la Cruz. I immediately recognized the downy mustache and the pleasant, slender face. He wasn't grimy with sweat and soot this time, nor was he wearing a buffcoat; he had on elegant city clothes, a fine cape and a hat with an embroidered hatband, and the sword he wore at his belt was clearly not that of a soldier. Nevertheless, he wore the same smile as he had at the sacking of Oudkerk.

"The boy's name," added Quevedo, "is Íñigo Balboa."

Pedro Calderón looked at me for a while, as if trying to place me.

"A comrade from Flanders, I believe," he said at last. "Isn't that right?"

His smile grew broader, and he placed a friendly hand on my shoulder. I felt like the luckiest young man in the world and savored the astonished look on the faces of Quevedo and my master. Calderón was claimed by some as the heir to Tirso and to Lope, and his star was beginning to shine brightly in the theaters and at the palace.

His play *The Mock Astrologer* had been performed with great success the previous year, and he was, at the time, putting the finishing touches to *The Siege at Breda*. No wonder, then, that don Francisco and my master were so astonished that this young playwright should remember a humble soldier's page who, two years before, had helped him save a library from the flames in a Flemish town hall. Calderón sat down with us, and for a while there was much pleasant conversation and more wine, which the new arrival accompanied with no more than a bowl of olives, for he did not, he said, have much appetite. Finally, we all got up and took a turn about the *mentidero*. An acquaintance, who had been reading something out loud to a group of guffawing idlers, came over to us with a few of his fellows in tow. He was holding a piece of manuscript paper.

"They say this was penned by you, Señor de Quevedo."

Quevedo cast a disdainful eye over the writing, enjoying the expectant hush. Then he smoothed his mustache and read out loud:

> *"The man in this dark tomb,*
> *Who lies here dead and doomed,*
> *Sold body and soul for a wager*
> *And even dead he's still a gamester . . .*

"No," he said, apparently grave-faced, but with tongue firmly in cheek. "That last line could do with a bit of work—if, of course, I had written it. But tell me, gentlemen, is Góngora such a broken man that people are already writing epitaphs for him?"

There were gales of flattering laughter, the same laughter that would have greeted a barb aimed by Góngora at Quevedo. The truth is that, although don Francisco preferred not to say so in public, he had, indeed, written those lines, just as he had many of the other anonymous verses that ran like hounds about the *mentidero*; although sometimes, other people's poems, however uninventive, were also attributed to him. As regards Góngora, that quip about his epitaph was not far off the mark. Quevedo had bought a house in Calle del Niño purely in order to evict Góngora; and that leader of the ranks of *culturanistas*, ruined by the vice of gaming and his desire to cut a fine figure, and so short of funds that he could only just afford a miserable carriage and a couple of maidservants, was forced to submit and retire to his native Córdoba, where he died, ill and embittered, the following year, when the disease afflicting him—apoplexy, some said—finally attacked his mind. Arrogant and aristocratic in manner, that Córdoban prebendary was as unlucky at cards as he was in his choice of friends and enemies; he clashed with Lope de Vega and with Quevedo, and placed his affections as mistakenly as he placed his bets, linking himself to the fallen Duke of Lerma, the executed don Rodrigo Calderón, and the murdered Count of Villamediana. And any hopes he had of receiving favors from the court and from the count-duke—whom he asked on numerous occasions for positions for his nephews and other members of his family—had died when Olivares famously announced: "The devil take those people from Córdoba." He had no better luck with his work. Out of pride, he had always refused to publish anything, preferring to distribute his poems amongst his friends for them to read and publicize; then, when necessity did finally force him to publish, he died before he saw his books leave the press, and the Inquisition immediately ordered them to be confiscated as suspicious and immoral. And yet, although I never warmed to the man and disliked his particular brand of Latinate gibberish—all triclinia and grottoes—I still say that don Luis de Góngora was an extraordinary poet who, paradoxically, along with his mortal enemy Quevedo, did much to enrich this beautiful language of ours. These two cultivated and spirited men, each writing in very different styles, but with equal skill, breathed new life into Castilian Spanish, one with his linguistic richness and the other with his intellectual swagger. It could be said that this fruitful, pitiless battle between two literary giants changed the Spanish language forever.

We left don Pedro Calderón with some relatives and friends of his and continued down Calle Francos to Lope's house— this was how everyone in Spain referred to it, with no need even to mention his glorious family name—for Quevedo had some messages to pass on to him from the palace. I turned to look behind me a couple of times, to see if we were being followed by that dark, cloakless ruffian; on the third time of looking, he had gone. A mistake perhaps, I told myself; my instinct, though, attuned to the violent mores of Madrid, told me that such mistakes smell of blood and steel on some dimly lit street corner. There were, however, other matters demanding my attention. One of these was the fact that don Francisco, as well as being commissioned by the count-duke to write a play, had been charged with composing a courtly ballad or two for the queen, to be performed at a party in the Salón Dorado—the Golden Room—in the Alcázar Palace. Quevedo had promised to take these ballads to the palace himself, because the queen wanted him to read them out loud to her and her ladies-in-waiting, and Quevedo, who was, above all, a good and loyal friend, had invited me to accompany him in the role of assistant or secretary or page or some such thing. I didn't mind what title I was given as long as I saw Angélica de Alquézar—the maid of honor with whom, as you will recall, I was deeply in love.

The other matter was this visit to Lope's house. Don Francisco de Quevedo knocked at the door and Lope's maidservant, Lorenza, opened it. I knew the house already, and later, over the years, visited it often because of the friendship that existed between don Francisco and Lope, and between my master and certain other frequent visitors to that Phoenix of Inventiveness, among them his close friend Captain Alonso de Contreras and another younger man who was, unexpectedly, about to enter the scene. We

walked into the hallway, down the passageway and past
the stairs leading up to the first floor, where the poet's
little nieces were playing. (Years later, it was discovered
that these were, in fact, Lope's daughters by Marta de
Nevares.) We emerged, at last, into the little garden where
Lope was sitting on a wicker chair beneath the shade of a
vine, next to the well and the famous orange tree that he
tended with his own hands. He had just finished eating,
and nearby stood a small table on which there were still the
remains of a meal, as well as cool drinks and sweet wine
in a glass pitcher for his guests. Lope was accompanied by
three other men, one of whom was the aforementioned
Captain Contreras, who wore the cross of Malta on his doublet and was always to be found at Lope's house whenever
he was in Madrid. My master and he were very fond of
each other, for they had sailed together in the Naples galleys, and had met before that as youths, almost boys, when
they both set off for Flanders with the troops of Archduke
Alberto. At the time, Contreras was something of a ruffian,
for at the tender age of twelve, he had already knifed one
of his own kind and subsequently deserted from the army
when the troops were only halfway to Flanders. The second
gentleman, don Luis Alberto de Prado by name, was a secretary in the Council of Castile; he was from Cuenca and
had a reputation as a decent poet; he was also a fervent admirer of Lope. The third was a handsome young nobleman

with a youthfully sparse mustache; he must have been about twenty years old or so and wore a bandage round his head. When he saw us, he sprang to his feet in surprise, an emotion I saw replicated on Captain Alatriste's face, for the latter immediately stopped where he was by the well and instinctively placed his hand on the hilt of his sword.

"Well," said the young man, "Madrid really is a small world."

It certainly was. Only the previous morning, he and Captain Alatriste, ignorant of each other's names, had fought a duel together. Even more remarkable, as everyone was about to discover, this young fighter's name was Lopito Félix de Vega Carpio and he was the poet's son, newly arrived in Madrid from Sicily, where he had served under the Marquis of Santa Cruz, having enlisted in the galleys when he was just fifteen. He was the illegitimate child—albeit acknowledged by Lope—from the latter's affair with the actress Micaela Luján; he had fought against Berber pirates, done battle with the French off the Îles d'Hyères, and taken part in the liberation of Genoa, and now he was in Madrid, hoping to sort out the papers that would confirm him in the rank of ensign. He was also, it turned out, keeping watch on a certain lady's window. Anyway, this present situation was damnably awkward. While Lopito gave a detailed account of what had happened, his bewildered father sat in his chair, his ecclesiastical gown still sprinkled with crumbs, and looked from one to the other, not knowing whether to be surprised or angry. Once recovered from their initial shock, Captain Contreras and don Francisco de Quevedo argued the case with reason and tact; my master, however, greatly upset, offered his apologies and made ready to leave at once, convinced that he would no longer be welcome in that house. Quevedo was saying:

"The boy is, in fact, to be congratulated. Crossing swords with the best blade in Madrid and coming away with only a scratch is either a mark of skill or very good luck."

Captain Contreras confirmed that this was so and gave further evidence. He and Diego Alatriste had been in Italy together, and he knew that the only reason Alatriste ever failed to dispatch an opponent was because he chose not to. This and other arguments continued to be exchanged, but my master was still preparing to leave. He courteously bowed to Lope, gave his word that he would never have unsheathed his sword had he known his adversary to be Lope's son, and then turned to go before Lope could say a word. At this point, Lopito de Vega intervened.

"Please, Father, allow the gentleman to stay," he said.

He bore him no ill feeling at all, because he had fought like a true hidalgo right from the start.

"And although that last knife-thrust may not have been exactly elegant—well, so few are—he didn't just leave me there like a dog. He bandaged my wound and was kind enough to send someone to fetch me and take me to a barber."

These dignified words calmed the situation. The father of the wounded man ceased frowning; Quevedo, Contreras, and Prado all praised the young ensign's discretion, which said much for himself and his purity of blood; Lopito described the incident in more detail this time and in jovial terms; and the conversation resumed its friendly tone, thus dissipating the heavy clouds that had been threatening to spoil that postprandial gathering and bring down Lope's displeasure on my master, something that the latter would have keenly regretted, for he was a great admirer of Lope and respected him as he did few men. Finally, the captain accepted a glass of sweet Málaga wine, concurred with everything the others had said, and Lopito and he became firm friends. They would remain so for eight years, until ensign Lope Félix de Vega Carpio met his unhappy fate when he drowned after his ship was wrecked on an expedition to Île Sainte-Marguerite. I will, however, have occasion to say more about him in this story, and possibly in a future episode, too, if I ever recount the role played by Lopito, Captain Alatriste, and myself, along with other comrades—some of whom you have met already and others whom you have not—in the attack on Venice launched by the Spanish for the second time in the century—an attempt to take the city and murder the doge and his cronies, who had given us so much trouble in the Adriatic and in Italy by ingratiating themselves with the pope and with Richelieu. But all in good time. Besides, Venice merits a book to itself.

We continued our pleasant conversation in the garden until late into the afternoon, and took advantage of this opportunity to observe Lope de Vega close to. I had met him once on the steps of San Felipe, when I was a young lad newly arrived in Madrid, and he had placed his hand on my head, almost as if in an act of confirmation. I imagine it must be difficult now to grasp just what an important figure the great Lope was in those days. He must have been about sixty-four then, and he still had a very gallant air about him, enhanced as it was by his elegant gray locks and his trim mustache and beard, which he continued to wear despite his clerical habit. He was a discreet man who spoke little, smiled a great deal, and sought to please everyone, and who concealed behind impeccable courtesy his pride at having reached such an enviable position. No one—apart from Calderón—enjoyed such fame in his lifetime, writing plays of a beauty, variety, and richness that were unequaled in Europe. He had been a soldier in his youth, seen action in a naval battle in the Azores, in Aragon, and in the war against England, and at the time of which I am speaking, he had written a good part of the more than one thousand five hundred plays and four hundred sacramental dramas that flowed from his pen. His status as a priest did not prevent him enjoying a long and scandalous life full of amorous intrigues, lovers, and illegitimate children, all of which meant, understandably enough, that despite his great literary reputation, he was never seen as a particularly virtuous man and so received none of the courtly benefits to which he aspired, such as the post of royal chronicler, which he always sought but never attained. Otherwise, he enjoyed both fame and fortune. And unlike good don Miguel de Cervantes, who died, as I said, poor, alone, and forgotten, Lope's funeral, nine years after the dates that concern us here, was a multitudinous display of homage such as had never before been seen in Spain. As for the basis for his reputation, much has been written about that, and I commend those books to the reader. I later had occasion to travel to England and learn the English tongue. I read and even saw performances of plays by William Shakespeare, and I would say that although the Englishman could plumb the depths of the human heart, and while his characters are perhaps more complex than Lope's, the Spaniard's sheer theatrical skill, inventiveness, and ability to keep an audience on tenterhooks, the brilliance of his intrigues and the captivating way in which each plot evolves are all incomparable. And even when it comes to characters, I'm not sure that the Englishman always succeeded in depicting the doubts and anxieties of lovers, or the crafty machinations of servants as ingeniously as Lope. Consider, if you will, his little-known work *The Duke of Viseu* and tell me if that tragic play is not the equal of any of Shakespeare's tragedies. Moreover, if it is true that Shakespeare's plays were in some way so universal that we can all recognize ourselves in them—only *Don Quixote* is as Spanish as Lope and as universal as Shakespeare—it is no less true that Lope, with his new approach to drama, held up a very faithful mirror to the Spain of our century, and that his plays were imitated everywhere, thanks to the fact that Spanish, then, was a language that bestrode two worlds, a language admired, read, and spoken by everyone. However, it must be said, too, that this was due in no small measure to the fact that it was also the language of our fearsome troops and our arrogant, black-clad ambassadors. Unlike other nations—and in this I happily include that of Shakespeare—only Spain has left such a clear record of its customs, values, and language, and all thanks to the plays of Lope, Calderón, Tirso, Rojas, Alarcón, and their ilk, which made such a lasting impression on the theaters of the world. At a time when Spanish was being spoken in Italy, Flanders, the Indies, and the remote seas of the Philippines, the Frenchman Corneille was imitating the work of Guillén de Castro in order to find success in his own land, and the land of Shakespeare was home only to a bunch of hypocritical pirates in search of excuses to prosper and, like so many others, nipping at the heels of the weary, old Spanish lion, who was, nonetheless, still capable of far greater things than they ever were. To quote Lope:

> *Forward, Spanish sea-dogs,*
> *In whose veins runs the blood of Goths,*
> *Fill your hands with gold,*
> *With slaves, with treasure,*
> *You've earned it, take full measure.*

During that conversation in the garden, we spoke about a little of everything. Captain Contreras brought news of various wars, and Lopito described to Diego Alatriste the current situation in the Mediterranean, where my master had once sailed and done battle. Then, inevitably, talk turned to literature. Luis Alberto de Prado read some of his own verse, which, to his great pleasure, drew praise from Quevedo, and Góngora's name was mentioned again.

"Apparently, the man's dying," Contreras told them.

"Good riddance," said Quevedo tartly, "there'll be plenty to replace him. Every day, eager for fame, as many overcultivated, turd-mongering poets spring up in Spain as mushrooms in the winter damp."

Lope smiled from his Olympian heights, amused and

tolerant. He could not bear Góngora either, although, paradoxically, he had also always hoped to draw him into his circle, because, deep down, he admired and feared him, so much so that he even wrote these lines:

> *Bright swan of Betis who so*
> *Sweetly and gravely tuned thy bow.*

Góngora—that prebendary-cum-swan—was, however, the kind of man who ate alone and never succumbed to blandishments. At first, he had dreamed of snatching the poetic scepter from Lope, even writing plays, but he failed in that as he did in so many things. For all these reasons, Lope always professed to loathe him, meanwhile mocking his own relative lack of knowledge of the classics—for unlike Góngora and Quevedo, Lope knew no Greek and could barely read Latin—as well as the success of his plays with ordinary people. Of his plays he wrote:

> *They are ducks who splash in the waters of Castile*
> *Which flow so easily from that vulgar stream*
> *And sweetly flood the lower slopes;*
> *From plain-born Lope expect no high-flown tropes.*

Lope, however, rarely stepped into the public arena. He did his best to get along well with everyone, and at that point in his life and his success, he was in no mood to become em-

broiled in disputes and rivalries. He contented himself instead with gentle, veiled attacks and left the really dirty
work to his friends, Quevedo among them, for the latter had
no qualms about pouring scorn on Góngora's *culturanista*
excesses or, indeed, on those of his followers. Góngora could
no longer hit back at the fearsome Quevedo, who was a past
master when it came to tongue-lashings.

"I read *Don Quixote* when I was in Sicily," remarked
Captain Contreras. "Not bad at all, I thought."

"Indeed," replied Quevedo. "It's already famous and
will, I'm sure, outlive many other works."

Lope raised a disdainful eyebrow, poured himself more
wine, and changed the subject. This is further evidence, as
I say, that in that Spain of never-ending envy and back-
stabbing, where a place on Parnassus was as sought-after as
Inca gold, the pen caused more blood to be shed than the
sword; besides, enemies in one's own profession are always the worst kind. The animosity between Lope and
Cervantes—the latter, as I said, had, by then, entered the
heaven reserved for just men and was doubtless seated at
the right hand of God—had gone on for years and was
still alive even after poor don Miguel's death. The initial
friendship between those two giants of Spanish literature
quickly turned to hatred when the illustrious one-armed
Cervantes, whose plays, like Góngora's, met with utter
failure—"I could," he wrote, "find no one who wanted

them"—fired the first shot, by including in Part One of his novel a caustic comment on Lope's work, in particular his famous parody of the flocks of sheep. Lope responded with these rough words: "I will say nothing of poets, for this is a good century for them. But there is none so bad as Cervantes and none so foolish as to praise *Don Quixote*." At the time, the novel was considered to be a minor art requiring little intellect and fit only to entertain young ladies; the theater brought money, but poetry brought luster and glory. This is why Lope respected Quevedo, feared Góngora, and despised Cervantes:

> *All honor to Lope, and to you only pain,*
> *For he is the sun and, if angered, will rain.*
> *And as for that trivial* Don Quixote *of yours,*
> *Its only use is for wiping your arse*
> *Or for wrapping up spices and all things nice,*
> *'Til it finds its just rest in the shit with the mice.*

. . . as he wrote in a letter, which, to rub salt in the wound, he sent to his rival without paying the one-*real* postage. Cervantes would write later: "What bothered me most was having to pay that one *real*." And so poor don Miguel was driven out of the theater, ground down by work, poverty, and prison, by a succession of humiliations and by many pointless hours spent waiting in anterooms, quite unaware that immortality was already riding toward him on the back of Rocinante. He, who never sought favors by shamelessly flattering the powerful, as Góngora, Quevedo, and Lope all did, finally accepted the illusion of his own failure, and, as honest as ever, wrote:

I who always strive and strain
To seem to have poetic grace
Though Heaven denies me again and again.

But then, that was the nature of the lost world I am describing to you, when the mere name of Spain made the earth tremble. It was all barbed quarrels, arrogance, ill will, cruelty, and poverty. As the empire on which the sun was setting was gradually crumbling, as we were being erased from the face of the earth by our misfortune and our own vile deeds, there, amongst the rubble and the ruins, lies the mark left by those remarkably talented men who, while they could not justify it, could at least explain that age of greatness and glory. They were the children of their time in the evil that they did—and they did a great deal— but they were also the children of the genius of their time in the brilliant works they wrote—and they wrote so much. No nation has given birth to so many men of genius at any one time, nor have the writers of any one nation recorded as faithfully as they did the tiniest details of their age.

Fortunately, they live on in libraries, in the pages of their books, within reach of whoever cares to approach and listen, astonished, to the heroic, terrifying roar of our century and our lives. Only thus is it possible to understand what we were and what we are. And then may the devil take us all.

Lope remained at his house, the secretary Prado left, and the rest of us, including Lopito, finished the evening in Juan Lepre's tavern, on the corner of Calle del Lobo and Calle de las Huertas, sharing a skin of Lucena wine. The talk grew animated. Captain don Alonso de Contreras, an extremely likable fellow, who enjoyed a good fight and good conversation, recounted tales of his life as a soldier and that of my master, including that business in Naples in the fifteenth year of this century, when, after my master had killed a man in a duel over a woman, it was Captain Contreras himself who helped him to elude justice and return to Spain.

"The lady didn't escape unscathed, either," he added, laughing. "Diego left her with a charming scar on her cheek as a souvenir. And by God, the hussy deserved it—and more."

"Oh, I know many such women who do," added Quevedo, ever the misogynist.

And on this theme, he regaled us with some lines that he had thought up there and then:

> *"Fly, thoughts, and tell those eyes*
> *That make my heart so glad:*
> *There's money to be had."*

I looked at my master, incapable of imagining him slashing a woman's face with a knife. He, however, remained impassive, elbows on the table, as he stared into his mug of wine. Don Franciso caught my look, cast a sideways glance at Alatriste, and said no more. What other things, I wondered, lay behind those silences. And I shuddered inside, as I always did when I got a glimpse of the captain's dark inner life. It is never pleasant to grow in years and understanding and thus penetrate into the more hidden recesses of one's hero's mind and life, and, as I grew more perceptive with passing time, I saw things in Diego Alatriste that I would have preferred not to see.

"But then, of course," said Contreras, who had also seen the expression on my face and feared perhaps that he had gone too far, "we were young and spirited. I remember one occasion, in Corfu it was . . ."

And he launched into another story. Along the way, he mentioned the names of various mutual friends, such as Diego, Duke of Estrada, a comrade of my master's during the disastrous attack on the Kerkennah Islands, where they both nearly lost their lives trying to save that of Álvaro de la Marca, Count of Guadalmedina. The count, of course, had since exchanged his soldierly accoutrements for the post of confidant to Philip IV and, according to Quevedo, now accompanied the king each night on his romantic sorties. Forgetting my earlier gloomy thoughts, I listened to them talk, fascinated by their accounts of galleys and ships being boarded, of slaves and booty. The way Captain Contreras told them, these events took on fabulous proportions: the famous incident when, with the Marquis of Santa Cruz, they set fire to the Berber fleet off La Goleta; the description of idyllic places at the very foot of Mount Vesuvius; the youthful orgies and acts of bravado, when Contreras and my master would spend in a matter of days the money they had earned from pursuing pirates around the Greek islands and the Turkish coast. Between swigs of the wine we were clumsily spilling all over the table, Captain Contreras felt moved to recite some lines written in his honor by Lope de Vega and into which he now introduced my master's name by way of a tribute:

> *"Contreras's valor was fully tested,*
> *And laurels hard won, in the fight for Spain.*
> *Alatriste and he were never bested*
> *During that bloody Turkish campaign.*
> *Even their slightest, most modest feat*

(For a blade of steel cannot deceive)
Brought them praise and honor sweet."

Alatriste still said nothing—his sword hanging from the back of his chair and his hat on the floor on top of his folded cloak—he merely nodded now and then, uttered the occasional monosyllabic comment, and managed a faint, courteous smile whenever Contreras, Quevedo, or Lopito de Vega mentioned his name. I listened and watched, drinking in the words, captivated by every anecdote and every memory, and feeling that I was one of them—and that I had every right to feel so, too. After all, I may have been only sixteen, but I was already a veteran of Flanders and some other rather murkier campaigns; I had both the scars to show for it and reasonable skills as a swordsman. This confirmed me in my intention to join the militia as soon as I could and to win my own laurels so that, one day, as I recounted my exploits at a tavern table, someone might recite a few lines of poetry in my honor, too. I did not know then that my wishes would be more than granted, and that the road I was preparing to take would also lead me to the farther side of glory and of fame. True, I had known war in Flanders, but had done so with the wide-eyed enthusiasm of the innocent, for whom the militia is a magnificent spectacle; the true face of war casts a dark shadow over heart and memory. I look back now from this interminable old age in which I seem to be suspended as I write these memoirs and—beneath the murmur of the flags flapping in the wind and the drumroll that marks the quiet passing of the old infantry whose long-drawn-out death I witnessed in Breda, Nördlingen, Fuenterrabía, Catalonia, and Rocroi—I find only the faces of ghosts and the lucid, infinite solitude of someone who has known the best and the worst of what that word "Spain" contains. And now, having myself paid the price demanded by life, I know what lay behind the captain's silences and his abstracted gaze.

The captain bade good night to everyone and set off alone up Calle del Lobo before crossing Carrera de San Jerónimo, wrapped in his cloak and with his hat pulled well down. Night had fallen, it was cold, and Calle de los Peligros was deserted; the only light came from a candle burning in a niche in the wall containing the image of a saint. Halfway along, he felt the need to stop for a moment. "Too much wine," he said to himself. He chose the darkest corner, drew back his cloak and unbuttoned his breeches. He was standing there in the corner, legs apart, relieving himself, when a bell tolled in the nearby convent of Bernardine nuns. He had plenty of time, he thought. It was half an hour until his rendezvous in a house farther up on the right, beyond Calle de Alcalá, where an old duenna, a seasoned bawd and matchmaker experienced in her profession, would have everything ready—bed, supper, washbowl, water, and towels—for his meeting with María de Castro.

He was buttoning up his breeches when he heard a noise behind him. This was, after all, Calle de los Peligros—the Street of Dangers—and there he was in the dark with his breeches unbuttoned. He really didn't want to end his days like this. He rapidly adjusted his clothing, all the time glancing over his shoulder, then he folded back his cloak so that his sword was unencumbered. Moving around at night in Madrid meant living in a state of permanent anxiety; anyone who could afford it hired an armed escort to light their way. If, on the other hand, your name was Diego Alatriste, you had the consolation of knowing that you could be just as dangerous, if not more, than whoever you might bump into. It was all a matter of temperament, and his had never been, shall we say, Franciscan.

For the moment, he could see nothing. It was pitch-black night, and the eaves of the houses left the façades and the doorways in deep shadow. Here and there, a domestic candle lit up a blind from within or a half-open shutter door. He stood motionless for a while, watching the corner of Calle de Alcalá like someone studying the slope of a fortification being swept by the fire of enemy harquebuses, then he walked warily on, taking care not to step in the horse dung or other filth that lay stinking in the gutter. He could hear only his own footsteps. Suddenly, where Calle de los Peligros narrowed and the convent wall ended, that sound seemed to find an echo. Still walking, he kept looking to either side, until he noticed a shape to his right that was keeping close to the walls of some tall houses. It might be some perfectly innocent passerby, or someone following him with evil intent; and so he continued on his way, never losing sight of that shape. He walked some twenty or thirty paces, remaining always in the middle of the street, and when the shape passed a lighted window, he saw a man wrapped in a cloak and wearing a broad-brimmed hat. The captain walked on, every sense alert now, and shortly afterward spotted a second shape on the other side of the street. Too many shapes and too little light, he thought. These were either hired killers or robbers. He un-clasped his cloak and unsheathed his sword.

Divide and conquer, he was thinking—if, that is, luck was with him. Besides, the early bird catches the worm. And so, wrapping his cloak around his free arm, he made straight for the shape on the right and dealt a blow with his sword before his adversary even had time to make a move. The man slumped to one side with a groan, his cloak and what lay behind it pierced through; then, with his cloak still wrapped about him, his sword unused in its sheath, he withdrew into the shadows of a doorway, moan-ing and breathing hard. Trusting that the second man would not be carrying a pistol, Alatriste spun round to face him, for he could hear footsteps running toward him down the street. A black cloakless silhouette was approaching, wearing, like his companion, a broad-brimmed ruffian's hat, and brandishing a sword. Alatriste whirled his cloak around in the air so that it wrapped about that sword, and while the other man was cursing and trying desperately to disentangle his weapon, the captain got in half a dozen short thrusts, dealt almost wildly, blindly. The last one hit home, causing his assailant to fall to the ground. The captain glanced behind him, in case he was in danger of attack from the rear, but the man in the cloak had had enough. Alatriste could see him disappearing down the street. He then picked up his own cloak, which stank from having been trampled in the gutter, put his sword back in its sheath, took out his dagger with his left hand, and, going over to his fallen opponent, held the point to his throat.

"Talk," he said, "or, by Christ, I'll kill you."

The man was breathing hard. He was in a bad way, but still capable of assessing the situation. He smelled of wine recently drunk, and of blood.

"Go to hell," he muttered feebly.

Alatriste scrutinized his face as best he could. A thick beard. A single earring glinting in the darkness. The voice of a ruffian. He was clearly a professional killer and, to judge by his words, a cool customer.

"Tell me the name of the person paying you," Alatriste said, pressing the dagger harder against the man's throat.

"I'm not saying," answered the man, "so slit my throat and be done with it."

"That's what I was thinking of doing."

"Fine by me."

Alatriste smiled beneath his mustache, aware that the other man could not see his face. The wily bastard had guts, and he clearly wasn't going to get anything out of him. He quickly searched the man's pockets, but found only a purse, which he kept, and a knife with a good blade, which he discarded.

"So you're not going to sing, then?" he asked.

"No."

The captain gave an understanding nod of the head and stood up. Amongst professionals like them, those were the rules of the criminal world. Trying to force the man to talk would be a waste of time, and if a patrol of catchpoles were to appear, he would be hard pushed to come up with an explanation, at that hour of the night and with a dead man lying at his feet. So he had better cut and run. He was just about to put away his dagger and leave, when he thought better of it, and instead, leaning forward again, he slashed the man across the mouth. It made a sound like meat being chopped on a butcher's board, and this time the man really did fall silent, either because he lost consciousness or because the blade had sliced through his tongue. Just in case. Not that the man had really made much use of it, thought

Alatriste, as he moved away. At any rate, if someone did manage to sew the man up and he survived, it would help Alatriste to identify him should they ever meet again in daylight. And even if they didn't, at least the man—or what remained of him after the wound to his body and that *signum crucis*—would certainly never forget Calle de los Peligros.

The moon rose late, forming halos on the glass panes of the window. Diego Alatriste had his back to the window and stood framed in the rectangle of silvery light that extended as far as the bed on which María de Castro lay sleeping. The captain was studying the shape of that woman and listening to her quiet breathing and the little moans she gave as she made herself more comfortable among the sheets that barely covered her. He sniffed his own hands and forearms: he had the smell of her on him, the perfume from her body that lay resting now, exhausted, after their long interchange of kisses and caresses. He moved, and his shadow seemed to slide like the shadow of a ghost over her pale naked body. By Christ, she was beautiful.

He went over to the table and poured himself a little wine. As he did so, he went from the mat to the flagstoned floor, and the cold sent a shiver over his weather-beaten soldier's skin. He drank, still keeping his eyes on the woman. Hundreds of men of all classes and stations, men of quality and with nice full purses, would have given anything to enjoy her for a few minutes; and yet there he was, sated with her flesh and her mouth. His only fortune was his sword and his only future, oblivion. How odd they are, he thought again, the mechanisms that move the minds of women. Or, at least, the minds of women like her. The killer's purse, which he had placed on the table without saying a word—doubtless the price of his own life—contained only enough for her to buy herself some fashionable new clogs, a fan, and some ribbons. And yet there he was. And there she was.

"Diego."

This was spoken in a sleepy murmur. The woman had turned over in bed and was looking at him.

"Come here, my love."

He put down his glass of wine and went over to her, sitting down on the edge of the bed and placing one hand on her warm flesh. My love, she had said. He didn't even have enough money to pay for his own funeral—an event he postponed each day with his sword—nor was he an elegant fop, or a gallant, cultivated man, the sort admired by women in the street or at evening parties. My love. He suddenly found himself remembering the last lines of a sonnet by Lope that he had heard that afternoon at the poet's house:

She loves you, loathes you, treats you well, then ill.
Like a leech or surgeon's knife, she's double-edged:
Sometimes she'll cure, but sometimes she will kill.

In the moonlight, María de Castro's eyes looked incredibly beautiful, and it accentuated the dark abyss of her half-open mouth. So what, thought the captain. My love or not my love. My love or someone else's love. My madness or my sanity. My, your, his heart. That night he was alive, and that was all that counted. He had eyes to see and a mouth to kiss with. And teeth to bite. None of the many sons of bitches who had crossed his path, Turks, heretics, constables, or bullies, had succeeded in stealing this moment from him. He was still breathing, although many had tried to stop him doing so. And now, as if to confirm this, one of her hands was caressing his skin, lingering over each old scar. "My love," she said again. Don Francisco de Quevedo would doubtless have got a good poem out of this, fitting it all into fourteen perfect hendecasyllables. Captain Alatriste, however, merely smiled to himself. It was good to be alive, at least for a while longer, in a world in which no one gave anything away for nothing, in which everything had to be paid for—before, during, and afterward. "I must have paid something," he thought. "I don't know how much or when, but I must have done so if life is rewarding me with the prize of having a woman look at me as she is looking at me now, even if only for a few nights."

3. THE ALCÁZAR DE
LOS AUSTRIAS

"I am *very* much looking forward to your play, Señor de Quevedo."

The queen was the extremely beautiful daughter of Henry IV of France, *le Béarnois*; she was twenty-three years old, pale-complexioned, and had a dimple in her chin. Her accent was as charming as her appearance, especially when, in her struggle to roll her *r*'s, she frowned a little, earnestly and courteously, as befitted such a refined and intelligent queen. She was clearly born to sit on a throne, and although she came from a foreign land, she reigned over Spain as a loyal Spaniard, just as her sister-in-law, Ana de Austria—sister of our Philip IV and wife of Louis XIII—reigned as a loyal Frenchwoman in her adoptive country. When the course of history brought the old Spanish lion into conflict with the young French wolf in a squabble over hegemony in Europe, both queens—brought up to fulfill the rigorous duties of honor and blood—unreservedly embraced the respective causes of their august husbands. In the harsh times that lay ahead, we Spaniards would find ourselves in the paradoxical position of coming to blows with a France ruled by a Spanish queen. Such are the vicissitudes of war and politics.

However, to return to that morning, to doña Isabel de Borbón and to the Alcázar Real, light was pouring in through the three balconies of the Room of Mirrors, gilding the queen's curled hair and making her two simple pearl earrings gleam. She was dressed in homely fashion, within the constraints of her rank, in a mauve gown of heavy watered camlet decorated with silver braid; and sitting, as she was, on a stool by the window of the central balcony, an inch of white stocking was visible above her satin shoes.

"I hope I will not disappoint, my lady."

"Oh, I am sure you will not. The court has complete confidence in your inventive talents."

She was angelic, I thought, from where I stood in the doorway, not daring to move so much as an eyebrow. I had several reasons for feeling petrified, and finding myself in the presence of the queen was only one, and not, by the way, the most important. I had put on new clothes for the occasion, a black doublet with a starched collar, black breeches, and a cap, all of which a tailor in Calle Mayor, a friend of Captain Alatriste, had made for me—on account, and in just three days—as soon as we knew that don Francisco de Quevedo would be taking me with him to the palace. As a favorite of the court, and held in high esteem by the queen, don Francisco had become a regular guest at all courtly functions. He amused our king and queen with his remarks; he flattered the count-duke, who, with his ever-growing number of political opponents, found it useful to have Quevedo's intelligent quill on his side; and he was adored by the ladies, who, at every party and every gathering, would plead with him to entertain them with his poetry or with some improvised verse. And so, astute and sharp as ever, the poet allowed himself to be loved; he exaggerated his limp so that others might forgive both his talent and his position as favorite; and he had no compunction about making the most of all this for as long as his luck lasted. There was evidently a favorable conjunction of the stars, but one that don Francisco's stoical skepticism—gleaned from the classics and from his own experience of changing fortunes—told him would not last forever. As he himself used to say, we are what we are until we cease to be so. This was especially true in Spain, where these things change overnight. The same people who applauded you yesterday and felt honored to know you and to be your friend will, today, for no apparent reason, throw you into prison or put a penitent's hat on your head and march you through the streets to the scaffold.

"Allow me, my lady, to introduce a young friend of

mine. His name is Íñigo Balboa Aguirre and he fought in Flanders."

Cap in hand, blushing furiously, I bowed so low that my forehead almost touched the floor. My embarrassment, as I have said, was due not only to finding myself in the presence of the wife of Philip IV. I was aware, too, of four pairs of eyes staring at me—the queen's four maids of honor. They were sitting nearby on the satin pillows and cushions arranged on the yellow-and-red tiled floor, next to Gastoncillo, the French jester whom doña Isabel de Borbón had brought with her at the time of her nuptials with our king. The glances and smiles of these young ladies were enough to turn anyone's head.

"So young," said the queen.

She smiled sweetly at me, then started chatting with don Francisco about the details of the ballads he had written, while I stayed where I was, cap in hand, eyes fixed on some point in the distance, and having to lean against the tiled frieze behind me in case my legs gave way. The girls were all whispering to each other, and Gastoncillo joined in. I scarcely knew where to look. The jester was, it is true, only three foot tall and as ugly as sin, and famed at court for his wicked tongue—you can imagine just how funny it would be to hear a French dwarf telling jokes—but the queen liked him and everyone laughed at his jests, even if only reluctantly and out of duty. Anyway, I stayed where I was, as still as one of the figures in the paintings that adorned the walls of the room, which had only been open since the very recent restoration work on the palace façade had been completed, for in that ancient building, dark rooms from the last century adjoined or flowed into entirely modern, newly decorated ones. I looked at Titian's representations of Achilles and Ulysses above the doors, at his very apposite allegory *Religion Succored by Spain*, at the equestrian portrait of the great emperor Charles at the battle of Mühlberg, and, on the opposite wall, at another of Philip IV, also on horseback, painted by Diego Velázquez. Finally, when I knew each and every one of those canvases by heart, I summoned up sufficient courage to turn and look at the real reason for my unease. I could not say whether the pounding inside me came from the hammering of the carpenters who were preparing the nearby Salón Dorado for the queen's evening party or from the blood pumping furiously through my veins and heart. However, there I stood, as if ready to withstand a charge from the Lutheran cavalry, and, opposite me, sitting on a red velvet cushion, was the blue-eyed angel-devil who simultaneously sweetened and soured my innocence and my youth. Needless to say, Angélica de Alquézar was watching me.

About an hour later, when the visit was over, and I was following don Francisco de Quevedo through the porticos of the Queen's Courtyard, the jester Gastoncillo caught up with me, tugged discreetly at the sleeve of my doublet, and pressed a tightly folded piece of paper into my hand. I stood for a moment studying it, as it lay unopened in my palm; then, before don Francisco saw the note, I slipped it into my purse. I looked around, feeling bold and gallant, the bearer of a secret message, like some character out of a cloak-and-sword drama. "Dear God," I thought, "life is beautiful and the court is a fascinating place." The palace, where decisions were made as to the fate of an empire that bestrode two worlds, reflected the pulse of the Spain which, just then, I found so intoxicating. The two courtyards, the queen's and the king's, were full of courtiers, suitors, and idlers who came and went between the palace and the *mentidero* outside, through the archway where, in the shadows or silhouetted against the light, I could see the checkered uniforms of the old guard. Don Francisco de Quevedo, who was, as I have said, very much in vogue at the time, was constantly being stopped by people greeting him deferentially or asking for his support for some plan or proposal. Someone sought a favor for his nephew, another for a son-in-law, someone else for his son or brother-in-law. No one offered anything in return, no one made any personal commitment. They were content—like pirates—to go around demanding favors, as if these were their right; and all of them, of course, claimed to have the blood of the Goths flowing in their veins; and all were in pursuit of the dream nurtured by every Spaniard: to live without doing a stroke of work, to pay no taxes, and to swagger about with a sword at their belt and a cross embroidered on their doublet. To give you an idea of just how far we Spaniards would go when it came to petitions and requests, not even the saints of the churches were free from such importunate demands; people placed letters of entreaty in the hands of statues, asking for this or that worldly grace, as if the images were mere palace functionaries. Indeed, at the church of the much-solicited Saint Anthony of Padua, a notice was placed underneath the saint, saying: "Closed for business. Please try Saint Gaetano."

Don Francisco de Quevedo was familiar with this game, for, in the past, he himself had felt no qualms about asking for favors—not all of which met with luck or good fortune—and now, like Saint Anthony of Padua, he listened and smiled and shrugged, never promising more than the bare minimum. "After all, I am only a poet," he would say as he made his escape. And, sometimes, grown weary of some particularly importunate supplicant and unable to find a polite way of getting rid of him, he would end up simply telling him to go to hell.

"Christ's blood," he would mutter, "we've turned into a nation of beggars!"

This was not so very far from the truth, and would become truer still in the years to come. Spaniards did not consider a favor to be a privilege but an inalienable right, so much so that the fact of not possessing something our neighbor possessed blackened both our bile and our soul. As for that proverbial, much-vaunted Spanish virtue *hidalguía*, or nobility—a lie that even Corneille and many others like him had swallowed whole—I will say only that it may have existed once, when our compatriots had to fight to survive and valor was only one of many virtues impossible to buy with gold, but no more. Too much water had flowed under too many bridges since the days when don Francisco de Quevedo himself wrote, by way of an epitaph:

Here lies virtue, rough as sin,
Less rich, 'tis true, but feared the more,
With the vanity and dreams it's buried in.

In the times I am describing, virtues, assuming always that they even existed, had almost all gone to the devil. We were left with nothing but the blind pride and lack of loyalty that would finally drag us into the abyss; and the little dignity we retained became the province of a few isolated individuals, or else appeared on the stages of our theaters—in the poetry of Lope and Calderón, and on the distant battlefields where our veteran troops were still fighting. It has always made me laugh to hear men declare, with a twirl of their mustaches, that ours is a dignified and gentlemanly nation. Well, I was, and am, a Basque and a Spaniard; I've lived my century from beginning to end, and along the way I've encountered many more Sancho Panzas than Don Quixotes, more base, despicable, wicked, ambitious people than valiant, honest folk. Our one virtue was that when there was no alternative, some, even the very worst of us, died like men, standing up with sword in hand. The truth is, though, that it would have been far better to live and work for the progress we so rarely enjoyed; alas, kings and royal favorites and priests obstinately denied us this possibility. Each nation is as it is, and what happened in Spain happened. Yet, since we all went down in the end, perhaps it was better like that, with just a few desperate men salvaging the dignity of the unspeakable rump—as if it were the tattered standard from the Terheyden redoubt—by praying, blaspheming, killing, and fighting to their last breath. And that, at least, is something. When anyone asks me what I admire about this poor, sad land of Spain, I always repeat what I said to that French officer in Rocroi: "Count the dead."

If you are gentleman enough to escort a lady, wait for me tonight at the Puerta de la Priora when the angelus is rung.

And that was all the note said; there was no signature. I read it several times, leaning against a column in the courtyard while don Francisco chatted with a group of acquaintances. Each time I read those words, my heart started pounding in my breast. During the time that Quevedo and I had been in the presence of the queen, Angélica de Alquézar had displayed no particular interest in me. She sat surrounded by her whispering companions, and even her smiles were subtle and contained, although, having said that, her blue eyes did occasionally fix on me with such intensity that I feared my legs might buckle. I was a handsome youth at the time, tall for my age, with bright eyes and thick black hair, and I cut quite a decent figure in my new clothes, and in the cap, complete with a red feather, that I was holding now in my hands. That is what had given me the courage to bear the scrutiny of my young lady, if the word "my" can be applied to the niece of the royal secretary Luis de Alquézar, for she was always herself alone, and even when I knew her mouth and her flesh—and I could not have imagined then how soon I would do so for the first time—I always felt like a temporary guest, an interloper, uncertain of the ground I was treading on and expecting, at any moment, that the servants should throw me out into the street. And yet, as I have said before, despite all that happened between us, despite the scar from the knife wound I bear on my back, I know—at least I want to believe that I do—that she always loved me. In her fashion.

. . .

We met the Count of Guadalmedina beneath one of the archways on the stairs. He had just emerged from Philip IV's apartments, where he came and went much as he pleased, and to which the king had just retired after a morning spent hunting in the woods around Casa del Campo. Hunting was one of the king's greatest pleasures, and it was known that he liked to hunt boar without the aid of dogs and could happily spend all day riding the hills in pursuit of his prey. Álvaro de la Marca was wearing a chamois leather doublet, mud-spattered gaiters, and a neat little hat adorned with emeralds. He was dabbing at his face with a handkerchief drenched in scented water as he made his way to the front of the palace, where his carriage awaited him. He looked even more handsome than usual in his hunting costume, which gave a spuriously rustic touch to his otherwise courtly appearance. It was hardly surprising, I thought, that the ladies of the court always fanned themselves more furiously and more ostentatiously whenever the count looked at them; and that even the queen had at first shown a certain fondness for him, without, of course, acting in any way that went against her high rank and person. And I say "at first" because, by this time, Isabel de Borbón was aware of her august husband's escapades and of the role that Guadalmedina played in these—as companion, escort, and procurer. She despised him for that, and although protocol obliged her to be polite—for as well as being her husband's servant, he was also a grandee of Spain—she always went out of her way to treat him with particular coldness. There was only one other person at court whom the queen hated quite as much, and that was the Count-Duke of Olivares, whose position as royal favorite never met with the approval of that princess brought up in the arrogant court of Marie de' Medici and Henry IV of France. Although loved and respected until her death, Isabel de Borbón would eventually lead the courtly palace faction which, a decade and a half later, would call a halt to the count-duke's absolute power, pushing him off the pedestal to which he had been elevated by his intelligence, ambition, and pride. The people had listened to, admired, and feared great Philip II, then quietly complained about Philip III, but, under Philip IV, they had become so broken and exhausted, so weary of financial ruin and disaster, that their feelings had begun to shift from respect to despair. To assuage those feelings, they had to be served up a political head:

You who think you'll never fall,
You who dare to swagger tall,
Remember this, be not deceived:
Troy finally fell, its power o'erheaved,
As did the Princesse de Bretagne.

That morning at the palace, when the Count of Guadalmedina spotted don Francisco and me, he came running down the last few stairs, elegantly sidestepping a small knot of petitioners—a retired captain, a cleric, a mayor, and three provincial hidalgos hoping for someone to breathe life into their pretensions. Then, having greeted the poet affectionately and clapped me cordially on the back, he took us to one side and came straight to the point.

"We have a problem," he said gravely.

He looked at me out of the corner of his eye, as if wondering whether he should say anything further in my presence. I had, however, already lived through many adventures with Captain Alatriste and don Francisco, such that my loyalty and discretion were proven beyond doubt. Glancing around him to make sure that no palace ears were listening, he touched his cap to a member of the Council of the Exchequer who was walking past beneath the arches—and after whom the group of petitioners scuttled like pigs to a maize field—then, lowering his voice to a whisper, said:

"Tell Alatriste to change mounts."

It took me a while to understand what he meant. Not so the ever-sharp don Francisco, who adjusted his glasses in order to study the count more closely.

"Are you serious?"

"I certainly am. Do I look as if I were in the mood for jokes?"

A silence. I was beginning to understand. Quevedo cursed quietly:

"Where women are concerned, I am, in every sense and tense, finished. You should give him the message yourself. If you have the balls for it, that is."

"You jest," Guadalmedina replied, shaking his head, unaffected by Quevedo's free manner of speaking. "I can't get involved in this."

"And yet you happily meddle in other affairs."

The count was stroking his mustache and beard, avoiding having to answer.

"That's enough, Quevedo. We all have our obligations, and I'm doing more than my part by warning him."

"What should I tell him, then?"

"I don't know. Tell him to aim less high. Tell him that Austria is besieging the same citadel as he."

A long and eloquent silence ensued, during which the two men regarded each other. One was wrestling with feelings of loyalty and prudence, the other with feelings of friendship and self-interest. Well placed as both men were at the time, and enjoying as they did the favor of the court, it would have been far safer, far more sensible, and more comfortable for the latter to say nothing and for the former not to listen. And yet there they were at the foot of the palace steps, exchanging anxious whispers about their friend. I was mature enough to appreciate their dilemma.

Finally, Guadalmedina shrugged and said:

"What do you expect? When the king wants something, there's nothing more to be said. He can say black is white."

I thought about this. How strange life is, I concluded. There was that lovely queen in the palace, an extremely beautiful woman who would, one would have thought, be enough to make any man happy, and yet, instead, the king chased after other women, and after mere riffraff, too: maids, actresses, serving wenches. I had no idea then that the king, despite his essentially kindly nature and his famed composure, or perhaps because of the same, was already succumbing to the two great vices which, in a few short years, would put paid to the prestige of the monarchy built up by his grandfather and great-grandfather: namely, an unbridled appetite for women and a complete indifference to affairs of state, both of which—appetite and affairs of state—he habitually left to panders and favorites to deal with.

"Is it an accomplished fact?"

"It will be in a day or so, I fear. Or before. The business with your play is helping greatly. The lady had already caught the king's eye at the theater, but then he watched the rehearsal of the first act—incognito, of course—and he was lost."

"What about the husband?"

"Oh, he knows all about it, naturally." Guadalmedina made a gesture as if patting his purse. "As keen as a knife he is, and with no scruples. This is the chance of a lifetime for him."

Quevedo shook his head sadly. He kept shooting me occasional worried glances.

"Dear God," he said.

His tone was somber, in keeping with the circumstances. I was thinking about my master, too. When it came to certain matters—and María de Castro might well be such a one—men like Captain Alatriste didn't care whether they were dealt a king or a knave.

The afternoon was drawing gently to a close, and the yellow sun's horizontal rays were casting long shadows along Carrera de San Jerónimo. At that hour, the cauldron of the Prado was seething with carriages: one caught glimpses of bejeweled hair and white hands fluttering fans, and many of the carriages were accompanied by gallant young horsemen. Opposite the garden of Juan Fernández, where the upper and lower Prado met, throngs of people were strolling about, enjoying the late sun: ladies—covered or half covered by their cloaks—clattered along in their clogs, although some were not ladies at all and never would be, whatever pretensions they might have. Likewise, many of the supposed hidalgos passing by—despite swords, capes, and the grand air they affected—had come straight from a cobbler's or a grocer's or a tailor's where they earned their daily bread with their hands. These were all perfectly honorable professions, but were, as I said, rejected as such by most Spaniards. There were, of course, genuine people of quality as well, but they were to be found near the little groves of fruit trees, the flower beds, the box maze, the waterwheel, and the garden's celebrated rustic arbor where, that afternoon, inspired by the success of Tirso's play, which was still being performed at the Corral de la Cruz, the Countesses of Olivares, Lemos, and Salvatierra and other ladies of the court had arranged to hold an informal picnic, with puff pastry cakes, made by the nuns from the Convento de las Descalzas Reales, and hot chocolate from the Augustinian monastery of Recoletos in honor of Cardinal Barberini, papal legate—and nephew— of His Holiness Urban VIII, who was visiting Madrid amidst much diplomatic salaaming from both parties and especially from him. After all, the Spanish troops were Catholicism's best defense, and, as in the days of the great Charles V, our monarchs, rather than be governed by heretics, were still prepared to lose everything—as, ultimately, they and we did. It does, nonetheless, seem paradoxical that while Spain was pouring blood and money into defending the one true religion, His Holiness was secretly undermining our power in Italy and in the rest of Europe, his agents and diplomats making pacts with our enemies. It would perhaps have concentrated minds had we sacked Rome again as the emperor's troops had done ninety-nine years before, in 1527, when we were still what we were and the mere word "Spaniard" could make the world hold its breath. Alas, these were very different times; Philip IV was certainly no match for his great-grandfather Charles; appearances tended to be preserved now through politics and diplomacy; and given the lean times ahead, it was hardly the moment for pontiffs to be hitching up their vestments and scurrying off to take refuge in Castel Sant'Angelo with the halberds of our Landsknecht soldiers tickling their arses. And that was a shame, because in the restless Europe I am describing—which contained young nations just coming into being, and older nations, like ours, with its century and a half of history—being loved would have brought us only a tenth of the advantages of being feared. Given the way things were, had we Spaniards opted to be loved, all those nations trying to cut the ground from beneath our feet—the English, the French, the Dutch, the Venetians, the Turks, et cetera—would long ago have destroyed us, and would have done so gratis. At least, by fighting for every foot of land, every league of sea, and every ounce of gold, we made the bastards pay dearly for it.

Anyway, let us return to Madrid and to his eminence, Cardinal Barberini. That afternoon, the most illustrious guests, including the pope's nephew, had long since left the gathering in the garden; however, there were still remnants of that party in the form of ladies and gentlemen of the court, people out for a stroll, enjoying the lovely gardens and the lawn near the waterwheel, and the cool drinks and dishes containing fruits and sweetmeats set out beneath the arbor awning. Outside, too, along the avenues and amongst the fountains, from San Jerónimo to Recoletos, people were promenading up and down or else taking their ease beneath the trees; there were carriages, respectable married couples, ladies of quality, doxies carrying lapdogs and pretending to be ladies, young wastrels, serving wenches from inns with nothing to lose, handsome young men on horseback, fops, vendors of limes and sweetmeats, maids and lackeys, and idle onlookers. Indeed, the scene was exactly as described, with his usual self-assurance, by an acquaintance and neighbor of ours, the poet Salas Barbadillo.

Married couples share this field,
All come t'enjoy its great appeal:
Both sexes truly like such days
When men can stare while women graze.

And we, too, were out for a leisurely afternoon stroll, the captain, don Francisco de Quevedo, and I, from the garden to the Torrecilla de la Música, where minstrels were playing, and then back up to the Prado again, beneath the shade cast by the three lines of tall poplars. My master and Quevedo were talking quietly about various private matters, and I have to confess that, although I normally listened carefully to what they said, on this occasion I had concerns of my own: that rendezvous near the palace at the hour of the angelus. This did not, however, prevent me from catching the drift of the conversation.

"You're risking your life," I heard don Francisco say, and a little farther on—the captain was walking beside him in silence, his eyes somber beneath the brim of his hat—he said it again:

"You're risking your life, you know. That particular cow bears someone else's brand."

They stopped, and I did too, by the parapet of the little bridge, in order to allow a few carriages to pass, carrying off ladies of the court and giving way to the trollops and whores who, with nightfall, would be out looking for likely lances to pierce their shields, and to loose young women, faces half covered, who, behind the backs of fathers or brothers, on the pretext of going to a late mass or on a charitable errand, and accompanied by an indulgent duenna, were off either to find or to meet some secret lover. Quevedo doffed his hat to an acquaintance in one of the carriages, then turned back to my master.

"It's as absurd as a doctor bothering to marry an old woman, when it's perfectly within his power to kill her."

The captain tugged at his mustache, unable to repress a smile, but still he said nothing.

"If you insist," said Quevedo, "you're as good as dead."

These words startled me. I studied my master's impassive aquiline profile silhouetted against the declining afternoon light.

"Well, I have no intention of simply surrendering," he said at last.

His friend looked at him, intrigued.

"Surrendering what? The woman?"

"No, my life."

There was another silence; then the poet, glancing around him, whispered something along the lines of: "You're mad, Captain. No woman is worth risking your neck for. This is a very dangerous game indeed." My master merely smoothed his mustache and said nothing more. And after uttering a few curses and "I'faith"s, don Francisco shrugged.

"Well, don't rely on me for help," he said. "I don't fight kings."

The captain looked at him again but made no comment. We walked back toward the garden's boundary walls, and shortly afterward, halfway between the Torrecilla and one of the fountains, we saw in the distance an open carriage drawn by two fine mules. I paid it no attention until I saw my master's face. I followed his gaze and saw, seated in the right-hand side of the carriage, María de Castro, all dressed up for the ride and looking very beautiful. To her left rode her diminutive husband, with his smiling, bewhiskered face; he was carrying an ivory-handled cane and wearing a gold-braided doublet and an elegant French-style beaver hat, which he was constantly having to remove to greet acquaintances along the way. He was clearly feeling delighted with life and with the excitement that he and his wife aroused.

"Were there ever two finer pairs of hands," commented don Francisco wryly, "hers for seducing and his for filching? A very elegant net for catching fish."

The captain said nothing. Some ladies clutching rosaries and wearing scapulars, robes, and full black skirts, were standing nearby with their husbands; they immediately drew into a knot, whispering and furiously fanning themselves as they shot glances at the carriage sharp as Berber arrows; meanwhile, their grave and equally black-clad husbands struggled to keep their composure, twirling their mustaches and staring at the carriage with barely concealed lust. As the actors approached, don Francisco told a story illustrating Cózar's blithe, inventive nature. In one particular scene during a performance in Ocaña, he had forgotten to bring on stage with him the dagger with which he was supposed to slit another actor's throat. When he realized his mistake, he had immediately snatched off his own false beard and pretended to strangle the other man with it. Afterward, the company had had to flee across the fields, pursued by furious townsfolk hurling stones at them.

"He's altogether a very jolly rascal," said Quevedo.

As the carriage drew nearer, Cózar recognized don Francisco and my master, and the rogue bowed very reverently, a bow in which I—trained now in courtly subtleties—saw a high degree of mockery. "With such courtesies, and with my wife," the gesture said, "I pay for my doublet and my hat, and your purse is my revenge." Or, in Quevedo's words:

> *He's more of a cuckold, he who pays,*
> *Than the man who takes the money,*
> *For I get to keep the lovely wife,*
> *The beehive, and the honey.*

As for the actor's spouse, the look and the smile that she directed at the captain spoke eloquently of very different things—complicity and promise. She made as if to cover her face with her cloak, but then did not, a gesture that was somehow more provocative than if she had done nothing; and I noticed that my master slowly and discreetly took off his hat and stood there with it in his hand until the carriage had borne the actors away down the avenue. Then he put his hat back on again, turned, and met the hate-filled gaze of don Gonzalo Moscatel, who, one hand resting on the hilt of his sword, was watching us from the other side of the avenue, angrily chewing the ends of his mustache.

"Ye gods," muttered don Francisco, "that's all we need."

The butcher was standing on the running board of a private carriage that was as elaborately decorated as a Flemish castle, with two dapple-gray mules between the shafts and a coachman on the driver's seat; inside, next to the open door on which don Gonzalo Moscatel was leaning, sat a young woman. She was the orphaned niece with whom he lived and whom he wished to see married to his friend, the lawyer Saturnino Apolo, a base and mediocre man if ever there was one, who apart from taking the bribes proper to his profession—and which were the origin of his friendship with the butcher—frequented Madrid's narrow little literary world and fancied himself a poet, which he wasn't, for his only skill lay in bleeding money out of successful authors, flattering them, and holding their chamber pot, if I may put it so, like someone playing for free in the gaming den of the Muses. He and Moscatel were as thick as thieves, and he liked to boast that he knew everyone in the world of the theater, thus fomenting the butcher's hopes with regard to María de Castro and wheedling more money out of him, meanwhile hoping to get the niece as well as her dowry. For that was his roguish specialty: living off other people's purses, so much so that don Francisco de Quevedo himself, seeing that all Madrid despised the wretch, dedicated a famous sonnet to him, which ended with these lines:

Never your lyre, always a purse you follow,
You offspring of Cacus, you bastard of Apollo!

Moscatel's young niece was very pretty, her suitor the lawyer utterly loathsome, and don Gonzalo, her uncle, absurdly jealous of her honor. The whole situation— niece, marriage, don Gonzalo's theatrical character and temperament, and his jealousy of Captain Alatriste regarding María de Castro—seemed more the stuff of plays than of real life; after all, Lope and Tirso filled the theaters with such plots. Then again, the theater owed its success precisely to the fact that it reflected what went on in the street, and the people in the street, in turn, imitated what they saw on the stage. Thus, in the thrilling, colorful theater that was my century, we Spaniards sometimes tricked ourselves out to play comedy, and sometimes to play tragedy.

"I bet *he* won't raise any objections," murmured don Francisco.

Alatriste, who was abstractedly studying Moscatel through half-closed eyes, turned to the poet.

"Objections to what?"

"To vanishing, of course, when he finds out he's been encroaching on the royal domain."

The captain smiled faintly but made no comment. From the far side of the avenue, the butcher, bristling with gravity and wounded pride, continued to shoot us murderous looks. He was wearing a short French cape, slashed sleeves, garters of the same vermilion red as the feather in his hat, and a very long sword with ornate guard and quillons. I looked at the niece. She was modest, dark-complexioned, and wore a full-skirted dress, a mantilla on her head, and a gold cross around her neck.

"I'm sure you'll agree," said a voice beside us, "that she is very pretty indeed."

We turned around, surprised. Lopito de Vega had come up behind us and there he was, thumbs hooked in the leather belt from which hung his sword, cloak wrapped about one arm, and his soldier's hat pushed slightly back over the bandage he still wore about his head. He was gazing adoringly at Moscatel's niece.

"Don't tell me," exclaimed don Francisco, "that she is *she*."

"She is."

We were all astonished, and even Captain Alatriste regarded Lope's son with a certain degree of interest.

"Does don Gonzalo Moscatel approve of your courtship?" asked don Francisco.

"No, on the contrary," the young man said, bitterly twisting the ends of his mustache. "He says his honor is sacred, et cetera. And yet half Madrid knows that as the city's supplier of meat, he's stolen money hand over fist. Nevertheless, Señor Moscatel cares only for his honor. You know—grandparents, coats of arms, ancestry . . . the usual thing."

"Well, given who he is and with a name like that, this Moscatel fellow must go back a long way."

"Oh, yes, as far back as the Goths, of course. Like everyone else."

"Alas, my friend," sighed Quevedo, "Spain the grotesque never dies."

"Well, someone should kill her, then. Listening to that fool talk, anyone would think we were still in the days of the Cid. He has sworn to kill me if he finds me loitering near his niece's window."

Don Francisco looked at Lopito with renewed interest.

"And do you or do you not loiter?"

"Do I look like a man who wouldn't loiter, Señor de Quevedo?"

And Lopito briefly described the situation to us. It was not a caprice on his part, he explained. He sincerely loved Laura Moscatel, for that was the young woman's name, and he was prepared to marry her as soon as he was given the post of ensign he was seeking. The problem was that, as a professional soldier and the son of a playwright—Lope de Vega may have been ordained as a priest, but his reputation as a rake placed the morality of the whole family in jeopardy—his chances of obtaining don Gonzalo's permission were remote indeed.

"And have you tried every possible argument?"

"I have, but without success. He refuses point-blank."

"And what if you were to stick a foot of steel through that turd of a suitor, that "Apollo"?" asked Quevedo.

"It would change nothing. Moscatel would simply engage her to another."

Don Francisco adjusted his spectacles in order to study

the young woman in the carriage more closely, then he said to the lovelorn gallant:

"Do you really wish to win her hand?"

"On my life, I do," replied the young man earnestly, "but when I went to Señor Moscatel to speak honestly and seriously with him, I was met by a couple of ruffians he had hired to frighten me off."

Captain Alatriste turned to listen, suddenly interested. This, to him, was familiar music. Quevedo arched his eyebrows in curiosity. He, too, knew a fair bit about wooings and sword fights.

"And how did you get on?" he asked.

"Quite well, really. Being a soldier and a swordsman has its uses. Besides, they weren't up to much, the ruffians. I drew my sword, which they weren't expecting; luck was on my side, and they both took to their heels. Don Gonzalo still refused to receive me, though. And when I returned that night to her window, accompanied this time by a servant who, as well as a guitar, was armed with a sword and a shield so that we would be equally matched, we found that there were now four ruffians."

"A prudent man, the butcher."

"He certainly is, and he has a large purse to pay for his prudence. They nearly sliced off my poor servant's nose, and after a few skirmishes, we decided to make ourselves scarce."

All four of us were now looking at Moscatel, who was most put out by our stares and by seeing in good company the two men who, from very different angles, were both hammering at his walls. He smoothed the fierce points of his mustache and paced back and forth a little, grasping the hilt of his sword as if he could barely keep himself from coming over and cutting us to pieces. In the end, he furiously fastened the curtain at the carriage window, thus hiding his niece from view, then gave orders to the coachman as he himself got into the carriage, drew up the running board, and drove off up the avenue, cutting a broad swathe through the crowds.

"He's a real dog in the manger," said Lopito sadly. "He doesn't want to eat, but he doesn't want anyone else to eat either."

Were all love affairs so difficult? I was pondering this question that very night, while I waited, leaning against the wall of the Puerta de la Priora, staring into the darkness that extended beyond the bridge toward the Camino de Aravaca and into the trees in the neighboring gardens. The nearness of Leganitos Stream and the river Manzanares had a cooling effect. I had my cloak wrapped about me—concealing the dagger tucked in my belt at the back and the short sword at my waist—but that wasn't enough to keep me warm. I preferred, however, not to move in case I caught the eye of some marauding group, whether curious or criminal, trying to scrape a living in that solitary place. And so there I stayed, like part of the shadow cast by the wall, alongside the door of the passageway that connected the Convento de la Encarnación, the Plaza de la Priora, and the riding school, linking the north wing of the Alcázar Real to the outskirts of the city. Waiting.

I was, as I said, pondering the problematic nature of love affairs, *all* love affairs it seemed to me then, and thinking how strange women were, capable of captivating a man and leading him to such extremes that he would risk money, honor, freedom, and life. There was I, no mere foolish boy, at dead of night, armed to the teeth like some lout from La Heria, exposed to all kinds of danger and not knowing what the devil the devil wanted of me, and all because a girl with blue eyes and fair hair had scribbled me two lines: *If you are gentleman enough to escort a lady* . . . Every woman knows how to look after herself. Even the most stupid woman can apply those skills, without even realizing that she is. No astute man of the law, no memorialist, no petitioner at court can better them when it comes to appealing to a man's purse, vanity, chivalry, or stupidity. A woman's weapons. Wise, experienced, lucid don Francisco de Quevedo filled pages and pages with words on the subject:

You are very like the blade of a sword:
You kill more when bare than clothed.

The angelus bell at the Convento de la Encarnación rang out, and this was immediately followed, like an echo, by the bell from San Agustín, whose tower could be seen among the dark rooftops, bright in the light of the half-moon. I crossed myself and, before the last chime had even faded away, heard the door to the passageway creak open. I held my breath. Then, very cautiously, I pushed back my cloak to free the hilt of my sword, just in case, and turning in the direction of the noise, glimpsed a lantern which, before it was withdrawn, lit up from behind a slender figure that slipped quickly out, shutting the door behind it. This confused me, because the figure I had seen was that of an agile young man, with no cloak, but dressed all in black and with the unmistakable glint of a dagger at his waist. This was not what I had expected, far from it. And so I did the only sensible thing I could at that hour of night and in that place: quick as a squirrel, I grabbed my dagger and pressed the point to the new arrival's chest.

"Another step," I whispered, "and I'll nail you to the door."

Then I heard Angélica de Alquézar laugh.

4. CALLE DE LOS PELIGROS

"We're getting close," she said.

We were walking along in the dark, guiding ourselves by the moonlight that filled the way ahead with the cut-out shapes of rooftops and projected our own shadows onto the rough ground that ran with streams of grubby water and filth. We were speaking in whispers, and our footsteps echoed in the empty streets.

"Close to what?" I asked.

"Close."

We had left behind us the Convento de la Encarnación and were approaching the little Plaza de Santo Domingo, presided over by the sinister bulk of the monastery occupied by the monks of the Holy Office. There was no one to be seen near the old fountain, and the fruit and vegetable stalls were, of course, bare. A guttering lamp above an image of the Virgin lit up the corner of Calle de San Bernardo beyond.

"Do you know the Tavern of the Dog?" asked Angélica.

I stopped and, after a few steps, so did she. By the light of the moon, I could see her man's costume, the tight doublet concealing all feminine curves, her fair hair caught up beneath a felt cap, the metallic glint of the dagger at her waist.

"Why have you stopped?" she asked.

"I never imagined I would hear the name of that inn on your lips."

"There are, I'm afraid, far too many things you have never imagined. But don't worry, I won't ask you to go in."

This reassured me somewhat, but not much. The Tavern of the Dog was a place even I would tremble to enter, for it was a meeting place for whores, ruffians, louts, and other passing trade. The quarter itself, Santo Domingo and San Bernardo, was a perfectly reputable area, inhabited by respectable people; however, the narrow alleyway where the inn was to be found—between Calle de Tudescos and Calle de Silva—was a kind of pustule that none of the neighbors' protests could burst.

"Do you know the inn or don't you?"

I said that I did, but avoided going into further detail. I had been there once with Captain Alatriste and don Francisco de Quevedo when the poet was in search of inspiration and looking for fresh material for his lighter verse. "The Dog" was the illustrative nickname given to the owner of the tavern, who sold hippocras, an infamous and extremely expensive cordial whose consumption was forbidden by various decrees, because, in order to make the drink more cheaply, its manufacturers routinely adulterated it with alum stone, waste matter, and other substances harmful to the health. Despite this, it continued to be drunk clandestinely, and since any prohibition brings wealth to those tradesman who flouts it, the Dog sold his particular brand of rat poison at twenty-five *maravedís* for half a quart—which was very good business indeed.

"Is there a place where we could keep watch on the tavern?"

I tried to remember. It was a short, gloomy street which at various points—by a crumbling wall, say, or around some hidden corner—would be pitch-black at night. The only problem, I explained, was that such places might be occupied by trulls.

"Trulls?"

"Whores."

I felt a kind of cruel pleasure in using such words, as if this gave me back a little of the initiative which she seemed determined to seize. Angélica de Alquézar did not, after all, know everything. Besides, she may have been dressed as a man, and be very brave indeed, but in Madrid, and at night, I was in my element and she was not. The sword hanging from *my* belt was not an ornament.

"Oh," she said.

This restored my composure. I might be head over heels in love, but this in no way diminished me, and, I concluded, it was no bad thing to make this clear.

"Tell me what exactly you're up to and where I fit in."

"Later," she said and set off with determined step.

I stayed where I was. After going only a short distance, she stopped and turned.

"Tell me," I insisted, "or you're on your own."

"You wouldn't do that."

She was standing there defiantly, a black shape in male costume, one hand resting casually on the belt on which she wore her dagger. I counted to ten, then spun round and strode away. Six, seven, eight steps. I was cursing inside and my heart was breaking. She was letting me leave, and I could not go back.

"Wait," she said.

I stopped, much relieved. I heard her footsteps approaching, felt her hand on my arm. When I turned, her eyes were lit by a ray of moonlight slipping between the eaves. I thought I could smell fresh bread. It was her. Yes, she smelled of fresh bread.

"I need an escort," she said.

"But why me?"

"Because there's no one else I can trust."

It sounded like the truth. It sounded like a lie. It sounded probable and improbable, possible and impossible, and the fact is, I didn't care. She was close. Very close. If I had reached out a hand, I could have touched her body, her face.

"There's a man I have to watch," she said.

I stared at her in astonishment. What was a maid of honor from the court doing out alone in the dangerous Madrid night, keeping watch on a man? On whose orders? The sinister figure of her uncle, the royal secretary, came into my mind. I was, I realized, getting drawn in again. Angélica was the niece of one of Captain Alatriste's mortal enemies; she was the same girl-woman who, three years before, had led me to the Inquisition's dungeons and, almost, to the stake.

"You must take me for a fool."

She said nothing, and the oval of her face was like a pale stain in the darkness, although there was still that glint of moonlight in her eyes. I noticed that she was edging closer and closer. Her body was so near now that the guard of her dagger was digging into my thigh.

"Once I told you that I loved you," she whispered.

And she kissed me on the mouth.

The only sources of light in the alleyway were a lit window and the grubby, smoky glow from a torch fixed in a ring on the wall next to the tavern door. Everything else lay in darkness, which meant that it was easy to melt into the shadow provided by a dilapidated wall that gave onto an abandoned garden. We positioned ourselves where we could see the door and window of the tavern. At the other end of the street, in the neighboring gloom of Calle de Tudescos, we could see a few ladies of the night casting their bait—with little success. Now and then, men, singly or in groups, would enter or leave the inn. Voices and laughter emerged from inside, and occasionally we caught a line from a song or the sound of a chaconne being strummed on a guitar. A drunk staggered over to where we were sitting in order to relieve himself and got the devil of a fright when I unsheathed my dagger, held it between his eyes, and told him in no uncertain terms to take himself and his bladder elsewhere. He must have assumed we were engaged in carnal business, because he said nothing, but stumbled off, weaving from one side of the street to another. Close by me, Angélica de Alquézar, vastly amused, was trying not to laugh.

"He took us for something we're not," she said, "and thought we were doing something we're not."

She seemed delighted with the whole situation—the strange place, the late hour, the danger. Perhaps, or so I wanted to believe, she was equally delighted to have me as her companion. Earlier, we had seen the night watch in the distance: a constable and four catchpoles armed with shields and swords and carrying a lantern. This had obliged us to take a different route, first, because the use of a sword by a boy of my years, just below the decreed limit, might be taken ill by the law. A far more serious danger, however, was the fact that Angélica's male costume would not have survived scrutiny by the catchpoles, and such an event, while pleasant and amusing in a stage play, could have grave consequences in real life. The wearing of men's clothes by women was strictly forbidden and was sometimes even banned in the theater. Indeed, it was only allowed if the actress was playing the part of a wronged or dishonored maiden—like Petronila and Tomasa in *The Garden of Juan Fernández* or Juana in *Don Gil of the Green Breeches* (both by Tirso), or Clavela in Lope's *The Little French Maid*, and other such delicious characters in similar situations—who had a genuine excuse for going in search of their honor and of marriage and were not disguising themselves for vicious, capricious, or whorish reasons.

> *Don't pretend to be so shocked,*
> *And take away that frown;*
> *I am a mermaid from the sea*
> *And thus a fish—waist down!*

This zealous desire to regulate clothing came not only from the prudes and hypocrites who later filled the bawdy houses (although that's another story) but from the Church, which, through the offices of royal confessors, bishops, priests, and nuns (and we have always had more of them than a muleteers' inn has bedbugs and ticks), was striving to save our souls and to stop the devil getting his own way, so much so that wearing men's apparel came to be considered an aggravating factor when sending women to the stake in autos-da-fé. Yes, even the Holy Office of the Inquisition had a hand in the matter, as it did—and, indeed, still has—in so many aspects of life in this poor wretched Spain of ours.

That night, however, I was not feeling in the least wretched, hidden there in the shadows with Angélica de Alquézar, opposite the Tavern of the Dog. We were sitting on my cloak, waiting, and now and then our bodies touched. She was looking at the door of the inn, and I was looking at her, and sometimes, when she moved, the spluttering torch on the wall opposite would illuminate her profile, the whiteness of her skin, a few locks of blond hair escaping from beneath her felt cap. In her tight-fitting doublet and breeches, she resembled a young page, but that impression was given the lie when a brighter light fell upon her pale, fixed, resolute gaze. Occasionally, she appeared to be studying me with great calm and penetration, peering into the innermost recesses of my soul. And when she had finished, and before she resumed her watch on the inn door, the lovely line of her mouth would curve into a smile.

"Tell me something about yourself," she said suddenly.

I placed my sword between my legs and sat for a while, nonplussed, not knowing what to say. Finally, I spoke about the first time I had seen her, in Calle de Toledo, when she was still little more than a child. I spoke about the Fuente del Acero, the dungeons of the Inquisition, the shame of the auto-da-fé, about her letter to me in Flanders, about how I had thought of her when the Dutch charged us at the Ruyter Mill and at the Terheyden barracks, while I was running after Captain Alatriste, carrying the flag, convinced that I was going to die.

"What is war like?"

She seemed to be paying close attention to my mouth, to me or to my words. I suddenly felt very grown-up. Almost old.

"Dirty," I said simply. "Dirty and gray."

She shook her head slowly, as if pondering this thought. Then she asked me to go on talking, and the dirt and the grayness were relegated to just one part of my memory. I rested my chin on the hilt of my sword and talked more about us—her and me. About our meeting in the Alcázar in Seville and the ambush she had led me into next to the pillars of Hercules. About our first kiss as I stood on the running board of her carriage, moments before I had to fight for my life with Gualterio Malatesta. That, more or less, is what I said. No words of love, no feelings. I merely described our meetings, the part of my life that had to do with her, and I did so with as much equanimity as possible, detail by detail, just as I remembered it and always would.

"Don't you believe that I love you?" she said.

We gazed at each other for what seemed like centuries, and my head started to swim as if I had drunk a potion. I opened my mouth to say something—although quite what I didn't know—or to kiss her perhaps. Not the kind of kiss she had given me in the Plaza de Santo Domingo, but a long, hard kiss, filled with a simultaneous desire to bite and caress, and with all the vigor of youth about to burst in my veins. And she smiled at me, her lips only inches from my mouth, with the serene certainty of someone who knows and waits and is capable of transforming mere chance into a man's inevitable fate, as if long before I was born, everything had been written down in an ancient book which she kept in her possession.

"Yes, I believe . . ." I started to say.

Then her expression changed. Her eyes shifted rapidly back to the tavern door, and I followed her gaze. Two men had come out into the street, hats pulled down low over their eyes; there was a furtive air about them as they put on their cloaks. One of them was wearing a yellow doublet.

We followed them cautiously through the dark city streets. We did our best not to make a noise as we walked, trying not to lose sight of their black shapes ahead of us. Fortunately, they suspected nothing and followed a clear route: from Calle de Tudescos to Calle de la Verónica, and from there to Postigo de San Martín, which they followed as far as San Luis de los Franceses. There they paused to doff their hats to a priest who was just coming out of the church, accompanied by an altar boy and a page bearing a lantern, obviously setting out to give someone the last rites. In the brief light cast by that lantern, I had a chance to study the two men we were following: apart from his eyes, the face of the man in the yellow doublet was entirely hidden by his black hat and cloak; he was wearing shoes and hose, and when he removed his hat, I noticed that he had fair hair. The other man was wearing a featherless hat, boots, and a gray cloak, which his sword lifted up behind; and as he was leaving the Tavern of the Dog, I caught a glimpse of his belt and noticed that, as well as the sword buckled on over his thick jerkin, he had a fine pair of pistols, too.

"They look like dangerous men," I whispered to Angélica.

"And does that worry you?"

I was too offended to reply. The men continued walking, and we followed behind. A little farther on, in San Luis, next to the stone cross that still marks the site of one of the city's old gates, we passed the stalls where they sold bread or food and drinks during the day; they were all closed and there was not a soul in sight. In Calle del Caballero de Gracia, the men stopped in a doorway to avoid a light advancing toward them; as the light passed us, we saw that it was a midwife hurrying to assist at a birth, her path lit by a nervous, harried husband. Then the two men continued on, always keeping to the part of the street where the moonlight did not reach. We pursued them for a fair distance through dark streets, past barred windows with shutters or lowered blinds, past startled cats, past the oily flames of candles in niches containing images of the Virgin or of saints, and, in the distance, we caught the occasional warning cry of someone emptying a chamber pot into the street. From an alleyway came the sound of clashing steel, of furious fighting, and the two men stopped to listen; the incident clearly held no interest for them, however, because they did not linger. When Angélica and I reached the same spot, a figure, his cloak masking his face, ran past us, sword in hand. I peered cautiously down the alley and saw nothing but more barred windows and flowerpots; then I heard someone at the far end moan. I sheathed my sword—I had whisked it out at the sight of the fugitive—and made as if to go to the aid of the wounded man, but Angélica gripped my arm.

"It's not our business."

"But someone might be dying," I protested.

"We'll all die one day."

And she strode off after the two men, obliging me to follow her through the dark city. For that was how it was in Madrid at night: dark, uncertain, and threatening.

We followed the men as far as a house in the narrow upper part of Calle de los Peligros, halfway between Calle del Caballero de Gracia and the Convento de las Vallecas. Angélica and I stood in the street, unsure what to do, until she suggested that we take shelter beneath an arcade. We sat down on a bench hidden behind a stone pillar. It was getting colder and so I offered her my cloak, which she had already refused twice. This time she accepted, on condition that it serve to cover us both. And so I placed it over my shoulders and hers, which meant, of course, that we had to sit very close. You can imagine my state of mind. Head spinning, I sat resting my hands on the guard of my sword, filled by an inner excitement that prevented me from stringing two thoughts together. She, with lovely ease, kept watch on the house opposite. She seemed tenser now, but still showed a serenity and self-control admirable in a girl of her age and social class. We talked quietly, our shoulders touching. She still would not tell me what we were doing there.

"Later," she would say each time I asked.

The roof of the arcade hid the moon, and her face was in shadow, a dark profile at my side. I was aware of the warmth of her body. I felt like someone who has willingly placed his neck in the hangman's noose, but I didn't care a jot. Angélica was beside me, and I would not have changed places with the safest, happiest man on earth.

"It isn't really important," I insisted. "I'd just like to know more."

"About what?"

"About this madness you're involved in."

A mischievous silence ensued. Then she said gleefully:

"And in which you're now involved too."

"That's precisely what worries me: not knowing what it is I'm involved in."

"You'll find out."

"I'm sure I will, but the last time that happened, I found myself surrounded by half a dozen killers, and the time before that, I ended up in one of the Inquisition's dungeons."

"I thought you were a bright, bold lad, Señor Balboa. Don't you trust me?"

I hesitated before responding. This is what the devil does, I thought, he toys with people, with ambition, vanity, lust, fear. Even with people's hearts. It is written: "All these things will I give you, if you fall down and worship me." An intelligent devil doesn't need to lie.

"Of course I trust you," I said.

I heard her laugh softly. Then she moved a little closer to me under the cloak.

"You're a fool," she concluded very sweetly.

And she kissed me again, or, to be exact, we kissed each other, not once, but many times; and I put my arm around her shoulders and tentatively caressed her neck and shoulders and then, when she offered no resistance, I ran my hand very gently over the female curves beneath her velvet doublet. She laughed softly, her lips still pressed to mine, coming closer, then drawing back when my desire grew too intense. I swear to you, dear reader, that even if I had seen the fires of hell before me, I would have followed Angélica without a tremor, wherever she chose to lead me, prepared to defend her with my sword and to snatch her from the arms of Lucifer himself. At the risk, or, rather, the certainty of eternal damnation.

All of a sudden she pulled away. One of the two men had come out into the street. I threw off the cloak and stood up in order to get a better view. The man remained utterly still, as if watching or waiting. He remained like that for a while, then began pacing up and down, and I feared he might see us. Finally, his attention seemed to focus on the far end of the street. I followed his gaze and saw the silhouette of someone approaching, wearing hat, long cloak, and sword. He was walking down the middle of the street, as if he distrusted the shadows cast by the walls. He kept walking until he reached the other man. I noticed that his pace gradually slackened until they were both standing face-to-face. There was something about the way the second man moved that was familiar to me, especially the way in which he folded back his cloak to free up his sword. I stepped forward slightly, keeping close to the stone pillar, so that I could see more clearly. In the moonlight, I was astonished to discover that the new arrival was Captain Alatriste.

The first man, the stranger, was still there in the middle of the street, his cloak enveloping his face so that only his eyes were visible beneath the brim of his hat. In response, Diego Alatriste folded his cloak back over his left shoulder. His hand was already lightly touching the hilt of his sword when he stopped in front of the man blocking his way. He studied him with a practiced eye, calm, silent. If he's alone, he decided, he's either very brave, a professional swordsman, or else he's carrying a pistol. Or perhaps all three. And at worst, he concluded, looking out of the corner of his eye, there are other men nearby. The question was this: Was he waiting for him or for someone else? At that hour, and outside that particular house, there was little doubt about the matter. It wasn't Gonzalo Moscatel.

The butcher was burlier and broader, and, in any case, he wasn't the kind of man to resolve these things in person. Perhaps the fellow was a hired killer earning his daily bread, although he must be very good indeed, Alatriste thought, if, knowing, as he must, who he was waiting for, he had brought no one with him to help.

"Come no farther, sir," said the stranger.

These words were spoken in a surprisingly educated and very polite voice, slightly muffled by the cloak.

"Says who?" asked Alatriste.

"Someone who can."

This was not a good start. The captain smoothed his mustache and then lowered his hand so that it rested on the large brass buckle of his belt. There seemed little point in prolonging the conversation. The only question was whether or not the rogue was alone. He cast another quick glance to right and left. There was something very odd about all this.

"To business, then," he said, unsheathing his sword.

The other man did not even push back his cloak. He stood very still with his back to the moonlight, looking at the captain's bare glinting blade.

"I don't want to fight with you," he said.

He did not bother to call him "sir" this time. He was either someone who knew him well or was foolish enough to provoke him by this lack of respect.

"Why not?"

"Because it doesn't suit me to do so."

Alatriste raised his sword and leveled the tip at the other man's face.

"Come on," he said, "fight, damn you."

Seeing the steel tip so near, the stranger retreated and folded back his cloak. His face was still concealed by the shadow cast by the brim of his hat, but Alatriste could now see what weapons he had on him. He had not one pistol at his waist, but two. And his jerkin appeared to be double in thickness. "He's either a fully fledged ruffian or an exceptionally prudent gentleman," Alatriste concluded. "He's certainly no lamb to the slaughter. If he so much as touches the handle of one of those pistols, I'll stick a foot of steel through his throat before he can say a word."

"I'm not going to fight with you, my friend," said the other man.

"He's making it very easy for me," thought the captain. "Now he's addressing me as 'friend.' He's giving me the perfect motive to skewer him, unless that familiar tone of voice has some justification and I know him well enough for him to poke his nose into my business and my nocturnal affairs and get away with it. Besides, it's late. Let's finish the business now."

He settled his hat more firmly on his head and undid the clasp of his cloak, letting his cloak fall to the ground.

Then he took a step forward, ready to attack, keeping a close eye on his opponent's pistols and meanwhile reaching with his left hand for his dagger. Seeing Alatriste closing on him, the other man took another step back.

"For heaven's sake, Alatriste," he muttered. "Do you still not know who I am?"

The tone this time was angry, even arrogant, and now the captain thought he recognized that voice, unmuffled now by the cloak. He hesitated and withheld the sword-thrust he was aching to make.

"Is that you, Count?"

"The same."

There was a long silence. It was Guadalmedina in person. Still keeping hold of sword and knife, Alatriste was trying to make sense of this new situation.

"And what the devil," he said at last, "are you doing here?"

"Trying to prevent you from ruining your life."

Another silence. Alatriste was thinking about what the count had just said. Quevedo's warnings and various other clues all fitted perfectly. Christ's blood! Given what a large place the world was, what bad luck to have met with such a rival. And as if that were not enough, there was Guadalmedina in the middle, as intermediary.

"My life is my business," he retorted.

"And that of your friends?"

"Tell me why I can't come any farther."

"I can't do that."

Alatriste shook his head thoughtfully, then looked at his sword and his dagger. "We are what we are," he thought. "My reputation is all, and I have no other."

"I'm expected," he said.

The count remained impassive. He was a skilled swordsman, as the captain knew all too well: steady on his feet and quick with his hand, and with that cold, scornful brand of courage favored by the Spanish nobility. Naturally, he wasn't as good as the captain, but chance and darkness always left room for the unexpected. In addition to which, he had two pistols.

"Your place has been taken," said Guadalmedina.

"I'd rather find that out for myself."

"You'll have to kill me first, or let me kill you."

He had said this with no hint of boastfulness or menace, he was simply stating an inevitable fact, like one friend confiding quietly in another. The count was also what he was, and had his and other people's reputations to protect.

Alatriste replied in the same tone:

"Don't make me do this."

And he took a step forward. The count stayed where he was, his sword still in its sheath, but with the two pistols in his belt clearly visible. And he knew how to use them. Alatriste had seen him do so only a few months before, in Seville, to dispatch a constable without even giving him time to make his confession.

"She's only a woman," said Guadalmedina. "There are

hundreds of women in Madrid." His tone was friendly, re-assuring. "Are you going to ruin your life for an actress?"

The captain took a while to reply.

"It doesn't matter who she is," he said at last. "That's the least of it."

The count gave a sad sigh, as if he had known what the captain's answer would be. Then he took out his sword and adopted the en garde position, his left hand hovering near the handle of one of his pistols. Alatriste raised both his weapons, resigned to his fate, knowing as he did so that the ground was opening up at his feet.

When I saw the stranger unsheathe his sword—at that distance, I still did not know who he was, even though his face was now uncovered—I took a step forward, but Angélica grabbed me and forced me to remain hidden behind the pillar.

"It's not our affair," she whispered.

I looked at her as if she were mad.

"What are you talking about?" I exclaimed. "That's Captain Alatriste."

She didn't appear in the least surprised. Her grip on my arm tightened.

"And do you want him to know that we've been spying on him?"

That gave me pause for thought. How could I explain to the captain what I was doing there at that hour of the night?

"If you leave, you'll be betraying me," added Angélica. "Your friend Batiste is quite capable of resolving his own affairs."

"What's going on," I asked myself, bewildered. "What's happening here, and what have I and the captain to do with it all? What has she got to do with it?"

"Besides, you can't leave me here alone," she said.

My mind fogged. She was still clinging to my arm, so close that I could feel her breath on my face. I felt ashamed not to go to my master's aid, but if I abandoned Angélica, or betrayed her presence there, I would feel another kind of shame. A wave of heat rushed to my face. I rested my forehead on the cold stone while, with my eyes, I devoured the scene being played out in the street. I was thinking about the pistols I had seen tucked in the belt of the man when he left the Tavern of the Dog, and that worried me greatly. Even the best blade in the world was helpless against a bullet fired from four feet away.

"I have to leave you," I said to Angélica.

"Don't even consider it."

Her tone had changed from plea to warning, but my thoughts were fixed now on what was going on there right before my eyes. After a pause during which both men, sword in hand, stared at each other without moving, my master finally took a step forward and they touched blades. At that point, I wrested myself from Angélica's grasp, unsheathed my sword, and went to the captain's aid.

Diego Alatriste heard footsteps running toward him and thought to himself that Guadalmedina was not, after all, alone, and that, what with the pistol the latter was now holding in his hand, things were clearly about to get very nasty indeed. "I'd better look sharp," he decided, "or I'll be done for." His opponent was defending himself with his sword and moving steadily backward, waiting for a chance to cock and fire the pistol he was holding in his other hand. Fortunately for Alatriste, this operation required two hands, and so he dealt a high slicing thrust to keep the count's right hand busy, while he considered the best way to wound and, if possible, not to kill. Those other footsteps were coming nearer; his next move would require great skill, for his life depended on it. He made a stabbing movement with his dagger, then pretended to step back, thus apparently giving Guadalmedina the space he needed; and just when the latter thought he had time to cock his pistol and lowered his sword hand in order to grip the barrel, the captain lunged at that arm, causing the pistol to fall to the ground and the count to go reeling backward, cursing. "I think I hit flesh," thought Alatriste; then again, the count was cursing rather than moaning, although in men of their kind, cursing and moaning were one and the same. Meanwhile, there was the third party in the dispute to deal with, a shadow running forward, a flash of steel in its hand; and Alatriste realized that Guadalmedina, who had another pistol in his belt, still posed a mortal danger. "I must finish it," he decided, "now." The count had also heard the approaching footsteps, yet he looked bewildered rather than cheered. He glanced behind him, losing precious time, and before he could compose himself, Alatriste—taking advantage of that moment, and still conscious of the other man running toward him—calculated the distance with expert eye, made a low feint toward Guadalmedina's groin, and when the count, caught off guard, desperately parried, he raised his sword again, ready to lunge forward either to wound or to kill, he no longer cared.

"Captain!" I shouted.

I didn't want him to run me through in the darkness, before he could recognize me. I saw him stop, sword raised, staring at me, and saw his opponent do the same. I pointed my blade at the latter, who, finding himself attacked from behind, drew aside, evidently confused, but still defending himself as best he could.

"For the love of God, Alatriste," he said, "what are you doing getting the boy involved in all this?"

I froze when I heard that voice. I lowered my sword, staring at my master's opponent, whose face I could now see in the moonlight.

"What are *you* doing here?" the captain asked me.

His voice sounded as sharp and metallic as his sword. I suddenly felt terribly hot, and beneath my doublet my sweat-drenched shirt stuck to my body. The night was spinning around and around inside and outside my head.

"I thought . . ." I stuttered.

"Just what did you think?"

I fell silent, embarrassed and incapable of saying another word. Guadalmedina was watching us in astonishment. He was clasping his sword under his right arm and painfully clutching the upper part of his left arm.

"You're mad, Alatriste," he said.

I saw the captain raise the hand holding the dagger, as if asking for time to think. From beneath the broad brim of his hat, his pale, steely eyes drilled into me.

"What are you doing here?" he asked again.

The tone in which he spoke was so murderous, I swear I felt afraid.

"I followed you," I lied.

I swallowed hard. I imagined Angélica hidden in the arcade, watching me from a distance. Or perhaps she had left already. My pathetic thread of a voice grew stronger.

"I was afraid something bad might happen to you."

"You're mad, both of you," commented Guadalmedina.

Nevertheless, he seemed relieved, as if my presence offered him an unexpected way out of this episode, an honorable solution, whereas before the only one had been for them to cut each other to pieces.

"It would," he said, "be in everyone's best interests to be reasonable."

"And what do you mean by that?" asked the captain.

The count glanced over at the house, which was still silent and in darkness. Then he shrugged.

"Let's leave things as they are for tonight."

That "for tonight" spoke volumes. I realized, sadly, that, for Guadalmedina, the house in Calle de los Peligros and the reason for the dispute were of little importance now. He and Diego Alatriste had exchanged sword thrusts, and that brought with it certain obligations. It broke certain rules and implied certain duties. The fight was postponed for the moment, but not forgotten. Despite their long friendship, Álvaro de la Marca was who he was, and his opponent was a mere soldier who possessed only his sword and not even a patch of ground to call his grave. After what had happened, anyone else in the count's position would have had the captain clapped in irons and thrown in a dungeon, or else consigned to the galleys, if, that is, he managed to resist the impulse to have him murdered. Álvaro de la Marca, however, was made of sterner stuff. Perhaps, like

Captain Alatriste, he thought that once words or blades have been unsheathed it was impossible simply to return them to the scabbard. It could all be sorted out later on, calmly and in the appropriate place, where they would have only themselves to consider.

The captain was looking at me, and his eyes still shone in the darkness. Finally, and very slowly, as if mulling something over, he put away both sword and dagger. He exchanged a silent look with Guadalmedina, then placed one hand on my shoulder.

"Don't do that again," he said sullenly.

His iron fingers were gripping my shoulder so tightly they hurt. He brought his face close to mine and looked at me hard, his aquiline nose prominent above his mustache. He smelled as he always did, of leather and wine and metal. I tried to free myself, but he did not loosen his grip.

"Don't ever follow me again," he said. "Ever."

And inside, I writhed in shame and remorse.

5. WINE FROM ESQUIVIAS

I felt even worse the following day as I watched Captain Alatriste where he sat at the door of the Tavern of the Turk. He was perched on a stool beside a table laid with a jug of wine, a plate of sausages, and a book—it was, I seem to remember, *The Life of Squire Marcos de Obregón*—which he had not opened all morning. He wore his doublet unfastened and his shirt open and was sitting with his back against the wall; his sea-green eyes, paler still in the morning light, were fixed on some indeterminate spot in Calle de Toledo. I was trying to keep my distance, for I still felt bitterly ashamed of having so disloyally lied to him, something that would never have happened had it not been for that woman, or girl, or whatever you wish to call her, who could so addle my brains that I no longer knew what I was doing. With my teacher Pérez—to whom the captain continued to entrust my education—I was, appropriately enough, currently engaged on translating the passage from Homer in which Ulysses is tempted by the Sirens. In short, I spent the morning avoiding my master and running various errands: buying candles, flint, and tinder for Caridad la Lebrijana, some sweet almond oil from Tuerto Fadrique's pharmacy, and visiting the nearby Jesuit college to take my teacher a basket of clean linen. Now, with nothing to do, I was loitering on the corner of Calle del Arcabuz and Calle de Toledo, watching the passing carriages and the carts carrying merchandise to the Plaza Mayor, the heavy-laden mules and the water-sellers' donkeys tethered to the railings at windows—both mules and donkeys, of course, depositing their excrement on the roughly paved street that was already running with filthy water from the sewers. I occasionally glanced over at the captain, but found him always in the same pose—motionless and thoughtful. Twice I saw La Lebrijana—bare-armed and in her apron—peer out at him, then go back inside again without saying a word.

As you know, these were not happy times for her. The captain responded to her complaints with only monosyllables or silence, and if the good woman ever raised her voice to him, my master would simply take hat, cloak, and sword and go for a walk. Once, he returned from such a walk to find the trunk containing his few possessions at the foot of

the stairs. He stood looking at it for a while, then went upstairs, closed the door behind him, and, after much talk, La
Lebrijana finally stopped shouting. Shortly afterward, the
captain, in his shirt, appeared on the gallery that gave onto
the courtyard and told me to bring the trunk up to him. I
did as he asked, and things appeared to return to normal,
for from my room that night, I heard La Lebrijana moan
like a bitch in heat. After a couple of days, though, her
eyes were once again red and tear-filled, and the whole
business started again and continued thus until the day I
am describing now, the day after my master's fight with Álvaro de la Marca in Calle de los Peligros. The captain and
I both suspected that a storm was brewing, but neither of
us could have imagined how seriously things were about to
go wrong. Compared with what awaited us, the captain's
rows with La Lebrijana were like one of those frothy in-
terludes penned by Quiñones de Benavente.

A burly, broad-shouldered shadow in hat and cape loomed
over the table just as Captain Alatriste was reaching for
the jug of wine.

"Good morning, Diego."

As usual, and despite the early hour, Martín Saldaña,
lieutenant of constables, was armed with sword and dagger. Both his profession and his own nature had taught him

not to trust even the shadow he himself had just cast over the table of his old comrade from Flanders, and so he had about him, as well as sword, dagger, and poniard, a couple of Milan pistols, too. This panoply of arms was completed by a thick buffcoat and the staff of office he wore stuck in his belt.

"Can we talk?"

Alatriste looked first at him, then at his own belt, which was lying on the ground, by the wall, wrapped around his sword and dagger.

"In your role as lieutenant of constables or as a friend?" he asked coolly.

"Christ's blood, Diego, be serious, man!"

The captain regarded his friend's bearded face, and the scars, which all had the same origin as his own. The beard, he remembered vividly, half concealed the mark left by a blow delivered twenty years before, during an attack on the city walls of Ostend. The scar on Saldaña's cheek and the one on Alatriste's forehead, above his left eyebrow, dated from that same day.

"All right," he said, "we can talk."

They walked up toward Plaza Mayor, under the arcade that occupies the latter part of Calle de Toledo. They were as silent as if they had both been hauled up before a notary, with Saldaña putting off saying what he had to say and Alatriste in no hurry to find out. The captain had fastened his doublet and put on his hat with its faded red feather; he wore the lower half of his cloak caught up and draped over his arm, and on his left side, his sword clanked against his dagger.

"It's a delicate matter," said Saldaña at last.

"I imagined it was from the look on your face."

They eyed each other intently for a moment, then continued on past some gypsy women who were dancing in the shade of the arcade. The Plaza Mayor—with its tall houses, lozenge-shaped roof tiles, and the gilded ironwork on the Casa de la Panadería glittering in the sunlight—was packed with whores and errand boys and ordinary passersby, who strolled amongst carts and crates of fruit and vegetables, past bread stalls with nets placed over the loaves to protect them from thieves, past barrels of wine— "No water added—guaranteed," cried the vendors. Shopkeepers stood at the doors of the shops and in front of the stalls that filled the areas under the arches. Rotten vegetables were piled up on the ground along with horse droppings, and the buzzing of swarms of flies mingled with the cries of those selling their various wares: "Eggs and milk—fresh today!" "Juicy cantaloupe melons!" "Asparagus—soft as butter!" "Buy some tender green beans and get a bunch of parsley free!" They headed over to the

right-hand side of the square, avoiding the sellers of hemp
and esparto, whose stalls filled the square as far as Calle
Imperial.

"I don't honestly know where to start, Diego."

"Just get straight to the point."

Saldaña, as slow as ever, took off his hat and ran one
hand over his bald pate.

"I've been told to give you a warning."

"Who by?"

"It doesn't matter who. What matters is that it comes
from high enough up for you to pay due attention. If you
don't, you could lose life or liberty."

"You're scaring me."

"This is no joke, damn it. I'm serious."

"And where do you fit in?"

Saldaña put his hat back on, waved distractedly to some
catchpoles chatting by the Portal de la Carne, and again
shrugged.

"Look, Diego. Possibly, despite yourself, you have friends
without whom you should by rights be lying in an alleyway
with your throat slit, or in prison somewhere with your legs
in irons. The matter was discussed in some detail very early
this morning, until someone recalled a service you had ren-
dered in Cádiz or somewhere. I've no idea what it was, nor do
I care, but I swear that if that someone hadn't spoken up in
your favor, I wouldn't be here on my own, but accompanied
by a lot of other men armed to the teeth. Do you follow?"

"I follow."

"Are you going to see that woman again?"

"I don't know."

"Oh, please, for the love of all that's holy, don't be so stupid."

They walked a little way in silence. Finally, outside Gaspar Sánchez's cake shop, next to the arch, Saldaña stopped and took a sealed letter from his purse.

"Enough talking. Let this letter speak for itself."

Alatriste took the note and studied it, turning it around in his fingers. There was nothing written on the outside, not a name or a word. He broke the seal, unfolded the piece of paper, and, when he recognized the handwriting, looked mockingly at his old friend.

"Since when have you acted as go-between, Martín?"

Saldaña frowned, stung.

"Christ's blood," he said. "Just shut up and read it, will you?"

And this is what Alatriste read:

I would be very grateful if, from now on, you refrained from visiting me. Respectfully, M. de C.

"I imagine," commented Saldaña, "that this will come as no surprise to you after what happened last night."

Alatriste thoughtfully folded up the note.

"And what do you know about last night?"

"Enough. I know, for example, that you were caught trespassing on the royal domain, and that you crossed swords with a friend."

"News travels faster than the post, I see."

"In certain circles, yes."

A mendicant friar from San Blas, with his bell and his little collecting box, came over to them and offered them the image of the saint to kiss. "Praised be the purity of Our Lady the Virgin Mary," he said meekly, shaking the box, then gave Saldaña such a fierce look that Saldaña thought better of it and walked on. Alatriste was thinking.

"I suppose this letter resolves everything," he concluded.

Saldaña was picking his teeth with a fingernail. He seemed relieved.

"I certainly hope so. If not, you're a dead man."

"In order for me to be a dead man, they'll have to kill me first."

"Just remember Villamediana. Not four paces from here they ripped his guts out. And he wasn't the only one, either."

Having said that, he stood vacantly watching some ladies who, escorted by duennas and maids carrying baskets, were eating sweet conserves, seated at the barrels of wine that served as tables outside the cake shop.

"So what it comes down to," he said suddenly, "is that you're just another sad soldier."

Alatriste laughed mirthlessly.

"As you once were," he retorted.

Saldaña gave a deep sigh and turned to the captain.

"You said it—*as I once was*. I was lucky. Besides, I don't ride other men's mares."

He looked away, embarrassed. Rather the opposite was true of him. Rumor had it that he had gained his staff of office thanks to certain friendships cultivated by his wife. And he had, it seemed, killed at least one man for making jokes on the subject.

"Give me the letter."

Alatriste, who was about to put it away, appeared surprised.

"It's mine."

"Not anymore. 'Let him read it, then take it straight back'—those were my orders. It was just so that you could see it with your own eyes—her hand and her signature."

"And what are you going to do with it?"

"Burn it—now."

He took it from the captain, who put up no resistance. Then, looking around, he decided to take advantage of the oil lamp positioned below the pious image a herbalist had placed outside his door, alongside a stuffed bat and a lizard. He held the paper to the flame.

"She knows what's for the best, and so does her husband," he said, returning to the captain's side holding the now burning letter between his fingers. "I expect someone dictated it to them."

They watched the flames consume the letter, then Saldaña dropped it and stamped on the ashes.

"The king's a young man," he said, as if this justified many things. Alatriste stared at him hard.

"And he is the king," he added in a neutral voice.

Saldaña was frowning now, one hand resting on the butt of one of his pistols. With the other hand, he was scratching his grizzled beard.

"Do you know something, Diego? Sometimes, like you, I really miss the mud and shit of Flanders."

Guadalmedina Palace stood on the corner of Calle del Barquillo and Calle de Alcalá, next to the Monastery of San Hermenegildo. The large door stood open, and so Diego Alatriste walked through into the ample hallway, where a liveried porter came to meet him. He was an old servant whom the captain knew well.

"I would like to see the count."

"Were you asked to come, sir?" asked the porter politely.

"No."

"I will see if His Excellency can receive you."

The porter withdrew, and the captain paced up and down before the wrought-iron gate that gave onto the immaculate garden with its lush fruit trees and ornamental shrubs, its stone cupids and classical statuary standing amongst the ivy and the clumps of flowers. He used the time to tidy himself up, straighten his collar, and fasten his doublet. He did not know what Álvaro de la Marca's reaction would be when they met face-to-face, although he assumed the count would be expecting the words of apology he had already prepared. The captain—as the count knew very well—was not a man to retract words or swords, and both had been bandied about the night before. However, he himself, when he analyzed his conduct, was not sure that he had acted fairly toward the count, who was, after all, fulfilling his duties with the same thoroughness he had applied to his own duties on the battlefield. "The king is the king," he reminded himself, "although there are kings and kings." And each man decides out of conscience or self-interest how he will serve his king. Guadalmedina received his pay in the form of royal favors, whereas Diego Alatriste y Tenorio—albeit little, late, and badly—had earned his in the army, as a soldier of that same king, and of his father and grandfather. Besides, Guadalmedina, despite his elevated social position, his noble blood, his courtly manners, and the complicated circumstances in which they found themselves, was a wise and loyal man. They had occasionally taken up arms together against a common enemy, but the captain had also saved the count's life in the

Kerkennah Islands, and subsequently turned to him for help when there was that problem with the two Englishmen. During the incident involving the Inquisition, the count's goodwill had again been proven, not to mention the matter of the Cádiz gold and the warnings given to don Francisco de Quevedo about María de Castro once she had piqued the royal fancy. Such things forged strong bonds—or so at least he hoped as he waited by the gate that led into the garden—bonds that might salvage the affection they both felt for each other. Then again, it might be that Álvaro de la Marca's pride would not allow for any reconciliation at all: the nobility does not care to be ill-treated, and that wound to the count's arm did not help matters. Alatriste was prepared to place himself entirely at the count's disposition, even if this involved letting him stick a few inches of steel through him at a time and place of his choosing.

"His Excellency does not wish to receive you, sir."

Diego Alatriste, who had been waiting, one hand on the hilt of his sword, was left dumbstruck by these words. The porter began ushering him out.

"Are you sure?"

The porter nodded scornfully, all trace of his earlier politeness gone.

"He recommends that you leave while you can."

The captain was not a man to be easily shaken, but he

could not help the wave of heat that rose to his face at finding himself so rudely treated. He shot another look at the
porter, sensing that the latter was secretly enjoying his dis-
comfiture. Then he took a deep breath and, repressing an
urge to beat the man roundly with the flat of his sword,
pulled his hat firmly down on his head, turned, and walked
out into the street.

He walked blindly up Calle de Alcalá, barely noticing
where he was going, as if there were a red veil before his
eyes. He was cursing and blaspheming under his breath.
Several times, as he strode along, he collided with other
passersby; however, when they protested—one man
even made as if to take out his sword—these protests van-
ished as soon as they saw his face. In this manner, he
crossed Puerta del Sol and got as far as Calle Carretas. He
stopped outside the Tavern of the Rock where he read
these words chalked on the door: *Wine from Esquivias.*

That same night, he killed a man. He chose him at random
and in silence from among the other customers crowding the bar—all as drunk as he was. In the end, he
slammed down a few coins on the wine-stained table
and staggered out, followed by the stranger, a braggart
who, along with two other men, was clearly determined
to pick a fight, and all because Alatriste kept staring at

him. The braggart—Alatriste never got his name—already had his sword unsheathed and was declaring loudly and coarsely to anyone who would listen that he wouldn't be stared at like that by any bastard, be he from Spain or from the Indies. Once outside, keeping close to the wall, Alatriste walked as far as Calle de los Majadericos, and there, under cover of darkness and safe from prying eyes, he waited until the footsteps following him grew nearer. Then he took out his sword, confronted the man, and ran him through there and then, making no pretense at observing fencing etiquette. The man dropped to the ground, with a wound to the heart, before he could utter a word, while his companions ran for their lives, crying: "Murder! Murder!" Standing next to his victim's corpse and leaning against the wall for support, his sword still in his hand, Alatriste vomited up all the wine he had drunk that night. Then he wiped the blade of his sword with the dead man's cloak, wrapped himself in his own, and made his way to Calle de Toledo, taking shelter in the shadows.

Three days later, don Francisco de Quevedo and I were crossing the Segovia bridge to go to the Casa de Campo, where Their Majesties were staying and taking advantage of the good weather; the king devoted himself to hunting and the queen to walking, reading, and music. We rode over the bridge in a carriage drawn by two mules and, leaving behind us the Ermita del Ángel and the beginning of the Camino de San Isidro, we proceeded along the right bank to the gardens that surrounded His Catholic Majesty's country retreat. To one side of us grew tall pine woods, and on the other, across the Manzanares, lay Madrid in all its splendor: with its innumerable church and convent towers, its city walls built on the foundations of the former Arab fortifications, and high up, large and imposing, the Alcázar Real, with its Golden Tower like the prow of a galleon looking out over the slender Manzanares River, whose shores were dotted with the white clothes hung out to dry on the bushes by the washerwomen. It was, in short, a splendid scene, and in response to my admiring remarks, don Francisco smiled kindly and said:

"Oh, yes, it's the center of the world all right—for the moment."

I did not then understand the clear-sighted caution that lay behind this comment. As a young man, I was so dazzled by everything around me that I was incapable of imagining an end to the magnificence of the court, to our ownership of the globe, to the empire which—if one included the rich Portuguese inheritance that we shared at the time—comprised not only the Indies in the West, Brazil, Flanders, Italy, but also our possessions in Africa, the Philippines, and other enclaves in the remote Indies of the

East. I could not conceive that one day this would all collapse when the men of iron were succeeded by men of clay incapable of sustaining such a vast enterprise with only their ambition, talent, and swords. For although Spain—forged out of glory and cruelty, out of light and dark—was already beginning to decline, the Spanish empire of my youth was still a mighty thing. It was a world that would never be repeated and that could be summed up, if such a thing is possible, in these old lines by Lorencio de Zamora:

> *I sing of battles and of conquests,*
> *Barbarous deeds, great enterprises,*
> *Sad events and grim disasters,*
> *Hatred, laughter, atrocities.*

So there we were that morning, don Francisco de Quevedo and I, outside the walls of what was then the capital of the world, stepping from a carriage into the gardens of the Casa de Campo, before the noble building with its Italianate porticos and loggias watched over by the imposing equestrian statue of the late Philip III, the father of our current king. And it was there—behind that statue, in the pleasant grove of poplars, willows, and other shrubs of Flemish origin that had been planted round the lovely three-tiered fountain—that our queen received don Francisco as she sat beneath a damask awning, surrounded by her ladies-in-waiting and her personal servants, including the jester Gastoncillo. She greeted the poet with a show of royal affection and invited him to say the angelus with her, for it was midday and the bells were tolling throughout Madrid. I doffed my hat and watched from a distance. Then the queen ordered don Francisco to sit by her side, and they talked for some time about the progress of his play, *The Sword and the Dagger*, from which he read the final lines, lines he claimed to have dashed off the previous night, although I knew that he had, in fact, drafted and redrafted them several times. The one thing that bothered her, she said, only half joking, was that the play was to be performed in El Escorial, for the somber, austere character of that vast royal edifice was repugnant to her cheerful French temperament. This is why, wherever possible, she avoided visiting the palace built by the grandfather of her august husband. It was one of the paradoxes of fate that eighteen years after the events I am describing, the poor lady—much to her chagrin, I imagine—ended up occupying a niche in the crypt there.

Angélica de Alquézar was not, as far as I could see, among the maids of honor accompanying the queen, and so while Quevedo, overflowing with wit and compliments, was delighting the ladies with his humor, I went for a stroll about the garden, admiring the uniforms of the Burgundy guards who were on duty that day. Feeling as pleased as a king with his revenues, I got as far as the balustrade that looked out over the vineyards and the old Guadarrama road, and from there I enjoyed a view of the orchards and market gardens of Buitrera and Florida, which were extraordinarily green in that season of the year. The air was soft, and from the woods behind the little palace came the distant sound of dogs barking and shots being fired, proof that our monarch, with his proverbial marksmanship—described ad nauseam by all the court poets, including Lope and Quevedo—was slaughtering as many rabbit, partridge, quail, and pheasant as his beaters could provide him with. If, during his long life, the king had shot heretics, Turks, and Frenchmen, rather than those small innocent creatures, Spain would have been a very different place.

"Well, well, well. Here's the man who abandoned a lady in the middle of the night to go off with his friends."

I turned around, thoughts and breath stopped. Angélica de Alquézar was by my side. Needless to say, she was looking very beautiful. The light of the Madrid sky lent an added brilliance to her eyes, which were now fixed ironically on me, eyes that were both lovely and deadly.

"I would never have expected such behavior from a gentleman."

Her hair was arranged in ringlets, and she was wearing a red silk taffeta basquine and a short bodice with a pretty little collar on which glittered a gold chain and an emerald-studded cross. A touch of rouge, after the fashion of the court, gave a faint blush to the perfect paleness of her face. She seemed older, I thought, more womanly.

"I'm sorry I abandoned you the other night," I said, "but I couldn't . . ."

She interrupted me impatiently, as if the matter were no longer important. She was gazing around her. Then she shot me a sideways glance and asked:

"Did it end well?"

Her tone was frivolous, as if she really didn't care either way.

"More or less."

I heard a trill of laughter from the ladies sitting around the queen and don Francisco, doubtless amused by some new witticism of his.

"This Captain Batiste, or Triste, or whatever his name is, doesn't have much to recommend him, does he? He's always getting you into trouble."

I drew myself up, greatly offended that Angélica de Alquézar, of all people, should say such a thing.

"He's my friend."

She laughed softly, her hands resting on the balustrade. She smelled sweet, of roses and honey. It was a delicious smell, but I preferred the way she had smelled on the night when we kissed. My skin prickled to remember it. Fresh bread.

"You abandoned me in the middle of the street," she said again.

"I did. How can I make it up to you?"

"By accompanying me again whenever I need you to."

"At night?"

"Yes."

"And with you dressed as a man?"

She stared at me as if I were an idiot.

"You can hardly expect me to go out dressed like this."

"In answer to your question," I said, "no, never again."

"How very discourteous. Remember: you are in my debt."

She was studying me again with the fixity of a dagger pointing at someone's entrails. I should say that I, too, was very smartly turned out that day: all in black, my hair freshly washed, and a dagger tucked in my belt, at the back. Perhaps that gave me the necessary aplomb to hold her gaze.

"I'm not that much in your debt."

"You're a lout," she said angrily, like a little girl who has failed to get her own way. "You obviously prefer the company of that Captain Sotatriste of yours."

"As I said, he's my friend."

She pulled a scornful face.

"Of course. I know the refrain: Flanders and all that, swords, cursing, taverns, and whores. The gross behavior one expects of men."

This sounded like a criticism, and yet I thought I heard a discordant note, as if, in some way, she regretted not being involved in that world herself.

"Anyway," she added, "allow me to say that with friends like him, you don't need enemies."

"And which are you?"

She pursed her lips as if she really were considering her answer. Then, head on one side, not taking her eyes off me for a moment, she said:

"I've already told you that I love you."

I trembled when she said this, and she noticed. She was smiling, as Lucifer might have smiled as he fell from heaven.

"That should be enough," she added, "if you're not a rogue, a fool, or a braggart."

"I don't know what I am, but I know that you're more than enough to get me burned at the stake or garrotted."

She laughed again, her hands folded almost modestly over the ample skirt and the mother-of-pearl fan that hung from her waist. I regarded the neat outline of her mouth. To hell with everything, I thought. Fresh bread, roses, and honey—and bare skin underneath. Had I not been where I was, I would have hurled myself upon those lips.

"You surely don't think," she said, "that you can have me for free."

.   .   .

Before matters became dangerously complicated, there was time for an agreeable interlude, one that would have played well on the stage. The plot was hatched during a meal at El León, offered by Captain Alonso de Contreras, who was his usual talkative, congenial, and slightly boastful self. He presided over the occasion, leaning back against a barrel of wine on which we had deposited our capes, hats, and swords. The other guests were don Francisco de Quevedo, Lopito de Vega, my master, and myself, and we were all happily dispatching some good garlic soup and a thick beef and bacon stew. Our host Contreras was celebrating having finally been paid a sum of money that had, he claimed, been owed to him since the battle of Roncesvalles. We ended up discussing Moscatel's steadfast opposition to Lopito and Laura's love, a situation only made worse by the butcher's discovery that Lopito and Diego Alatriste were now friends. The young man told us forlornly that he could only see his lady in secret—when she went out with her duenna to make some purchase, or else at mass in the church of Our Lady of the Miracles, where he, kneeling on his cloak, would observe her from afar. Sometimes, he even managed to approach and exchange a few tender words while he held, cupped in his hand—O supreme happiness—the holy water with which she made the sign of the cross. Given that Moscatel was determined to marry his niece to that vile pettifogger Saturnino Apolo, the poor girl had only two options: marriage to him or the nunnery, and so Lopito had about as much chance of marrying her as he would of finding a bride in the seraglio in Constantinople. Twenty men on horseback wouldn't change her uncle's mind. Besides, these were turbulent times, and what with the to-ings and fro-ings of both Turks and heretics, Lopito could, at any moment, be called on to resume his duties to the king, and that would mean losing Laura forever. This, as he admitted to us, had often led him to curse the similarly tangled situations described in his own father's plays, because they were of no help whatsoever in resolving his problems.

This remark gave Captain Contreras a bold idea.

"It's perfectly simple," he said, crossing his legs. "Kidnap her and marry her—in good soldierly fashion."

"That wouldn't be easy," replied Lopito glumly. "Moscatel is still paying several ruffians to guard the house."

"How many?"

"The last time I tried to see her, there were four."

"Good swordsmen?"

"On that occasion, I didn't stay long enough to find out."

Contreras smugly twirled his mustache and looked around, letting his eyes linger in particular on Captain Alatriste and don Francisco.

"The greater the number of Moors to fight, the greater the glory, don't you agree, Señor de Quevedo?"

Don Francisco adjusted his spectacles and frowned, for it ill became a court favorite to get involved in a scandal involving kidnappings and sword fights. However, the presence of Alonso de Contreras, Diego Alatriste, and Lope's son made it very hard for him to refuse.

"I'm afraid," he said in resigned tones, "there's nothing for it but to fight."

"It might provide you with matter for a sonnet," remarked Contreras, already imagining himself the hero of another poem.

"Or, indeed, a reason to spend a further period in exile."

As for Captain Alatriste, who was leaning on the table before his mug of wine, the look he exchanged with his old comrade Contreras was an eloquent one. For men like them, such adventures were merely part of the job.

"And what about the boy?" asked Contreras, meaning me.

I felt almost offended. I considered myself a young man of considerable experience and so I smoothed my nonexistent mustache, as I had seen my master do, and said:

"The 'boy' will fight too."

The way in which I said this brought me an approving smile from the *miles gloriosus*—the boastful soldier Contreras—and a glance from Diego Alatriste.

"When my father finds out," moaned Lopito, "he'll kill me."

Captain Contreras roared with laughter.

"Your illustrious father knows a thing or two about kidnappings and elopements. The Phoenix was always a great one for the ladies!"

There followed an embarrassed silence, and we all stuck nose and mustache in our respective mugs of wine. Even Contreras did so, suddenly remembering that Lopito himself was the illegitimate child born of just such an affair, even though, as I mentioned before, Lope had subsequently acknowledged him. The young man, however, did not appear offended. He knew his father's reputation better than anyone. After a few sips of wine and a diplomatic clearing of the throat, Contreras took up the thread again:

"There's nothing like a fait accompli; besides, that's what we military men are like, isn't it? Direct, bold, proud, straight to the point. I remember once, in Cyprus it was . . ."

And he immediately launched into another story. When he had done, he took a long draft of wine, sighed nostalgically, and looked at Lopito.

"So, young man, are you truly willing to join yourself in holy matrimony to that woman, until death do you part, et cetera?"

Lopito held his gaze unblinking.

"As long as God is God, and beyond death itself."

"No one's asking that much of you. If you stick with her until death, you'll be doing more than your duty already. Do we gentlemen here have your word as a gentleman?"

"On my life, you do."

"Then there's nothing more to be said." Contreras gave the table a satisfied thump. "Can anyone resolve matters on the ecclesiastical side?"

"My Aunt Antonia is abbess of the Convento de las Jerónimas," Lopito said. "She'll gladly take us in. And Father Francisco, her chaplain, is also Laura's confessor and knows Señor Moscatel well."

"Will he agree to help if he's needed?

"Oh, yes."

"And what about the young lady? Will your Laura be prepared to be put to the test like this?"

Lopito said quite simply that she would, and there was no further discussion of the matter. Everyone agreed to take part, we all drank to a happy conclusion, and don Francisco de Quevedo, as was his wont, contributed a few appropriate lines of verse, not his this time, but Lope's:

> "Once she's in love, the most cowardly woman
> (More so if she's a maid)
> Will gladly tread her family's honor
> Mud-deep where she is laid."

Everyone drank to this as well, and eight or ten toasts later, using the table as a map and the mugs of wine as the main protagonists, Captain Contreras—his speech now slightly uncertain, but his resolution firm—invited us to pull up our chairs so that he could lay out his plan to us. His assault tactics, as he termed them, were as detailed as if we were preparing to send a hundred lancers into Oran rather than plotting a small-scale attack on a private house in Calle de la Madera.

A house with two doors is always difficult to guard, and don Gonzalo Moscatel's house had two doors. A couple of nights later, we, the conspirators, our faces muffled by our cloaks, were standing in the shadows of a nearby arcade opposite the main door. Captain Contreras, don Francisco de Quevedo, Diego Alatriste, and I stood watching the musicians who, by the light of the lantern one of them had brought with him, were taking up their positions before the barred window of the house in question, on the corner of Calle de la Madera and Calle de la Luna. The plan was a bold and simple one: a serenade at one door, attracting protests and alarm, followed by a skirmish with swords, while escape was made via the other door. Military planning aside, due attention had also been paid to preserving the lady's honor. Since Laura Moscatel was free neither to choose whom she would marry nor to leave her house, the only way of bending the will of her stubborn uncle was a kidnapping followed immediately by a wedding to make amends. The abbess aunt and the chaplain-cum-family-friend—the latter's pastoral scruples having been soothed by a purseful of doubloons—had both been forewarned by Lopito and were, at that moment, waiting in the Convento de las Jerónimas, where the bride would be taken as soon as she was freed, so that everything could be seen to be proper and aboveboard.

"An excellent adventure, praise God," muttered a gleeful Captain Contreras.

He was doubtless recalling his youth, when such adventures were more common. He was leaning against the wall, his face concealed by hat and cloak, between Diego Alatriste and don Francisco de Quevedo, who were equally well disguised, so that only the glint of their eyes could be seen. I was watching the street. In order to reassure don Francisco somewhat and to preserve appearances, our arrival on the scene had been made to look like mere coincidence, as if we were a group of men who just happened to be passing. Even the poor musicians, hired by Lopito de Vega, had no idea what was about to occur. They only knew that they had been paid to serenade a certain lady—a widow, they had been told—at eleven o'clock at night, outside her window. There were three musicians, the youngest of whom was fifty if he was a day. They were standing ready with guitar, lute, and tambourine, the latter played by the singer, who launched without further ado into the famous song:

> *"I worshipped you in Italy,*
> *In Flanders died of love,*
> *I come to Spain still passionate,*
> *My* madrileña *dove . . ."*

Not the most original of sentiments, it has to be said, but this was, nevertheless, a very popular ditty at the time. The singer got no further than these lines, however, for no sooner had he concluded that first verse than lights were lit inside the house, and don Gonzalo Moscatel could be heard swearing by all that's holy. Then the front door was flung open and there he stood, sword in hand, wildly threatening the musicians and their progenitors and declaring that he would skewer them like capons. This, he roared, was no time to be disturbing honest households. He was accompanied—they were presumably spending the evening together—by the lawyer Saturnino Apolo, who was armed with a short sword and was carrying the lid of an earthenware jar as buckler. At this point, four nasty-looking individuals came bursting out of the coach house and immediately fell upon the musicians. The latter, who had done nothing wrong, found themselves being roundly punched and beaten with the flat of their assailants' swords.

"Right," said Captain Contreras, almost licking his lips with delight, "to business."

And we all emerged at once from the arcade, just as if we had turned the corner and happened on the scene by chance. Don Francisco de Quevedo, meanwhile, was murmuring philosophically to himself from beneath his cloak:

> *"Don't make your life so miserable,*
> *Don't fret, stop taking pains,*
> *For nothing's more impossible*
> *Than to keep a woman in chains."*

The musicians were now huddled against the wall, poor things, surrounded by the swords of the hired ruffians and with their instruments shattered. Gonzalo Moscatel had picked up their lantern from the ground and was holding it high, still with his sword in his right hand. He was furiously bawling questions at them: Who had sent them to disturb him at such an hour? How? Where? When? At this point, as we passed by, hats down over our eyes, our cloaks up to our noses, Captain Contreras said out loud something along the lines of: "A pox on these wretches troubling our streets, a pox on them and the devil who lights their way," and he said this loudly enough for everyone to hear. Moscatel happened to be the person lighting the way of his four hired bully-boys—in the dim lantern glow we could see their sinister mugs, the lawyer Apolo's porcine features, and the terrified expressions on the musicians' faces—and he clearly felt that with the backing of his armed retinue, he could afford to strut and crow. He therefore addressed Captain Contreras in surly fashion— he had no idea who we were, of course—and told him to go to hell and not to stop en route. If we didn't, he declared, by Saint Peter and by all the saints in the calendar, he would cut off our ears there and then. As you can imagine, these words suited our designs perfectly. Contreras laughed in Moscatel's face and said with great aplomb that he had no idea what was going on there nor what the quarrel was about, but if it was a matter of cutting off anyone's ears, *really* cutting off their ears, the fool who had just said that and the whore who bore him were very welcome to try. He laughed again and was still laughing, still without uncovering his face, as he took out his sword. Captain Alatriste, sword unsheathed, was already lunging at the nearest ruffian. Seemingly almost in the same movement, he slashed at Moscatel's arm, causing him to drop the lantern and start back as if he had been stung by a scorpion. The light went out as it hit the ground, leaving us all in darkness. The terrified shadows of the three musicians scampered away like hares, and we fell with glee upon the remaining men—and it was like the Fall of Troy all over again.

Great God, but I enjoyed myself. The idea was that while doing our utmost not to kill anyone—we didn't, after all, want to cast a pall on the marriage—amidst the general confusion and with the help of the duenna, whose palm had been greased with doubloons drawn from the same purse that had bribed the chaplain, we would allow time for Lopito de Vega to escape with Laura Moscatel by the back door and carry her off to the Convento de las Jerónimas in the carriage he had hired for the purpose. While all this was going on at the back door, blows were raining down in the pitch dark at the front door. Moscatel and his men fought like Turks, while Saturnino Apolo, from behind his shield, urged them on from a safe distance. Men as skilled as Alatriste, Quevedo, and Contreras had only to parry and thrust, which they did with a will, and I did not acquit myself badly either. I could hear the heavy breathing of the ruffian I took on above the clang of steel. This was no time for fancy flourishes because we were all fighting together and at close quarters, and so I resorted to a trick Captain Alatriste had taught me on board the *Jesús Nazareno* on the voyage home from

Flanders. I made an upward thrust, drew back as if to cover my side, but instead spun round and, swift as a hawk, dealt my opponent a low slashing blow, which, given the sound it made and the position of my blade, must have sliced through the tendons at the back of his knee. My adversary fled, hopping and blaspheming against every saint in heaven, while I, feeling excited and very pleased with myself, looked around to see how I could best assist my comrades. The four of us had started to advance boldly on the six of them, muttering "Yepes, Yepes"—like the wine—which was the password we had decided upon so that we could recognize each other if we had to fight in the dark. Things were already tipping in our favor, however, because the lawyer Apolo had taken to his heels after taking a jab to the buttocks, and don Francisco de Quevedo—who made sure to keep his face covered by his cloak so that he would not be recognized—was repelling the particular ruffian it had fallen to him to fight.

"Yepes," he said to me, as if he had done quite enough for one night.

For his part, Alonso de Contreras was still fighting—his man was putting up rather more resistance than his fellows—and they were still furiously battling it out, the other man retreating down the street, but not as yet running away. The fourth man was a motionless shape on the ground: he came off worst, for the thrust the captain had

dealt him in the initial chaos was to prove deadly; as we
learned afterward, three days later he was given the last
rites and on the eighth day died. Having seen off one
ruffian and wounded Moscatel in the arm, my master,
making sure to keep his hat pulled well down and his
face covered so that he would remain unrecognized by
Moscatel, was now harrying the butcher with his sword,
while that fool, who had long since ceased his strutting,
was stumbling backward in search of the door to his
house—something my master was doing his best to
prevent—and calling for help to defend himself against
these murderers. Moscatel finally fell to the ground, where
Captain Alatriste spent some time kicking him in the ribs,
until Contreras returned, having finally chased off his
opponent.

"Yepes," he said, when, at the sound of his footsteps, my
master spun round, sword in hand.

Gonzalo Moscatel lay on the ground moaning, and his
neighbors, woken by the clamor, were beginning to appear
at their windows. At the far end of the street a light glim-
mered, and someone yelled something about calling out
the constables.

"Can we please leave now?" grumbled don Francisco de
Quevedo from behind his cloak.

The suggestion seemed a reasonable one, and so we
made our exit as if we were carrying in our pocket the

king's patent. An ebullient Alonso de Contreras affectionately patted my cheek and called me "son," and Captain
Alatriste, after giving Moscatel one last kick in the ribs, followed after, sheathing his sword. Three or four streets farther on, when we made a halt in Calle de Tudescos to
celebrate, Contreras was still laughing.

"Od's my life," he declared. "I haven't enjoyed myself
so much since the sack of Negroponte, when I had some
Englishmen hanged."

Lopito de Vega and Laura Moscatel were married four
weeks later in the church of the Jerónimas, in the absence
of her uncle, who was going about Madrid with fourteen
stitches in his face and his arm in a sling, blaming both
injuries on a certain "Yepes." Lopito's father was not present either. The marriage was a very discreet affair, with
Captain Contreras, Quevedo, my master, and I as witnesses.
The young couple moved into a modest rented house in
Plaza de Antón Martín, where they intended to await
Lopito's promotion to ensign. As far as I know, they
lived there happily for three months. Then, due to some
infection of the air or a corruption of the water caused
by the terrible heat ravaging Madrid that year, Laura
Moscatel died of a malign fever, after being bled and
purged by incompetent doctors; and her young widower, his

heart broken, returned to Italy. And so ended the strange adventure of Calle de Madera, and I, too, learned something from that whole sad affair: Time carries everything away, and eternal happiness exists only in the imaginations of poets and on the stage.

6. THE KING IS DEAD, LONG LIVE THE KING

Angélica de Alquézar had again asked me to meet her at the Puerta de la Priora. As she put it in her brief note: *I require an escort.* I would be lying if I said that I had no reservations about accepting; on the other, hand, I never for a moment considered not going. Angélica had entered my blood like a quartan fever. I had tasted her lips, touched her skin, and seen too many promises in her eyes; my judgment grew blurred whenever she was involved. Nevertheless, however in love I may have been, I was not totally bereft of all common sense, and so this time, I took proper precautions, and when the door opened and that same agile shadow joined me in the darkness, I was reasonably well prepared for what might lie ahead. I had on a thick buff-coat made by a leatherworker in Calle de Toledo out of an old one belonging to the captain, and had my sword at my left side and my dagger tucked into my belt at the back. Covering and disguising all these things, I was wearing a gray serge cloak and a black hat with no feather or band. I had also washed with soap and water, and was sporting the soft down on my upper lip which I kept shaving in the hope that this would encourage it, one day, to reach the impressive dimensions of Captain Alatriste's mustache; this it never did, by the way, for I never had much of a mustache or a beard. Before leaving, I scrutinized myself in La Lebrijana's mirror, and was quite pleased with what I saw, and on my way to the rendezvous, whenever I passed beneath a torch or a lantern, I would admire my own shadow. I recall this now and smile, and I'm sure that you, dear readers, will understand.

"Where are you taking me this time?" I asked.

"I want to show you something," replied Angélica. "It will be useful for your education."

I did not find these words in the least reassuring. I had seen something of life by then and knew that anything "useful for one's education" was only ever acquired with damage to one's own ribs or with the kind of bloodletting not administered by a barber. So, once again, I prepared myself for the worst, or, rather, resigned myself—sweetly and fearfully. As I have said before, I was very young at the time and in love with the devil.

"You seem to like dressing as a man," I said.

This continued both to fascinate and shock me. As I mentioned earlier, a woman adopting male attire in order to find manly glory or to seek a solution to troubles of the heart had been a commonplace in the theater since the early Italian plays and, indeed, since Ariosto, but the truth is that, plays and legends apart, such a figure never appeared in real life, or not at least in my experience. Angélica laughed softly, as if to herself, more Marfisa than Bradamante, for I would soon learn the extent to which she was moved less by love than by war.

"Surely," she said mischievously, "you wouldn't want me running around Madrid in skirt and farthingale."

She completed this thought by placing her lips so close to my ear that they touched it, making the skin all over my body prickle; then she whispered these bold lines by Lope:

"How could he ever love me, he who saw me,
  Bloodstained, beat down a wall of Turks?"

And, wretch that I was, the only thing that prevented me from kissing her, whether stained in blood or not, was the fact that she suddenly turned away and set off at a brisk pace. The journey, this time, was shorter. Following the walls of the Convento de María de Aragón, we walked through dark and near-deserted streets to the orchards and vegetable gardens of Leganitos, where I felt the cold and damp penetrate my serge cloak. In her mannish black clothes and with her dagger at her waist, she was only lightly dressed yet she did not appear to feel the cold. She strode resolutely into the night, determined and confident. When I paused to get my bearings, she carried on, without waiting, and I had no option but to go after her, casting cautious glances to right and left. She wore a page's cap tucked into her belt so that she could cover her hair should this prove necessary, but meanwhile, she wore it loose, and the pale smudge of her fair hair guided me through the darkness toward the abyss.

There wasn't a light to be seen anywhere. Alone in the dark, Diego Alatriste stopped and, with professional prudence, looked around him. Not a soul in sight. Again he touched the folded piece of paper he was carrying in his purse.

> *You deserve an explanation and a proper good-bye.*
> *Meet me at eleven o'clock in Camino de las*
> *Minillas. The first house.*
> *María de Castro*

He had hesitated right up until the last moment. Finally, when there was only just enough time, he had downed a quart of brandy to keep out the cold. Then, having equipped himself properly as regards weapons and clothing—including, this time, his buffcoat—he set off toward Plaza Mayor and from there to Santo Domingo before following Calle de Leganitos to the outskirts of the city. This was where he was now, standing by the bridge near the walls surrounding the orchards, watching the road that lay steeped in shadow. In common with all the other houses bordering the river, no lights were lit in the first house. These houses, each with its own orchard and fields, were often used as cool summer retreats. The one that interested Alatriste had been built against the wall of a ruined convent, whose cloister served as a small garden, its roofless pillars holding up the starry vault of the sky.

A dog barked in the distance and another answered. Then the barking stopped and silence was restored. Alatriste stroked his mustache as he again looked about him before proceeding. When he reached the house, he pushed back his cloak and folded it over his left shoulder so as to leave his sword free. He knew what might happen. He had thought about it all evening as he sat on his bed, staring at his weapons where they hung from a nail on the wall. Then he made his decision and set off. Oddly, this decision had nothing to do with desire. Or rather, if he was honest with himself, he did still desire María de Castro, but this wasn't why he was standing now in the dark, listening intently, his hand hovering over the hilt of his sword, as he sniffed out possible perils like a boar scenting the presence of the huntsman and his pack of hounds. There was another reason, too. "The royal domain," Guadalmedina and Martín Saldaña had said, but he had a perfect right to be there if he chose. He had spent his life defending the royal domain, as his scarred body bore witness. Like all good men, he had done his duty a hundred times, but king and pawn were equal when naked and in a woman's bed.

The door stood ajar. He slowly pushed it open; beyond lay a dark hallway. "You might die here," he said to himself. "Tonight." He took out his dagger, smiled a crooked, dangerous, wolfish smile, then advanced into the darkness, the point of his blade foremost. With his free hand he groped his way along the bare walls of a corridor. An oil lamp was burning at the far end, lighting up the rectangle of a door that led to the cloister. A bad place for a fight, he thought—narrow and with no escape route. Nevertheless, placing one's head in the lion's mouth had its fascination, its own dark, distorted pleasure. In that unhappy Spain, which he had loved and which he now despised with a lucidity acquired through time and experience, one could buy honors and beauty as easily as one might buy plenary indulgences, but even in Spain, there were still some things that could not be bought. And he knew what those things were. There came a point when the gift of a gold chain, presented to him, in passing, in a palace in Seville, was not enough to bind Diego Alatriste y Tenorio, old soldier and paid swordsman. "After all," he concluded, "if worst comes to worst, the only thing anyone can take from me is my life."

"We've arrived," said Angélica.

We had walked through the orchards along a narrow path that snaked between the trees, and before us lay a small garden that formed part of the ruined cloister of a convent. On the other side, among the stone pillars and fallen capitals, hung an oil lamp. I did not like the look of this at all; prudently, I stopped.

"*Where* have we arrived?" I asked.

Angélica did not reply. She was standing motionless at my side, looking in the direction of the light. She was breathing fast. After a moment of indecision, I made as if to go on, but she grabbed my arm to hold me back. I turned to look at her. Her face was a shadowy shape outlined by the tenuous light in the cloister.

"Wait," she whispered.

She sounded less assured now. After a while, she moved forward, still gripping my arm and guiding me across the neglected garden; our feet swished through the grass and weeds.

"Don't make so much noise," she said.

When we reached the first of the cloister pillars, we stopped again and took shelter there. We were closer to the lamp now and I could see my companion more clearly; her face was utterly impassive, her eyes intent on what was going on around. She was obviously agitated, though, for her breast rose and fell beneath her doublet.

"Do you still love me?" she asked suddenly.

I looked at her, bewildered, openmouthed.

"Of course I do," I answered.

Angélica was looking at me with such intensity that I trembled. The light from the oil lamp was reflected in her blue eyes, and it was Beauty itself that kept me nailed to the spot, incapable of thought.

"Whatever happens, remember that I love you, too."

And she kissed me, not a light kiss or a peck, but pressing her lips slowly and firmly to mine. Then, still looking into my eyes, she drew back and indicated the lamp at the far end of the cloister.

"May God go with you," she said.

I looked at her, confused.

"God?"

"Or the devil, if you prefer."

She stepped backward into the shadows. And then, in the lamplight, I saw another figure appear in the cloister—Captain Alatriste.

. . .

I confess that I felt afraid, more afraid than Sardanapalus himself. I didn't know the purpose of this ambush, but whatever it was, I, and my master, too, were clearly up to our necks in it. I went anxiously over to him, with all these new events buzzing in my head. I shouted a warning to him, although without knowing quite what I was warning him against.

"Captain! It's a trap!"

He was standing next to the lamp, dagger in hand, and staring at me in stupefaction. I reached his side, unsheathed my sword, and looked around for hidden enemies.

"What the devil . . ." the captain began.

At this point, as if at a prearranged signal and just as happens on stage, a door opened and a well-dressed young man, startled by our voices, appeared in the cloister. Beneath his hat we could see his fair hair; he wore his cape folded over his arm, his sword in its sheath, and a yellow doublet that seemed strangely familiar. The most remarkable thing, however, was that I knew his face, and so did my master. We had seen it at public ceremonies, in the streets of Calle Mayor and El Prado, and at much closer quarters, too, only a short time before, in Seville. His Hapsburg profile appeared on gold and silver coins.

"The king!" I exclaimed.

Terrified, I took off my hat, about to kneel down, not knowing what to do with my unsheathed sword. At first, the king seemed as confused as us, but quickly became his usual erect, solemn self again and regarded us without saying a word. The captain had doffed his hat and sheathed his dagger, and the look on his face could only be described as thunderstruck.

I was about to put away my sword as well, then I heard someone in the shadows whistle a tune. *Ti-ri-tu ta-ta.* And my blood froze in my veins.

"How very pleasant!" said Gualterio Malatesta.

Dressed in black from head to toe, his eyes as hard and bright as jet, he had appeared out of the night as if he and it were one and the same. I noticed that his face had changed since the adventure aboard the *Niklaasbergen.* Now he bore an ugly scar above his right eyelid, which gave him a slight squint.

"Three pigeons," he went on in the same smug tone, "caught in the same net."

I heard a metallic hiss at my side. Captain Alatriste had taken out his sword and was pointing it at the Italian's chest. Still bewildered, I raised my blade too. Malatesta had said three pigeons, not two. Philip IV had turned to look at him. He remained august and imperturbable, but I realized that this new arrival was not on his side.

"It's the king," my master said slowly.

"Of course it's the king," replied the Italian coolly. "And this is no hour for monarchs to be out sniffing around women."

I must say that, to his credit, our young king was dealing with the situation with due majesty. He kept his sword in its sheath and a firm control on his emotions, whatever they might have been; he stood gazing at us as if from a distance, inexpressive, impassive, face averted from earthly things and from danger, as if none of what was happening had anything to do with him. Where the devil, I wondered, was the Count of Guadalmedina, his usual companion on these nighttime forays, and whose duty it was to help him out in such situations; instead, more shadows began to emerge from the darkness. They were advancing through the cloister and gradually surrounding us; by the light of the lamp, I could see that they were not exactly elegant figures and were, therefore, fitting companions for Gualterio Malatesta. I counted six men swathed in cloaks and with taffeta masks covering their faces; they wore broad-brimmed hats pulled down low over their eyes, had a bow-legged gait, and as they moved, there was a clank of metal. Hired killers, without a doubt. And their fee for such an exploit must have been exorbitant. In their hands I saw the glint of steel.

Captain Alatriste seemed, at last, to understand the situation. He took a few steps toward the king, who, seeing him approach, lost just a drop of his sangfroid and placed his hand on the hilt of his sword. Taking no notice of this royal gesture, my master turned toward Malatesta and the others, describing a semicircle with the blade of his sword, as if marking an impassable line in the air.

"Íñigo," he said.

I joined him and made the same movement with my sword. For a moment, my eyes met those of the king of both worlds, old and new, and I thought I saw in them a flicker of gratitude. "Although," I said to myself, "he might at least open his mouth to thank us." The seven men were now tightening the circle around us. "This," I thought, "is as far as we go, the captain and I. And if what I fear will happen happens, it's as far as our king goes, too."

"Let's see what the boy has learned," said Malatesta mockingly.

I took my dagger in my left hand and prepared myself. The Italian's pockmarked face was a sarcastic mask, and the scar above his eye accentuated his sinister air.

"Old scores to settle," he said in his harsh voice and gave a hoarse laugh.

Then they fell upon us. All of them. And as they did so, my courage rose. Our situation might be desperate, but we would not go like lambs to the slaughter. And I stood my ground and fought for my pride and my life. The years and the century I lived in had trained me for this, and dying here was as good as dying anywhere else—at my age, only a little earlier than expected. A matter of luck. And I only hope, I thought, fleetingly, as I fought, that the great Philip unsheathes his sword too and throws in his lot with us; it is, after all, his illustrious skin that's at stake. I did not have time to find out whether he did or not. Thrusts and lunges were raining down upon my sword, my dagger, and my buffcoat, and out the corner of my eye I glimpsed Captain Alatriste withstanding the same deluge, without giving an inch. One of his opponents leapt back, cursing, dropping his sword and clutching his belly. At the same moment, I felt a steel blade cut into my buffcoat; without it, the blade would have sliced open my shoulder. I drew back, alarmed, avoiding as best I could the various sharp points and edges seeking my body. I stumbled as I did so and fell backward, striking my head on the fallen capital of a pillar, and my mind suddenly filled up with night.

The voice pronouncing my name gradually wormed its way into my consciousness. I lazily ignored it. It was good there, in that peaceful torpor, without past or future. Suddenly, the voice sounded much closer, almost in my ear, and a pain seared down my backbone from top to bottom.

"Íñigo," said Captain Alatriste again.

I sat up, remembering the glinting swords, my fall backward, the darkness filling everything. I moaned as I did so—my neck felt stiff and my brain as if it were about to burst—and when I opened my eyes, I saw my master's face only a few inches away. He looked very tired. The light from the oil lamp lit up his mustache, his aquiline nose, and the anxious look in his green eyes.

"Can you move?"

I gave a nod which only intensified the pain, and the captain helped me to remain in a sitting position. His hands left bloody stains on my buffcoat. In alarm, I started feeling my own body, but could find no wound. Then I saw the cut to his right thigh.

"Not all the blood is mine," he said.

He gestured toward the motionless body of the king, lying at the foot of a pillar. His yellow doublet was badly slashed and, in the light from the lamp, I could see a dark stream spreading out over the flagstoned floor of the cloister.

"Is he . . . ?" I began, but stopped, incapable of uttering the terrifying word.

"He is."

I felt too stunned to take in the magnitude of the tragedy. I looked to either side, but saw no one else, not even the man I had seen the captain run through with his sword. He had disappeared into the night, along with Gualterio Malatesta and the others.

"We must go," said my master urgently.

I picked up my sword and my dagger. The king was lying face up, his eyes wide open, locks of his fair, bloodied hair sticking to his skin. He no longer looked very dignified, I thought. No dead man does.

"He fought well," remarked the captain, ever objective.

He was pushing me toward the garden and the shadows. I still hesitated, confused.

"What about us? Why are we still alive?"

My master glanced about him. I saw that he still had his sword in his hand.

"They need us. He was the one they wanted dead. You and I are merely scapegoats."

He paused for a moment, thinking.

"They could have killed us," he added, "but that isn't why they came." He eyed the corpse gravely. "They fled as soon as they had killed him."

"What was Malatesta doing here?"

"Hang me if I know."

On the other side of the house, in the street, we heard voices. The hand resting on my shoulder tensed, digging steely fingers into me.

"They're here," said the captain.

"You mean they've come back?"

"No, these are different men . . . worse."

He continued to propel me away from the light and out of the cloister.

"Run, Íñigo."

I stopped. I was confused. We had almost reached the shadows of the garden now and I couldn't see his face.

"Run and keep running. And remember, whatever happens, you weren't here tonight. Do you understand? You weren't here."

I resisted for a moment. "And what about you, captain?" I was about to ask, but there was no time. When I did not obey immediately, he gave me a shove, sending me several paces into the long grass.

"Go, damn it!" he said.

The entrance to the corridor leading to the cloister was lit up now with torches, and there was the sound of clanking weapons and people talking. "In the name of the king," said a distant voice. "In the name of the law." And that cry in the name of a dead king made my scalp creep.

"Run!"

And by my life, I did. Running because you want to run is not the same as having to run. I swear to God that if a precipice had opened up before me, I would have leapt unhesitatingly over it. Blind with panic, I ran through the undergrowth, past trees, across fields, jumping fences and walls, splashing through the stream and climbing out and up toward the city. And only when I was safe, far from that accursed cloister, did I drop to the ground, half mad with horror and fear, heart pounding, lungs burning, and a thousand pins and needles pricking neck and temples. Only then did I stop to wonder what may have happened to Captain Alatriste.

He limped over to the wall, looking for the best path to follow. Fighting with so many men at once had worn him down; the cut to his thigh was not that deep, but it was still bleeding. Besides, knowing the identity of the corpse lying in the cloister was enough to shake anyone's composure and lower his spirits. Despite his wound, fear—had he felt any—might have lent wings to his feet, but he did not feel afraid, only a grim sense of desolation at the trick played on him by Fate. A black, despairing melancholy. The utter certainty that his luck had finally run out.

The lights were filling the cloister now. He could see them glinting through the trees and the undergrowth. Voices and shadows everywhere. "Tomorrow," he thought, "the whole of Europe and the world will tremble when they learn what has happened."

He took a run at the wall, about five cubits high. He tried twice, but failed. Christ's blood! The pain from the wound in his leg was too much.

"Here he is!" cried a voice behind him.

He turned slowly around, resigned, his sword held firmly in his hand. Four men were coming toward him through the garden, lighting their way with torches. He had no difficulty in recognizing the Count of Guadalmedina, who had his arm in a sling. The others were Martín Saldaña and a couple of constables. Behind them, he saw catchpoles moving about in the cloister.

"Give yourself up, in the name of the king."

These words brought a wry smile to Alatriste's lips. In the name of what king, he felt like asking. He looked at Guadalmedina, who was standing there, sword sheathed, hand on hip, regarding him, as he never had before, with utter scorn. The splint on his arm was clearly a souvenir from their encounter in Calle de los Peligros. More unfinished business.

"Only some of this is my doing," said Alatriste.

No one seemed to believe him. Martín Saldaña was grave-faced. He had his staff of office tucked in his belt, his sword in one hand and a pistol in the other.

"Give yourself up," he warned again, "or I'll kill you."

The captain reflected for a moment. He knew the fate that awaited regicides: he would be tortured to death and his body quartered. Not a very pleasant prospect.

"It would be better if you killed me."

He was looking at the bearded face of the man who, up

until that night, had been his friend—he was losing friends at an alarming rate—and he saw him hesitate, just for a moment. They both knew that Alatriste had no wish to be taken prisoner. Saldaña exchanged a rapid glance with Guadalmedina, and the latter almost imperceptibly shook his head. We need him alive, the gesture said, so that we can try to get him to talk.

"Disarm him," ordered Guadalmedina.

The two catchpoles carrying the torches stepped forward, and Alatriste raised his sword. Martín Saldaña's pistol was pointing straight at his stomach. "I could force him to fire," he thought. "I just need to meet the barrel full on and with a little luck . . . True, a bullet in the gut hurts more than one in the head, and you take longer to die, but there's no alternative. Martín might not refuse me that."

Saldaña himself seemed to be pondering the matter deeply.

"Diego," he said suddenly.

Alatriste looked at him, surprised. It sounded like an introduction to a longer speech, and his comrade from Flanders was not the most verbose of men, certainly not in a situation like this.

"It isn't worth it," added Saldaña after a pause.

"What isn't worth it?"

Saldaña was still thinking. He raised his sword hand and scratched his beard with the cross-guard, then said:

"Letting yourself get killed for no good reason."

"Leave any explanations for later," Guadalmedina said brusquely.

Alatriste leaned against the wall, confused. There was something that didn't quite fit. Saldaña, his pistol still leveled at Alatriste, was looking at Guadalmedina now, frowning.

"Later might be too late," Saldaña said sullenly.

Guadalmedina paused to think, head to one side. Then he stood studying them both for a while. Finally, he seemed convinced. His eyes fell on Saldaña's pistol and he sighed.

"It wasn't the king," he said.

Through the left-hand window of the carriage, on the hills overlooking the orchards and the Manzanares River, he could just make out the dark shape of the Alcázar Real. Accompanied by half a dozen constables and catchpoles on foot, all bearing torches, they were on their way to Puente del Parque. Alongside the coachman sat another two guards, one of whom was carrying a harquebus with the match lit. Guadalmedina and Martín Saldaña were in the coach, sitting opposite Captain Alatriste. The latter could hardly believe the story they had just told him.

"We've been using him as a double for His Majesty for eight months now; the likeness was quite astonishing," concluded Guadalmedina. "The same age, the same blue eyes, a similar mouth . . . His name was Ginés Garcia-millán and he was a little-known actor from Puerto Lumbreras. He stood in for the king for a few days during the recent visit to Aragon. When we heard that something was being planned for tonight, we decided that he should play the role once more. He knew the risks, but agreed to take part anyway. He was a loyal and valiant subject."

Alatriste pulled a face.

"A fine reward he got for his loyalty."

Guadalmedina regarded him in silence, faintly irri-tated. The torches outside illuminated his aristocratic pro-file, his neat beard and curled mustache. Another world and another caste. He was supporting his splinted arm with his good hand to protect it from the jolting of the carriage.

"It was doubtless a personal decision," he said lightly. After all, compared with a monarch, the late Ginés Garcia-millán mattered little to him. "His orders were not to appear until we arrived to protect him, but he was deter-mined to play his role to the hilt and he didn't wait." He shook his head disapprovingly. "Playing a king was prob-ably the high point of his career."

"He played the part well, too," said the captain. "He remained dignified throughout and fought without once uttering a word. I doubt a king would have done the same."

Martín Saldaña listened impassively, never taking his

eyes off Alatriste, his pistol in his lap, cocked and ready. Guadalmedina had removed one glove and was using it to flick away the dust on his fine breeches.

"I don't believe your story," he said. "At least not entirely. It's true, as you say, that there are signs of a fight and there must have been more than one assassin, but who's to say that you weren't in league with them?"

"My word."

"And what else?"

"You know me well enough."

Guadalmedina snorted, one glove hanging limp in his hand.

"Do I? You haven't proved very trustworthy of late."

Alatriste stared hard at the count. Up until that night, no one who said such a thing would have lived long enough to repeat it. Then he turned to Saldaña.

"Don't you believe me either?"

Saldaña kept his mouth shut. It was clear that it was not his business to believe or disbelieve anything. He was simply doing his job. The actor was dead, the king was alive, and his orders were to guard the prisoner. He kept his thoughts to himself. Any debating he would leave to inquisitors, judges, and theologians.

"It will all become clear in the fullness of time," said Guadalmedina, drawing on his glove again. "The fact is, you received orders to stay away."

The captain looked out of the window. They had passed the Puente del Parque, and the carriage was taking them past the city wall, along the dirt road that led to the south side of the Alcázar.

"Where are you taking me?"

"To Caballerizas," said Guadalmedina.

Alatriste studied Martín Saldaña's inexpressive face and noticed that he was now gripping the pistol more firmly and pointing it at his chest. "The sly fox knows me well," he thought. "He knows it was a mistake to give me that information." Caballerizas, better known as the Slaughterhouse, was the small prison next to the Alcázar stables where prisoners guilty of lèse-majesté were sent to be tortured. It was a sinister place where neither justice nor hope was to be found. There were no judges or lawyers, only torturers, strappado, and a scribe to note down each scream. Two interrogations were enough to leave a man crippled for life.

"So this is as far as I go."

"Yes," agreed Guadalmedina. "This is as far as you go. Now you'll have time to explain everything."

"I might as well be hanged for a sheep as a lamb," thought Alatriste. And never better said. Taking advantage of another sudden jolt of the carriage, he flung himself on Saldaña just as the latter's pistol was pointing slightly away from him. With the same impetus, he delivered a vicious headbutt to Saldaña's face and felt the other man's nose crunch beneath the impact. *Cloc*, it went. Thick, red blood flowed forth, pouring down Saldaña's beard and chest. By then, Alatriste had snatched the pistol from him and was pointing it straight at Guadalmedina.

"Your weapon," the captain said.

Taken completely by surprise, Guadalmedina was about to open his mouth to call for help from those outside, when Alatriste hit him hard in the face with the pistol, just a moment before relieving him of his sword. Killing them wouldn't solve anything, he decided. He glanced at Saldaña, who was barely moving, like an ox felled by a blow to the back of the neck. He again struck Álvaro de la Marca hard, and the count, unable to defend himself, his arm in a sling, slid between the seats. "You're damn well not taking me to the Slaughterhouse," thought the captain. A blood-spattered Saldaña was gazing at him with dazed eyes.

"I'll see you again, Martín," said Alatriste.

He took Saldaña's second pistol and stuck it in his belt. Then he kicked open the carriage door and jumped out, a pistol in his right hand and a sword in his left. "I just hope my wounded leg doesn't let me down," he thought. A catchpole was already there, shouting to his comrades that the prisoner was trying to escape. The man was holding a torch and struggling, single-handed, to unsheathe his sword, and so, without thinking twice, Alatriste shot him point-blank in the chest; the blast lit up the man's face as it hurled him backward into the shadows. Alatriste's military instinct alerted him to the smell of a harquebus lit and ready to fire. Its owner was on the coachman's seat; there was no time to lose. He threw down the discharged pistol and took out the second one in order to shoot the man above. At that moment, however, another catchpole came running toward him, brandishing a sword. Alatriste had to choose. He pointed the pistol and stopped the running man in his tracks. The man was still clinging to a wheel of the carriage for support as Alatriste raced to the edge of the road and hurled himself down the slope that led to the stream and the river. Two men made as if to follow him, and a shot from a harquebus blazed forth from on top of the carriage: the bullet whistled past him and was lost in the darkness. He scrambled to his feet among the under-growth, his face and hands all scratched, ready to start run-ning again despite his painful leg, but his pursuers were on him already. Two black shapes came panting and stum-bling their way through the bushes, shouting: "Halt! Halt! Give yourself up in the name of the king!" Two of them at once and so near as well. He had no alternative but to turn and face them, his sword at the ready; and when the first one reached him, he did not wait, but lunged straight at him, driving his blade into the man's chest. The catchpole screamed and fell to the ground, while the other man hung back, prudently. Alatriste could see several more torches approaching down the path now. He set off running into the darkness, downhill, keeping close to the trees, guided by the sound of the nearby river. He found himself at last in the reedbeds and felt the mud beneath his boots. Luckily, the river was still full after the recent rains. He stuck his sword in his belt, waded in until the water was shoulder high, and then let himself be carried along by the current.

He swam downriver as far as the little islands, and from there returned to the shore. He walked through the reedbeds, splashing through the mud, until he was nearly at the Segovia bridge. He rested awhile to recover his breath, tied a handkerchief around the wound in his thigh, and then, shivering in his drenched clothes—he had lost cloak and hat in the scuffle—passed underneath the stone arches, avoiding the sentry box at the Puerta de Segovia. From there he walked slowly up to the heights of San Francisco, where, via a small stream that was used as a kind of drain, he could enter the city unseen. At that hour, he thought, there would be a swarm of constables out looking for him. He obviously couldn't go back to the Inn of the Turk, nor to Juan Vicuña's place. Taking refuge in a church would serve no purpose either, not even with Master Pérez's Jesuit brethren. In any matter involving a king, Saint Peter's jurisdiction was no match for that of the sword. His one chance lay in the poorest areas, where royal justice would not dare to venture at that hour of the night, and even during the day would do so only in a large band. Taking shelter in the shadows, he cautiously made his way as far as Plaza de la Cebada, and from there—taking the very narrowest of streets, and hurrying across the broader thoroughfares of Calle de Embajadores and Calle del Mesón de Paredes—he got as far as the fountain of Lavapiés, where Madrid's lowest inns and taverns and bawdy houses were to be found. He needed a place where he could hide away and think—he found Gualterio Malatesta's presence in Camino de las Minillas disconcerting in the extreme—but he had not a single doubloon with which to pay for such a haven. He mentally reviewed the friends he had in that area, weighing up which of them would be loyal enough not to betray him for thirty pieces of silver when a price was put on his head the next day. Immersed in these black thoughts, he turned and walked as far as Calle de la Comadre, where, at the door of the various whorehouses, lit by the torches and the little lanterns in the hallways, half a dozen prostitutes were plying their sad trade. Then he said to himself: "Perhaps God does exist and doesn't merely content himself with watching from afar while chance or the devil play fast and loose with mankind." For who should he see outside one of the taverns, slapping a whore about the face and looking every inch the ruffian, with the brim of his hat pulled down over one bushy eyebrow, but Bartolo Cagafuego.

7. THE FENCER'S ARMS

Don Francisco de Quevedo angrily threw down his cloak and hat on a stool and unfastened his ruff. The news could not be worse. "There's nothing to be done," he said, unbuckling his sword. "Guadalmedina refuses even to talk about the matter."

I stared out of the window. The threatening, gray clouds filling the Madrid sky above the rooftops of Calle del Niño made everything seem even grimmer. Don Francisco had spent two hours with Guadalmedina, trying, unsuccessfully, to convince the king's confidant of Captain Alatriste's innocence. Álvaro de la Marca had said that even if Alatriste were the victim of a conspiracy, his flight from justice had complicated everything. Quite apart from killing two catchpoles and badly wounding a third, he had left Saldaña with a broken nose and inflicted further injuries on the count himself.

"In short," concluded don Francisco, "he's determined to see him hanged."

"But they were friends," I protested.

"No friendship could withstand this. Furthermore, this really is a very strange affair."

"I hope at least *you* believe his story."

The poet sat down in the armchair made of walnut in which the late Duke of Osuna used to sit when he visited the house. On the table next to it lay paper and quills, a copper inkwell and sandbox, as well as a snuffbox and several books, among them a Seneca and a Plutarch.

"If I didn't believe the captain," he said, "I wouldn't have gone to see Guadalmedina."

He stretched out his legs and crossed his ankles. He was looking abstractedly at a sheet of paper, the top half of which bore his own clear, vigorous handwriting—the first four lines of a sonnet which I had read while I was waiting.

He that denies me what's only gained by stealth
Acts quite rightly and deprives me of nothing,
For low ambition, brought to pass with loathing,
Brings with it much dishonor, naught of wealth.

I went over to where don Francisco kept his wine—a sideboard decorated with a frieze made of squares of green glass, beneath a painting depicting Troy ablaze—and poured a large glass of wine. Don Francisco took a pinch of the snuff. He was not a great smoker, but he was fond of that powder made from leaves brought from the Indies.

"I've known your master for a long time, my boy," he went on. "He may be stubborn, he may sometimes go too far, but I know he would never raise his hand against the king."

"The count knows him too," I said, handing him the glass.

He nodded, having first sneezed twice.

"True. And I would bet my gold spurs that he knows the captain had nothing to do with it. However, there are only so many insults a nobleman can take: Alatriste's impertinence, the wound he dealt him in Calle de los Peligros, the beating he received the other night . . . Guadalmedina's pretty face still bears the marks left by your master before he escaped. Such things are hard to accept when you're a grandee of Spain. It's not so much the blow as not being able to make a fuss about it."

He took a sip of his wine and sat looking at me, meanwhile still fiddling with the canister of tobacco.

"It's lucky the captain got you out of there in time."

He continued to regard me thoughtfully. Then he put down the canister and took a longer drink of wine.

"Whatever made you go after him?"

I muttered something about a boy's curiosity, a liking for intrigues, et cetera. I knew that anyone trying to justify his actions tends to talk too much, and that too many explanations are always worse than a prudent silence. On the one hand, I was ashamed to admit that I had let myself be led into a trap by the poisonous young woman with whom, despite all, I was deeply in love. On the other hand, I considered Angélica de Alquézar to be my affair alone. I wanted to be the one to resolve that particular situation, but as long as my master was safely hidden away—we had received a discreet message from him through a safe channel—all explanations could wait. What mattered now was keeping him out of the hands of the torturers.

"I'm going to tell him what you've told me," I said.

I buttoned up my doublet and picked up my hat. Rain had started speckling the windows, and so I put on my serge cloak as well. Don Francisco watched as I concealed my dagger amongst my clothes.

"Be careful no one follows you."

There was every likelihood that someone would. The constables had questioned me at the Inn of the Turk, until I managed to convince them, by lying shamelessly, that I knew nothing about what had happened in Camino de las Minillas. La Lebrijana had been of no use to them either, even though they threatened and abused her, albeit only verbally. No one told her the real reason for the captain's disappearance. It was attributed to a sword fight in which someone had died, but no further details were offered.

"Don't worry. The rain will help to disguise me."

I was less concerned about the officers of the law than I was about the people behind the conspiracy, because they, I imagined, would certainly be watching me. I was about to take my leave when the poet raised one finger, as if an idea had just occurred to him. Getting up, he went over to a small desk by the window and removed what looked like a jewelry box.

"Tell the captain that I'll do whatever I can. It's a shame poor don Andrés Pacheco passed away so recently, and that Medinaceli is in exile and the Admiral of Castile has fallen from grace. All three were very fond of me and they would have been perfect as intermediaries."

It grieved me to hear this. Monsignor Pacheco had been the highest authority in the Spanish Inquisition, higher even than the Court of the Inquisition, which was presided over by our old enemy, the fearsome Dominican friar Emilio Bocanegra. As for Antonio de la Cerda, Duke of Medinaceli—who in time would become a close friend of don Francisco's and my protector—his impulsive young man's blood meant that he was now exiled from the court after using force to try to free a servant of his from prison. And the fall of the Admiral of Castile was public knowledge. His arrogance had caused unease in Catalonia during the recent visit to Aragon, after he had squabbled with the Duke of Cardona over who should sit next to the king when the latter was received in Barcelona. (His Majesty, by the way, returned without having extracted a single doubloon from the Catalans, for when he asked them for money for Flanders, they replied that they would uncomplainingly lay down life and honor for the king, as long as it involved no other expense, and declared that the treasury was the patrimony of the soul, and the soul belonged only to God.) The Admiral of Castile's misfortunes were compounded at the public washing of feet on Maundy Thursday, when Philip IV stripped him of the privilege he normally enjoyed of handing the king a towel on which to dry his hands, asking the Marquis of Liche to do so instead. Humiliated, the admiral had protested to the king, asking his permission to withdraw. "I am the first knight of the kingdom," he said, forgetting that he was standing before the first monarch of the world. And the king, annoyed, not only gave him permission to withdraw, he went even further. The admiral was to stay away from court, he said, until he received orders to the contrary.

"Do we have no one else?"

Don Francisco accepted that "we" as perfectly natural.

"Not of the stature of an Inquisitor General, a grandee of Spain, or a friend of the king, no, but I've asked for an audience with the count-duke. At least he doesn't allow himself to be taken in by appearances. He's intelligent and pragmatic."

We exchanged a none too hopeful look. Then don Francisco opened the small box and took out a purse. He counted eight *doblones de a cuatro*—more or less half of what was there, I noticed—and handed them to me.

"The captain might well have need of that powerful gentleman, Sir Money," he said.

How fortunate my master was, I thought, to have a man like don Francisco de Quevedo show him such loyalty. In our wretched Spain, even one's closest friends tended to be freer with words or sword-thrusts than with money. Those five hundred and twenty-eight *reales* were minted in lovely pale gold; some bore the cross of the true religion, others the head of His Catholic Majesty, and others that of his late father, Philip III. And each and every one of those coins would have been quite capable of blinding one-eyed Justice and buying a little protection—as indeed would coins bearing the Turk's crescent moon.

"Tell him I'm only sorry I can't give him double the amount," added the poet, returning the box to the desk, "but I'm still eaten up by debts. There's the rent on this house—which I was fool enough to buy simply in order to evict that vile sodomite, Góngora—and that alone drains forty ducats and my life's blood from me, and even the paper I write on has just had a new tax slapped on it. Oh well. Tell him to be very careful and not to go out into the street. Madrid has become an extremely dangerous place as far as he's concerned. Of course, he might console himself by meditating on the thought that he is the sole author of his woes:

It's the mark of both a miser and a louse
To want to buy but not to pay the price.

Those lines made me smile. Madrid was a dangerous place for the captain and for others as well, I thought proudly. It was all a question of who drew his sword first, and hunting a hare was not at all the same thing as hunting a wolf. I saw that don Francisco was smiling too.

"Then again, the most dangerous thing about Madrid is perhaps Alatriste himself," he said drily, as if he had guessed what I was thinking. "Don't you agree? Guadalmedina and Saldaña soundly beaten, a couple of catchpoles dead, another well on the way, and all in less time than it takes to say 'knife.'" He picked up his glass of wine and looked at the rain falling outside. "That's what I call killing."

He sat for a moment, staring thoughtfully into his glass, then raised it to the window as if drinking a toast to the captain.

"Your master," he concluded, "doesn't carry a sword in his hand but a scythe."

. . .

God was hurling the rain down in torrents on every inch of His good earth as I, wrapped in my cloak and with my hat dripping, walked to Lavapiés along Calle de la Compañía, seeking shelter beneath arcades and eaves from the water that was falling now as if every dyke in Holland had burst over my head. And although I was soaked to the skin and up to my gaiters in mud, I walked unhurriedly through the curtain of rain and the drops that were riddling the puddles like musket fire. Zigzagging up various streets, just to see if anyone was following me, I finally reached Calle de la Comadre, jumping over rivulets of mud and water to do so, and after one last prudent glance around me, entered the inn, where I shook myself like a wet dog.

The inn smelled of sour wine, damp sawdust, and grime. The Fencer's Arms (which bore its owner's nickname) was one of the most disreputable drinking dens in Madrid. The landlord had been an out-and-out knave and a cheat—he was also said to have been a thief, notorious for his skill as a picklock—until old age caught up with him. Worn down by a lifetime of poverty and hardship, he had opened the inn and turned it into a receiving house for stolen goods—hence his nickname, the Fencer—sharing any profit he made with the thieves. The inn was a large, dark house built around a courtyard and surrounded by other crumbling edifices; its many doors led to twenty or so sordid bedrooms and to a grimy, smoke-stained dining room where one could eat and drink very cheaply. It was, in short, the perfect place for pilferers and ruffians in search of a little privacy. In their attempts to scrape a living, the criminal world came and went at all hours, swathed in cloaks, swords clanking, or laden down with suspicious bundles. The place was filled with roughs and purloiners and captains of crime, with nimble-fingered pickpockets and ladies of the night, with every kind of no-good bent on dishonoring the Castiles, Old and New, and who all flocked there as happily as rooks to a wheatfield or scribes to a lawsuit. The powers that be were nowhere to be seen, partly so as not to stir up trouble and partly because the Fencer—a wily man who knew his trade—was always generous when it came to greasing the palms of constables and buying the favor of the courts. Furthermore, he had a son-in-law serving in the house of the Marquis of Carpio, which meant that seeking refuge in the Fencer's Arms was tantamount to taking sanctuary in a church. The other denizens, as well as being the cream of the criminal classes, were also blind, deaf, and dumb. No one there had a name or a surname, no one looked at anyone else, and even saying "Good afternoon" could be a reason for someone to slit your throat.

I found Bartolo Cagafuego sitting next to the fire in the kitchen, where the coals beneath the cooking pots were filling half the room with smoke. He was drowning his sorrows with sips from a mug of wine and some quiet talk with a comrade; he was, at the same time, keeping a watchful eye on his doxy, who, with her half-cloak draped over her shoulders, was agreeing on terms with a client. Cagafuego showed no sign of recognizing me when I went over to join him and to dry my wet clothes, which immediately began to steam in the heat. He continued his conversation, the subject of which was a recent encounter with a certain constable. This, he was explaining, had been resolved not with blood or shackles, but with money.

"Anyway," Cagafuego was saying in his *potreño* accent, "I goes over to the chief rozzer, gets out my purse, takes out two nice gold ducats of eleven *reales* each, and I says to the man, winkin' like, I says: 'I swear on these twenty-two commandments that the man you're lookin' for ain't me.' "

"And who was he, this rozzer?" asked the other man.

"One-eyed Berruguete."

"A decent son of a bitch, he is. And accommodatin' too."

"You're tellin' me, my friend. Anyway, he pocketed the cash and that was that."

"And the pigeon?"

"Oh, he was tearin' his hair out, sayin' as how it was me what stole his purse and that I had it on me still. But Berruguete, good as his word, just turned a deaf ear to him. That were a year ago now."

They continued for a while in quiet and distinctly un-Góngoresque fashion. Then, after a while, Bartolo Caga-fuego glanced across at me, put down his mug, stood up very casually, and stretched and yawned extravagantly, thus displaying the inside of his mouth with its half-dozen missing teeth. Then in buffcoat and breeches, his sword sheathed, he swaggered over to the door with all his usual bluff and bravado. I went to join him in the gallery of the courtyard, where our voices were muffled by the sound of the rain.

"No one at your heels, was there?" he asked.

"No one."

"You sure?"

"As sure as there's a God."

He nodded approvingly, scratching his bushy eyebrows, which met in the middle on his scarred face. Then, without a word, he set off down the gallery, and I followed. We hadn't seen each other since he'd had his sentence as a galley slave lifted after the attack on the *Niklaasbergen* and was granted a pardon, courtesy of Captain Alatriste. Caga-fuego had pocketed a tidy portion of that Indies gold, which allowed him to return to Madrid and continue in his chosen criminal career as ruffian or pimp or protector of prostitutes. For all his solid build and fierce appearance, and although he had acquitted himself well in Barra de Sanlúcar and slit many a throat, exposing his own throat to danger wasn't really his line. The fierce air he adopted was more for show than anything else, ideal for striking fear into the hearts of the unwary and for earning a living from women of the street, but not when it came to confronting any real toughs. So profound was his ignorance that only two or three of the five Spanish vowels had reached his notice, yet despite this—or perhaps precisely because of it— he now had a woman posted in Calle de la Comadre and had also come to an arrangement with the owner of a bawdy house, where he kept order by dint of a great deal of swearing and cursing. In fact, he was doing very well. With a record like his, though, it seemed to me even more remarkable that such a tavern-bound tough should risk his neck to help Captain Alatriste, for he had nothing to gain and a great deal to lose if anyone went bleating to the law. However, since their first meeting, years before in a Madrid dungeon, Bartolo Cagafuego had shown a strangely steadfast loyalty toward my master, the same loyalty I had observed often amongst people who had dealings with the captain, be they army comrades, people of quality, or heartless delinquents, or even, occasionally, enemies. Every now and then, certain rare men emerge who stand out from their contemporaries, not perhaps because they are different exactly, but because, in a way, they encapsulate, justify, and immortalize the age in which they live; and those who know such men realize or sense this, and take them as arbiters of how to behave. Diego Alatriste may well have been one of those unusual individuals, but even if he wasn't, I would say that anyone who fought at his side or shared his silences or met with a look of approval in his green eyes, felt bound to him forever by strong ties. It was as if gaining his respect made you respect yourself more.

"There's nothing to be done," I said. "You'll just have to wait until the air clears."

The captain had listened intently, not saying a word. We were sitting next to a rickety table spattered with candle wax and on which stood a bowl containing some leftover tripe, a jug of wine, and a crust of stale bread. Bartolo Cagafuego was standing a little apart, arms folded. We could hear the rain on the roof.

"When is Quevedo going to see the count-duke?"

"He doesn't know yet," I replied. "But *The Sword and the Dagger* is going to be performed in a few days' time at El Escorial, and don Francisco has promised to take me with him."

The captain ran a hand over his unshaven face. He seemed thinner, more haggard. He was wearing darned stockings, a collarless shirt beneath his doublet, and breeches made from cheap cloth. He did not look well, but his soldier's boots were standing in one corner, newly polished, and his new sword-belt on the table had just been freshly treated with horse grease. Cagafuego had bought him a hat and cloak from an old-clothes shop, as well as a rusty dagger that now lay sharpened and gleaming next to the pillow on the unmade bed.

"Did they give you much trouble?" the captain asked.

"No, not much," I said with a shrug. "Besides, no one can prove I was involved."

"And what about La Lebrijana?"

"The same."

"How is she?"

I gazed down at the puddle of water on the floor, beneath the soles of my boots.

"You know what she's like: lots of tears and threats. She swears blind that she'll be there in the front row when they hang you. But she'll get over it." I smiled. "She's softer than molasses, really."

Cagafuego nodded gravely, as if he knew exactly what I meant. He looked as if he were about to offer his views on women and their jealousies and affections, but restrained himself. He had too much respect for my master to butt into the conversation.

"And is there any news of Malatesta?" asked the captain.

The name made me fidget in my seat.

"No, not a word."

The captain was thoughtfully stroking his mustache.

Now and then he studied my face closely, as if hoping to read in it anything I might be keeping from him.

"I might know where to find him," he said.

These words suggested to me some mad plan.

"You mustn't run any unnecessary risks."

"We'll see."

"As the blind man said," I commented bluntly.

He looked at me again, and I rather regretted my impertinence. Out of the corner of my eye, I caught Bartolo Cagafuego's reproving glance, but it was true that this was no time for the captain to be prowling the streets or lurking in the shadows. Before he did anything that might compromise him further, he should wait and see what progress don Francisco de Quevedo could make. And I, for my part, urgently needed to talk to a certain maid of honor, for whom I had been watching out for days now, without success. As regards the information I was keeping from my master, any remorse I might feel was somewhat tempered by the thought that, while it was true that Angélica de Alquézar had led me into the trap, that trap would never have been possible without the captain's stubborn or suicidal collaboration. I had sufficient judgment to make these distinctions, and when you are nearly seventeen years old, no one is entirely a hero, apart from yourself, of course.

"Is this place safe?" I asked Cagafuego, as a way of changing the subject.

Cagafuego gave a fierce, gap-toothed smile.

"Tight as a drum. The law wouldn't come around here, not even if you paid them. And if some snitch was to peach on him, the captain can always climb out of the window and onto the roof. The captain's not the only one in trouble around here. If any bluebottles was to turn up, there's comrades aplenty to sound the alarm. And if that happens, he just has to scarper."

My master had not ceased looking at me all this time.

"We have to talk," he said.

Cagafuego raised one huge hand to his eyebrows by way of a farewell.

"While you're talkin' and if you don't need anythin' else, Captain, this here herdsman's goin' to take a turn around his pastures to see how Maripérez is gettin' on with the little bit of business she's got in hand. Like they say, the eye of the master fattens the mare."

He opened the door and stood silhouetted for a moment against the gray light of the gallery.

"Besides," he said, "and I mean no disrespect, you never can tell when you might run headfirst into the law and however plucky you might be and however hard you hold out when they plays you like a guitar, it's always easier to keep quiet about what you don't know than to keep quiet about what you do know."

"An excellent philosophy, Bartolo," the captain said with a smile. "Aristotle couldn't have put it better."

Cagafuego scratched the back of his neck.

"I don't know how brave or not that don Aristotle was, nor how he would stand up to three turns on the rack and never say 'Nones,' as is set down by a scribe that yours truly here once did. But you and I know tormentors what could make a stone sing."

He left, closing the door behind him. I took out the purse that don Francisco de Quevedo had given me and placed it on the table. With an absent air, my master piled up the gold coins.

"Tell me what happened," he said.

"What do you mean?"

"Tell me what you were doing the other night in Camino de las Minillas."

I swallowed hard and again stared down at the puddle of rainwater forming around my feet, then back at the captain. I felt as stunned as a wife in a play does when she discovers her husband in the dark with his mistress.

"You know what I was doing, Captain. I was following you."

"Why?"

"I was worried about . . . "

I stopped. The expression on my master's face had grown so somber that the words died on my lips. His pupils, which had been very dark in the dim light from the window, grew suddenly so small and steely that they seemed to pierce me like knives. I had seen that look on other occasions, occasions that often ended with a man bleeding to death on the ground. I felt afraid.

Then I gave a deep sigh and told him everything, from start to finish.

"I love her," I said when I had done.

And I said this as if it entirely justified my actions. The captain had got up and was standing at the window, watching the rain.

"Very much?" he asked pensively.

"Too much to put into words."

"Her uncle is the royal secretary."

I understood the implications of these words, which were more warning than reproach. However, they showed on what slippery ground we stood. Apart from the matter of whether or not Luis de Alquézar did or didn't know—Malatesta had, after all, worked for him before—the question was whether or not Angélica was part of the conspiracy, or whether her uncle or others, without being directly involved themselves, were trying to take advantage of the situation and climbing aboard a wagon that was already in motion.

"She is also," added the captain, "one of the queen's maids of honor."

This, it was true, was no small thing either. Then I

suddenly caught what he meant by these last words and froze. The idea that our queen could have anything to do with the intrigue was not so very ridiculous. Even a queen is a woman, I thought. She can feel jealousy just as keenly as a kitchen maid.

"But then why involve you?" the captain wondered out loud. "I was more than enough."

I thought for a while.

"I don't know," I said. "It would provide the executioner with another head to chop off, I suppose. But you're right, if the queen were involved, it would make sense if one of her maids of honor was too."

"Or perhaps someone simply wants to make it seem that way."

I looked at him, startled. He had gone over to the table and was studying the little pile of gold coins.

"Hasn't it occurred to you that someone might want to lay the blame for the incident on the queen?"

I stared at him, openmouthed, aghast at the sinister implications of such an idea.

"After all," the captain went on, "as well as being a deceived wife, she's also French. Imagine the situation: the king dies, Angélica disappears, you're arrested along with me, and on the rack you reveal that it was one of the queen's maids of honor who lured you into the trap . . ."

I pressed my hand to my heart, offended.

"I would never betray Angélica."

He looked at me and smiled the weary smile of a veteran.

"Just imagine that you did."

"Impossible. I didn't give you away to the Inquisition, did I?"

"True."

He was still looking at me, but he said no more. I knew what he was thinking, though. Dominican friars were one thing, but royal justice another. As Cagafuego had said, there were torturers capable of loosening the tongue of even the bravest man. I considered this new variant to the plot, and could see that it was not unreasonable. Thanks to our strolls through Madrid's *mentideros*, or gossip-shops, and to conversations with the captain's friends, I was up to date on all the latest news: the struggle between Richelieu, the minister of France, and our Count-Duke of Olivares was already sounding the drum of future wars in Europe. No one doubted that once our froggy neighbors resolved the problem with the Huguenots in La Rochelle, the Spanish and the French would go back to killing each other on the battlefield. Implying that the queen was involved, regardless of whether this was true or false, was therefore not so very outlandish and could prove very useful to certain people. There were those who loathed Isabel de Borbón—Olivares, his wife, and followers among them—and there were those inside and outside Spain—England, for example, as well as Venice, the Turk, and even the pope in Rome—who wanted us to go to war with France. An anti-Spanish plot implicating the sister of the French king was all too credible. On the other hand, it might be an explanation that concealed others.

"It's time, I think," said the captain, looking at his sword, "for me to pay a little visit."

It was a shot in the dark. Three years had passed, but there was no harm in trying. In his drenched cloak and dripping hat, Diego Alatriste studied the house carefully. By curious chance, the house was only two streets from his hiding place, or perhaps it wasn't chance. That area of Madrid was one of the worst in the city, home to the lowest taverns, bars, and inns. And if, he concluded, it was a good place for him to hide, then it would be for others as well.

He looked around. Behind him, the Plaza de Lavapiés was veiled by a translucent gray curtain of rain that almost concealed the stone fountain. Calle de la Primavera—"Spring Street, indeed," he thought with some irony. At that moment it couldn't have been a less appropriate name, what with the muddy unpaved street awash with filth. The house, formerly the Landsknecht Inn, was directly opposite him; thick trails of water poured from the roof down the façade, where some much-darned white bed linen, put out to dry before the rains came, hung like shrouds from the windows.

He watched for one long hour before deciding to act. He crossed the road and went through the archway into a courtyard that stank of horse manure. There was no one to be seen. A few bedraggled chickens were pecking around beneath the galleries, and as he went up the wooden stairs, which creaked beneath his feet, a fat cat engaged in devouring a dead rat eyed him impassively. The captain unfastened his drenched cloak, which weighed too heavily on him. He also took off his hat, because the brim was so sodden it was obscuring his view. Thirty or so steps took him up to the top floor, and there he paused to think. If his memory served him well, the door was the last one on the right, in the corner of the corridor. He went over and pressed his ear to the door. Not a sound. Only the cooing of the pigeons sheltering in the dripping roof of the gallery. He put his cloak and hat down on the floor and took from his belt the weapon for which, that very afternoon, he had paid Bartolo Cagafuego ten *escudos*: a flintlock pistol, almost new, with a damascus barrel two spans long and the initials of an unknown owner on the butt. He checked that it was still primed despite the damp, then cocked the hammer—*clack*. He held it firmly in his right hand and, with his left, opened the door.

It was the same woman. She was sitting in the light from the window, mending the clothes in the basket on her lap. When she saw the intruder enter, she stood up, threw down her work, and opened her mouth to cry out, and only failed to do so because a slap from Alatriste propelled her backward against the wall. Better to hit her once now, thought the captain, than several times later on, when she's had time to collect her thoughts. There's nothing like that initial shock and fear. And so, once he had slapped her, he grabbed her violently by the throat, then, releasing his grip, covered her mouth with his left hand and pressed the pistol to her head.

"Not a word," he whispered, "or I'll blow your face off."

He felt the woman's damp breath on the palm of his hand, her body trembling against his, and while he held her in his grasp, he looked about him. The room had barely changed: the same miserable bits of furniture, the chipped crockery on the table, the same rough table-cloth. Nevertheless, everything was tidy. There was a copper brazier and a rug on the floor. A bed, separated off from the rest of the room by a curtain, was neatly made and clean, and a cooking pot was boiling in the hearth.

"Where is he?" he asked the woman, slightly easing his grip on her mouth.

Another shot in the dark. She might have nothing to do

with the man he was looking for, but it was the only trail he had to follow. As he recalled, and according to his hunter's instinct, this woman was not an insignificant player in the game. He had only seen her once before, years ago, and only for a matter of moments, but he remembered the expression on her face and her anxiety, her disquiet for the man who, at the time, was defenseless and under threat. Even snakes need company, he thought with a sardonic smile; yes, even snakes have their other half.

She said nothing, simply stared at the pistol out of the corner of her eye, terrified. She was a slender, ordinary-looking young woman, neither pretty nor ugly, but with a good figure; the dark hair caught back at her neck fell in loose locks about her face. She was wearing a skirt made of some cheap fabric and a sleeveless blouse that left her arms bare, her shawl having slipped off in the struggle. She smelled slightly of the food steaming in the pot, and of sweat, too.

"Where is he?" asked the captain again.

She focused her terrified gaze on him again, breathing hard, but still she said nothing. Alatriste could feel her agitated bosom rise and fall beneath his arm. He glanced around for some sign of a male presence: a short black cape hanging from a hook, a man's shirts in the basket she had dropped, two clean collars, newly starched. Although, of course, it might not be the same man. Life goes on, and women are women; men come and go. These things happen.

"When will he be back?" he asked.

She remained dumb, staring at him with fearful eyes. Now, however, he saw in them a glimmer of comprehension. "Perhaps she recognizes me," he thought. "At least she'll realize that I mean her no harm."

"I'm going to let you go," he said, sticking the pistol back in his belt and taking out his dagger. "But if you scream or try to run away, I'll slit your throat like I would a sow's."

At that hour, the gambling den in the Cava de San Miguel was in full swing. The place was packed with gamblers and cheats, and with hangers-on hoping that the winners might toss them a fraction of their winnings. The atmosphere was, in short, thick with possibilities. Juan Vicuña, the owner, came over to me as soon as I walked through the door.

"Have you seen him?" he asked in a low voice.

"The wound in his leg has healed up. He's well and sends you greetings."

The former sergeant of horse, maimed in the dunes at Nieuwpoort, nodded, pleased. His friendship with my master went back a long way. Like other denizens of the

Inn of the Turk, he was concerned about Captain Alatriste's fate.

"And what about Quevedo? Is he talking to people at the palace?"

"He's doing what he can, but that isn't very much."

Vicuña sighed deeply and said nothing more. Like don Francisco de Quevedo, Master Pérez, and Licentiate Calzas, Vicuña believed not a word of what was being said about the captain, but my master didn't want to go to any of them for help in case he implicated them, too. The crime of lèse-majesté was far too serious to involve one's friends; it ended on the scaffold.

"Guadalmedina is inside," he said.

"Alone?"

"No, with the Duke of Cea and a Portuguese gentleman I've never seen before."

I handed him my dagger, as everyone did, and Vicuña gave it to the guard on the door. In that city of proud people who all too easily reached for sword or dagger, it was forbidden to bear arms when entering gambling dens or whorehouses. Despite that precaution, however, it was still not uncommon for cards and dice to end up stained with blood.

"Is he in a good mood?"

"Well, he's just won a hundred *escudos*, so, yes, but you'd better be quick because they're talking about going to the

Soleras bawdy house, where they've arranged a supper and a few girls."

He squeezed my shoulder affectionately and left me. Vicuña had behaved like a loyal friend by advising me of the count's presence there that night. After my talk with Captain Alatriste, I had spent a long time pondering a possibly desperate plan—desperate, but one to which I could see no alternative. Then I trudged across the city in the rain, visiting friends and weaving my web as I went. I was now soaked to the skin and exhausted, but I had flushed out my prey in the most propitious of places, something I could never have done at the Guadalmedina residence or in the palace itself. After giving it much thought, I had decided to go through with my plan, even if it cost me my liberty or my life.

I walked across the room, beneath the yellowish light from the tallow lamps hanging from the ceiling. As I said, the atmosphere was as heavily weighted as the dice they used in some of the games. Money, cards, and dice came and went on the half-dozen tables around which sat the players. At one table, cards were being dealt, at another, dice were being rolled, yet another rang with curses—"A pox on't," "Damn my luck," "Od's my life"; and at every table, sharpers and swindlers, skilled at palming an ace or weighting a die, were trying to fleece their fellow men, either by a slow bloodletting, one *maravedí* at a time, or by a single fulminating blow, of the sort that left the poor dupe plucked and singed, and all his cargo gone.

A pox on you, vile card—
Accursed, cruel, ill-starred—
Which, with rigor fierce and rash
Has left me cards, but no cash.

Álvaro de la Marca was not one to be fleeced. He had a good eye and even better hands, and was himself a master at cozening, beguiling, and duping. If the fancy took him, he could have gulled any gambler worth his salt. I saw him at one of the tables, in good spirits and still winning. He was as elegantly dressed as ever: gray doublet embroidered with silver thread, breeches, and turned-down boots, with a pair of amber-colored gloves folded and tucked in his belt. With him, along with the Portuguese gentleman Vicuña had referred to—and whom I found out later to be the young Marquis of Pontal—was the Duke of Cea, grandson of the Duke of Lerma and brother-in-law of the Admiral of Castile, a young man of the best family who, shortly afterward, won fame as the bravest of soldiers in the wars in Italy and Flanders, before dying with great dignity on the banks of the Rhine. I made my way discreetly through the throng of hangers-on, gawpers, and cheats, and waited until the count looked up from the table, where he had just beaten two other dice players by throwing a double six. When he saw me, he looked half surprised, half annoyed. Frowning, he returned to the game, but I stood my ground, determined not to move until he took proper notice of me. When he glanced at me again, I gestured knowingly to him and moved away a little, hoping that, if he didn't have the decency to greet me, he might at least feel curious about what I had to tell him. In the end, albeit reluctantly, he gave in. I saw him pick up his winnings from the table, give a tip to a couple of the hangers-on, and put the rest in his purse. Then he came toward me. On the way, he made a sign to one of the serving boys, who hurried over to him with a mug of wine. The rich never lack for minions to fulfill their hedonistic desires.

"Well," he said coldly, taking a sip of his wine. "What are you doing here?"

We went into the small room that Juan Vicuña had set aside for us. There were no windows, just a table, two chairs, and a burning candle. I closed the door and leaned against it.

"Be brief," said Guadalmedina.

He was looking at me suspiciously, and the coolness of his manner and his words saddened me greatly. The captain must have offended him greatly, I thought, for him to have forgotten that he saved his life in the Kerkennahs, that we attacked the *Niklaasbergen* out of friendship for him and in the king's service, and that one night, in Seville, we saw off a patrol of catchpoles together outside a bawdy house. Then, however, I noticed the purplish marks still visible on his face, the awkward way he moved the arm injured in Calle de los Peligros, and realized that we all have our reasons for doing what we do or don't do. Álvaro de la Marca had more than enough reason to bear my master a grudge.

"There's something you should know," I said.

"Something? Too many things, you mean. But time will tell . . ."

Like an evil omen, or a threat, he left those last words floating in the wine that he raised to his lips. He had not sat down, as if to convey that he intended to get the conversation over with as quickly as possible, and he maintained his lofty pose, mug of wine in one hand, the other hand planted nonchalantly on his hip. I looked at his aristocratic face, his wavy hair, curled mustache, and fair beard, at his elegant white hands and at the ring which, alone, was worth the ransom of some poor captive in Algeria. The Spain he inhabited, I concluded, was another world, one endowed with power and money from the cradle onward. For someone in Álvaro de la Marca's position, there were certain things that could never be contemplated with equanimity. Nevertheless, I had to try. It was my last chance.

"I was there that night, too," I said.

Darkness had descended. Outside, the rain was still falling. Diego Alatriste remained motionless, sitting at the table, observing the woman sitting equally still in the other chair, her hands tied behind her back and a gag in her mouth. He did not like having to do this, but he felt he had his reasons. If the man he was waiting for was who he thought, it would be too dangerous to leave the woman free to move or cry out.

"Is there nothing I can light the candle with?" he asked.

She did not stir. She kept staring at him, her mouth covered by the gag. Alatriste got up and rummaged around in the larder until he found a match and a few wood shavings, which he threw onto the coals in the kitchen, where he had hung his cloak and hat to dry. While he was there, he removed the pot from the fire and found that the contents had boiled half away. With the match, he lit a candle on the table. Then he emptied some of contents of the pot into a bowl; the lamb and chickpea stew had rather too strong a flavor, was overcooked and very hot, but he ate it anyway, along with some bread and a pitcher of water, and wiped the plate clean. Then he glanced at the woman.

He had been there for three hours, and in all that time, she had uttered not a single word.

"Don't worry," he lied. "I just want to talk to him."

Alatriste had used the time to confirm to himself that he was in the right place. Besides observing the short black cape, the shirts, collars, and other clothes in the house, all of which might have belonged to anyone, he had opened a chest and found a pair of good pistols, a flask of gunpowder, a small bag of bullets, a knife as sharp as a razor, a coat of mail, and a few letters and documents evidently giving coded place names and itineraries. There were also two books which he was now leafing curiously through, having first loaded the two pistols and placed them in his belt, leaving Cagafuego's on the table. One of the books was, surprisingly enough, an Italian translation of Pliny's *Natural History*, printed in Venice, which, for a moment, made the captain doubt that the owner of the book and the man he was waiting for could be the same person. The other book was in Spanish and the title made him smile: *God's Politics, Christ's Governance*, by don Francisco de Quevedo y Villegas.

There was a noise outside. Fear flickered in the woman's eyes. Diego Alatriste picked up the pistol from the table and, trying not to make the floorboards creak, positioned himself to one side of the door. Everything happened with extraordinary simplicity: the door opened and in walked Gualterio Malatesta, shaking his sodden cloak and hat. Then, ever so gently, the captain pressed the barrel of the pistol to Malatesta's head.

8. OF MURDERERS
AND BOOKS

"She has nothing to do with any of this," said Malatesta.

He put his sword and dagger down on the floor, kicking them away from him as Alatriste ordered. He was looking at the woman who was still sitting, bound and gagged, on the chair.

"It doesn't matter," said the captain, keeping the pistol pressed to Malatesta's head. "She's my trump card."

"Well played, I must say. Do you kill women, too?"

"If necessary. As do you, I imagine."

Malatesta nodded thoughtfully. His pockmarked face remained impassive, although the scar above his right eye gave him a slight squint. Finally, he turned to look at the captain. In the dim light from the candle, Alatriste could see his black clothes, sinister air, and cruel, dark eyes. A smile appeared beneath Malatesta's mustache.

"This is your second visit here."

"And it will be my last."

Malatesta paused before replying:

"You had a pistol in your hand on that occasion, too."

Alatriste remembered it well: the same bed, the same miserable room, the wounded man's eyes like those of a dangerous snake. The Italian had commented then: "With luck I'll arrive in hell in time for supper."

"I've often regretted not using it," retorted Alatriste.

The cruel smile grew wider. "We're in agreement there," the smile seemed to say, "pistol-shots are full stops and doubts are dangerous ellipses." He noticed and recognized the two pistols the captain had found in the chest and which he was now wearing in his belt.

"You shouldn't go wandering about on your own in Madrid, you know," he remarked with grim solicitude. "They say your skin isn't worth a Ceuta penny."

"Who says?"

"I don't know. It's just a rumor."

"Worry about your own skin."

Malatesta gave that same pensive nod, as if he appreciated the advice. Then he looked at the woman, whose terrified eyes kept shifting from him to Alatriste.

"There's just one thing in all this that I find rather insulting, Captain. The fact that you didn't simply shoot me as soon as I came through the door means that you think I'm going to blab."

Alatriste did not reply. Some things one took for granted.

"I can understand you feeling curious, though," added the Italian after a moment. "But perhaps I *can* tell you something without detriment to myself."

"Why me?" Alatriste asked.

Malatesta made a gesture with his hands as if to say "Why not?" and then indicated the pitcher of water on the table and asked for a little to slake his parched throat. The captain shook his head.

"For various reasons," Malatesta went on, resigned to going thirsty. "You have unfinished business with a number of people, not just me. Besides, your affair with the Castro woman was like a gift from the gods." His malicious smile grew wider. "How could we miss the opportunity of putting it all down to jealousy, especially with a man like you involved, always so ready to reach for his sword? It's just a shame they played that trick on us, replacing the king with an actor."

"Did you know who the man was?"

Malatesta tutted glumly, like a professional disgusted at his own ineptitude.

"I thought I did," he said, "although, afterward, it turned out that I didn't."

"You certainly had your sights set very high."

Malatesta regarded Alatriste almost with surprise, almost ironically.

"High or low, crown or bishop, it's all the same to me," he said. "The only king I value is the one in a pack of cards, and the only God I know is the one I use to blaspheme with. It's a great relief when life and the passing years strip away certain things. Everything is so much simpler, so much more practical. Don't you feel that? Ah, no, of course, I am forgetting. You're a soldier. Or, rather, you pay lip service to such things; because people like you need words like "king," "true religion," "my country," and all that, just to get by and to feel you're doing the decent thing. I find it hard to believe, really, in a man of your experience, and given the times we're living through."

Having said this, he stopped and looked at the captain, as if expecting him to reply.

"Then again," he added, "your exemplary loyalty as a subject didn't prevent you from getting into a squabble with His Catholic Majesty over a woman. But then a hair from a quim has done in far more men than the noose ever has. *Puttana Eva!*"

He sneered mockingly and fell silent, before whistling his usual little tune through his teeth. Ignoring the pistol pointing at him, he gazed distractedly about the room. He was, of course, only pretending to be distracted. Alatriste knew that the Italian's wary eyes would miss nothing. "If I drop my guard for a moment," he thought, "the bastard will be on me."

"Who's paying you?"

Malatesta's hoarse, discordant laugh filled the room.

"Fie on you, Captain. Such a question is hardly appropriate between men like us."

"Is Luis de Alquézar involved?"

Malatesta remained silent, his face expressionless. He was looking at the books Alatriste had been leafing through.

"I see you've taken an interest in my reading matter," he said at last.

"Yes, I was surprised," agreed the captain. "I didn't know you were such an educated son of a whore."

"I see no contradiction."

Malatesta glanced at the woman who was still sitting motionless in the chair. Then he touched the scar over his right eye.

"Books help you to understand life, don't you think? You can even find in them a justification for lying and betraying . . . for killing."

He had placed one hand on the table as he spoke. Alatriste drew back prudently, and with a movement of the pistol indicated that the Italian do the same.

"You talk too much, but not about what interests me."

"What do you expect? We men from Palermo have our rules."

He had obediently moved a few inches away from the

table and was studying the barrel of the pistol gleaming in the candlelight.

"How's the boy?"

"Fine. At least he's alive and well."

Malatesta's smile broadened into a knowing grimace.

"Yes, I see you managed to leave him out of it. I congratulate you. He's a plucky lad, and good with a sword, too. However, I fear you may be leading him astray. He'll end up like you and me. And speaking of endings, I suppose my life is about to end here and now."

This was neither a lament nor a protest, merely a logical conclusion. Malatesta again looked at the woman, for longer this time, before turning back to Alatriste.

"A shame," he said serenely. "I would have preferred to have this conversation elsewhere, sword in hand, with time to spare. But I don't somehow think you're going to give me that chance." He held Alatriste's gaze, the expression on his face half inquisitive, half sarcastic. "Because you're not, are you?"

He was still calmly smiling, his eyes fixed on the captain's.

"Have you ever thought," he said suddenly, "how very alike we are, you and I?"

A likeness, thought Alatriste, that would last for only a few seconds more, and with that, he steadied his hand, and prepared to squeeze the trigger. Malatesta had read this sentence as clearly as if it had been written on a poster and placed before his eyes.. His face tensed and his smile froze on his lips.

"I'll see you in hell," he said.

At that moment, the woman—hands tied behind her, eyes wild, the gag muffling a cry of fierce desperation—stood up and hurled herself headfirst at Alatriste. He stepped lightly aside to avoid her and, just for an instant, lowered the pistol. For Gualterio Malatesta, however, that instant meant the slender difference between life and death. The woman fell at Alatriste's feet, and in the precious moment Alatriste spent avoiding her and trying to readjust his aim, Malatesta knocked the candle off the table with one swipe of his hand—thus plunging the room into darkness—and immediately crouched down to pick up his discarded weapons. The pistol shot broke the windowpanes above his head, and the flash lit up the gleaming steel blade already in his hand. "Christ's blood," thought Alatriste, "he's going to escape. Either that or kill me."

The woman lay groaning on the floor, thrashing about like a wild thing. Alatriste leapt over her, threw down the discharged pistol, and unsheathed his sword. He would just have time to stab Malatesta before he got to his feet—if, that is, he could find him in the darkness. He lunged several times, but met only thin air. As he wheeled around, a blow came from behind, hard and fast, piercing his jerkin and only failing to pierce his flesh because it caught him sideways. The sound of a chair scraping the floor helped him to orient himself better, and he headed in that direction, blade foremost, and this time his sword found the enemy. "So there you are," he thought, reaching with his left hand for one of the pistols. Malatesta, however, had noticed the pistols already and was in no mood to let him fire. He hurled himself violently upon the captain, lashing out and striking him with the guard of his sword. No words were spoken, no insults or threats exchanged. The two men were saving their breath for the struggle, and all that could be heard were grunts and panting. "If he's had time to pick up his dagger," thought the captain suddenly, "I'm done for." He forgot about his pistol and felt for his own knife. Malatesta guessed what he was up to and reached out to try and stop him; they rolled across the floor with a great clatter of furniture and broken crockery. At such close quarters, there was no room for swords. Finally, Alatriste managed to free his left hand and take out his own dagger. He drew back and stabbed wildly twice. The first stab slashed his opponent's clothes, the second struck nothing at all, and there was no time for a third blow. There came the sound of the door being wrenched violently open and, for a moment, he saw the fleeing figure of the Italian framed in a rectangle of light.

I was feeling very happy. It had stopped raining; over the city's rooftops, the day was dawning, bright and sunny, with a clear blue sky; and I was going in through the palace door, at the side of don Francisco de Quevedo. We had walked across the square, pushing our way through the idlers who had been assembling there since before daybreak and were being kept in check by the uniformed lancers standing guard. The curious, talkative people of Madrid were ingenuously loyal to their monarchs, always ready to forget their own miseries and take inexplicable delight in applauding the luxury in which those who governed them lived. On that particular morning, they were happily waiting to see the king and queen, whose carriages stood outside the Alcázar. Any royal journey always brought out the crowds and, inevitably, involved legions of courtiers, gentlemen of the household, handmaids, servants, and carriages. Rafael de Cózar and his theater company, including María de Castro, would also be setting off for El Escorial, if, indeed, they had not done so already, for *The Sword and the Dagger* was to be performed in the gardens of that palace-cum-monastery at the beginning of the following week. As for the members of the royal entourage, they were—despite the strict sumptuary laws in force—all competing with one another in ostentation and lavishness of dress. Assembled outside the palace was a colorful collection of coaches emblazoned with coats of arms; there were good mules and even better horses, liveried footmen, silks, brocades, and other adornments, for both those with the means and those without would gladly spend their last *maravedí* on cutting a fine figure at court. In that world of pretense and appearances, nobles and plebeians would have pawned their own coffin to prove that they were of pure blood and better than their neighbor. As Lope said:

Tie me up and burn me
If I couldn't make a million
Out of taxing every would-be don
Just one maravedí.

"It still amazes me," said don Francisco, "that you managed to convince Guadalmedina."

"I didn't convince him of anything," I said. "He convinced himself. I merely told him what had happened, and he believed me."

"Perhaps he wanted to believe you. He knows Alatriste and knows precisely what he would and wouldn't do. The idea of a conspiracy makes much more sense. It's one thing to dig your heels in about a woman, but quite another to kill a king."

We were walking past the granite pillars to the main staircase. The queen's courtyard, where a large number of courtiers were waiting for the king and queen to come down, was filled by the golden light of the rising sun that glinted on the capitals and on the two-headed eagles above the arches. Don Francisco politely doffed his hat to a few court acquaintances. He was dressed, as usual, entirely in black grosgrain, with a ribbon as hatband, a red cross on his breast, and a gold-hilted court sword at his waist. I was no less elegant in my light woolen costume and my cap, my dagger stuck crosswise in my belt at the back. A manservant had placed my traveling case, containing my day-to-day clothes and a pair of clean undergarments neatly folded by La Lebrijana, in the carriage occupied by the Marquis of Liche's servants, with whom don Francisco had arranged transport for me. He had a seat in the marquis's carriage, a privilege which, as usual, he justified in his own way:

I'll not bend the knee to a noble house,
For as the ancient saying goes:
If the king's of pure blood, then so's his louse.

"The count knows that the captain is innocent," I said once we were alone again.

"Of course," replied the poet, "but the captain's insolence and that cut to the arm are hard to forgive, even more so with the king involved. Now, though, the count has an opportunity to resolve the matter honorably."

"He hasn't gone that far," I objected. "He's merely promised to arrange for the captain to meet the count-duke."

Don Francisco looked around him and lowered his voice.

"That's no small thing," he said. "Although it's only

natural, of course, that, as a courtier, he'll try to turn things to his advantage. The affair has gone beyond a simple spat over a woman, so he's quite right to place it all in the count-duke's hands. Alatriste is an invaluable witness if the conspiracy is to be uncovered. They know he'll never talk under torture, or can be reasonably sure that he won't. To do so voluntarily would be a different matter."

I felt a pang of remorse. I had not told Guadalmedina or don Francisco about Angélica de Alquézar, only the captain. Whether my master chose to give her away or not was a matter for him, but I would not be the one to tell others the name of the young woman with whom, despite everything, and to the damnation of my soul, I was still deeply in love.

"The problem," the poet continued, "is that, after all the commotion created by his escape, Alatriste can't just wander about as if nothing were amiss, at least not until he's spoken to Olivares and Guadalmedina at El Escorial. But that's seven leagues away."

I nodded anxiously. I myself, with don Francisco's help, had hired a good horse so that the captain could set off the following morning for El Escorial, where he was due to present himself that night. The horse, which I had left in Bartolo Cagafuego's care, would be waiting, saddled and ready, next to the Ermita del Ángel on the other side of the Segovia bridge.

"Perhaps you should speak to the count, just in case anything unexpected should happen."

Don Francisco placed one hand on the cross of Santiago he bore on his chest.

"Me? Absolutely not. I have so far managed to keep out of the affair without betraying my friendship with the captain. Why spoil things at the last moment? You're doing a fine job."

He gave another nod of greeting to passing acquaintances, then smoothed his mustache and rested the palm of his left hand on the hilt of his sword.

"You have, I must say, behaved like a proper man," he concluded fondly. "Approaching Guadalmedina really was tantamount to stepping into the lion's den. You showed real courage."

I did not respond. I was looking around me, for I had made a rendezvous of my own before traveling to El Escorial. We were near the broad staircase that stood between the respective courtyards of the queen and the king, beneath the large allegorical tapestry that presided over the main landing where four German guards, armed with halberds, stood motionless. The most noble members of the court, with the count-duke and his wife at their head, were waiting for the king and queen to descend in order to greet them. They provided a spectacular display of fine fabrics and jewels, of perfumed ladies and gentlemen with waxed mustaches and curled hair. I heard don Francisco murmur:

"See them all decked out in purple,
Hands beringed with glittering gems?
Inside, they're naught but putrefaction,
Made of mud and earth and worms."

I turned to him. I knew something of the world and of the court. I remembered what he had said about the king and the louse, too.

"And yet you, Señor Poet," I said smiling, "will be traveling in the Marquis of Liche's carriage."

Don Francisco imperturbably returned my gaze, looked to left and right, then gave me a discreet nudge.

"Hush, you insolent boy. To everything its season. I had hoped you might give the lie to that magnificent line— penned by myself—which says: "Young ears are no fit recipient for the truth." And in the same quiet voice, he continued:

"Evil and evil doers? Leave them well alone.
Let us live as witnesses not accomplices,
So the Old World to the New makes moan."

However, the New World, namely me, had ceased listening to the Old World. The jester Gastoncillo had just appeared amongst the throng and was gesturing toward the servants' stairs behind me. When I looked up, I caught a glimpse, above the carved granite balustrade, of Angélica de Alquézar's fair ringlets. A letter I had written the previous afternoon had clearly reached the person to whom it was addressed.

"I believe you have some explaining to do," I said.

"Not at all. And I have very little time. The queen is about to go down to the courtyard."

She was resting her hands on the balustrade, watching the comings and goings below. That morning, her eyes were as cold as her words. She was no longer the affectionate young woman, dressed as a man, whom I had held in my arms.

"This time you've gone too far," I said. "You, your uncle, and whoever else is mixed up in all this."

She was playing distractedly with the ribbons adorning the bodice of her silk-embroidered dress.

"I don't know what you're talking about, sir. Nor what my uncle has to do with your ravings."

"I'm talking about the ambush in Camino de las Minillas," I replied angrily. "About the man in the yellow doublet. About the attempt to kill the—"

She placed a hand on my lips, just as she had placed a kiss on them a few nights before. I shivered, and again she noticed. She smiled.

"Don't talk nonsense."

"If all is revealed," I said, "you'll be in great danger."

She regarded me with interest, almost as if she found my disquiet intriguing.

"I can't imagine you ever taking a lady's name in vain."

I felt as if she had guessed what I was thinking. I drew myself up, embarrassed.

"No, *I* might not, but there are other people involved."

She looked at me as if she could not believe the implication behind my words.

"Have you told your friend Batatriste?"

I said nothing and averted my gaze. She read my reply on my face.

"I thought you were a gentleman," she said disdainfully.

"I am," I protested.

"I also thought that you loved me."

"I do love you."

She bit her lower lip as she pondered my words. Her eyes were like very hard blue polished stone. Finally, she asked bitterly:

"Have you betrayed me to anyone else?"

There was such scorn in that word "betrayed" that I could not speak for shame. Eventually, I composed myself and opened my mouth to utter a new protest. "You surely don't think I could keep all this secret from the captain," I began to say, but the sound of trumpets echoing through the courtyard drowned out my words. Their Majesties had appeared on the other side of the balustrade, at the top of the main staircase. Angélica glanced around, catching up her skirt.

"I have to go." She seemed to be thinking as fast as she could. "I will see you again perhaps."

"Where?"

She hesitated, then gave me a strange look, so penetrating that I felt quite naked before it.

"Are you going to El Escorial with don Francisco de Quevedo?"

"I am."

"I'll see you there."

"How will I find you?"

"Don't be silly. I'll find you."

This sounded more threat than promise, or both things at once. I watched as she walked away and as she turned once to smile at me. I thought again, "By God, she's beautiful. And frightening, too." Then she disappeared behind the columns and went down to join the king and queen, who were already at the foot of the stairs, where they were greeted by the Count-Duke of Olivares and the other courtiers. Then they all went out into the street. I followed behind, plunged in dark thoughts. I recalled with some unease the lines of poetry that Master Pérez had once made me copy out:

Averting one's gaze from evident deceit,
When poison foul gives off a honey'd smell
And pain is loved and pleasures all retreat,
Then, one believes that heaven's found in hell
And body and soul are at illusion's behest,
Such is love—as he who tastes it can attest.

Outside, the sun was shining, and the scene it lit up was splendid indeed. The king was bowing to the queen and offering her his arm, and both were wearing sumptuous traveling clothes. The king had on a riding outfit sewn with silver thread, a crimson silk taffeta sash, as well as sword and spurs, a sign that, being the bold, young rider he was, he would make part of the journey on horseback, escorting the queen's carriage, which was drawn by six magnificent white horses and followed by another four coaches carrying the queen's twenty-four handmaids and maids of honor. In the square, among the courtiers and other people crowding the area, the monarchs were greeted by Cardinal Barberini, the papal legate, who would be traveling in the company of the Dukes of Sessa and Maqueda, and so the greetings and salutations continued. With the royal party was the Infanta María Eugenia—only a few months old and in the arms of her nurse—the king's brothers, the Infante Don Carlos, and the Prince of Wales's impossible love, the Infanta Doña María, as well as the

Cardinal-Infante Don Fernando, who had been Archbishop of Toledo since he was a boy and would eventually become general and governor of Flanders. Under his command, a few years later, Captain Alatriste and I would find ourselves battling hordes of Swedes and Protestants at Nördlingen. Amongst the courtiers closest to the king, I spotted the Count of Guadalmedina, wearing an elegant cape and French boots and breeches. Farther off, don Francisco de Quevedo was standing next to the count-duke's son-in-law, the Marquis of Liche, reputed to be the ugliest man in Spain and married to one of the most beautiful women at court. And as the king and queen, the cardinal, and the nobles took their seats in their respective carriages, and the drivers cracked their whips and the cortège set off toward Santa María la Mayor and Puerta de la Vega, the people, delighted with the spectacle, applauded constantly. They even cheered the carriage in which I was sitting with the Marquis of Liche's servants, but then, in this unhappy land of ours, we Spaniards have always been prepared to cheer almost anything.

The bell of the Hospital de los Aragoneses was ringing for matins. Diego Alatriste, who was awake and lying in his bed at the Fencer's Arms, got up, lit a candle, and started pulling on his boots. He had more than enough time to get to the Ermita del Ángel before daybreak, but crossing

Madrid and the Manzanares River in the current circumstances was a very complicated enterprise indeed. Better to be there an hour before than a minute late, he thought. And so, once he had pulled on his boots, he poured some water into a bowl, washed his face, ate a morsel of bread to settle his stomach, and finished dressing, donning his buffcoat, buckling on dagger and sword, and wrapping the dagger in a piece of cloth so that it would not bang against his sword guard; and for that same reason, he put his metal spurs in his purse. Stuck in his belt behind and concealed by his cloak, he had the booty from his eventful visit to Calle de la Primavera—Gualterio Malatesta's two pistols, which he had loaded and primed the previous evening. Then he put on his hat, glanced around in case he had forgotten anything, doused the light, and made his way out into the street.

He drew his cloak about him against the cold. Then, orienting himself in the dark, he left behind him Calle de la Comadre and reached the corner of Calle del Mesón de Paredes and the Cabrestreros fountain. He stood there for a moment, motionless, thinking that he could hear something moving in the shadows, then he continued on, taking a shortcut along Embajadores to San Pedro. Finally, once past the tanneries, which were, of course, closed at that hour, he emerged onto the little hill of the Rastro, where, beyond the cross and the fountain, rose the somber bulk of the new abattoir, which stood out clearly in the light of a lantern in Plaza de la Cebada. The stench of rotten meat made it easy to recognize even in the dark. He was about to walk on when—and he had no doubts this time—he heard footsteps behind him. This could either be someone who simply happened to be there at the same time or someone who was following him. In case the latter proved to be the case, he sought refuge by the wall, folded back his cloak, shifted one of his pistols around to the front of his belt, and got out his sword. He stood for a while, utterly still, holding his breath to listen, until he could be sure that the footsteps were coming in his direction. Taking off his hat so as to be less noticeable, he leaned cautiously out and saw a shape approaching slowly. It could still be mere coincidence, he thought, but this was not the moment to leave anything to chance. He put on his hat again, and when the figure drew alongside him, stepped out, sword foremost.

"Damn your eyes, Diego!"

The last person Alatriste was expecting to see in that place and at that hour was Martín Saldaña. The lieutenant of constables—or rather the sturdy shadow to whom the voice belonged—had started back in fright, swiftly unsheathing his sword; there was a metallic whisper and a faint glint of steel as he moved the blade from side to side, covering his guard like a veteran. Alatriste checked that the ground beneath his feet was smooth and unimpeded by loose stones, then he leaned his left shoulder against the wall to protect that side of his body. His right hand, however, remained free to wield his sword, thus complicating matters for Saldaña, who, if he attacked, would find *his* right hand blocked by the wall.

"What the hell are *you* doing here?" asked Alatriste.

Saldaña did not respond at once. He was still standing alert and ready. He was doubtless aware that his former comrade might try a trick they had both often used before—attacking an opponent while he was speaking. Talking was a distraction, and between men like them, an instant was all it took to find yourself with a foot of steel through your chest.

"You wouldn't want me to let you slip the net that easily, would you?" said Saldaña at last.

"Have you been watching me for long?"

"Since yesterday."

Alatriste thought for a moment. If this were true, Saldaña would have had ample time to surround the inn and have a dozen or so catchpoles on hand to arrest him.

"Why are you alone?"

Saldaña paused a long time before answering. He was a man of few words and appeared to be searching hard for them now. Finally, he said:

"This isn't official business. It's private—between you and me."

The captain carefully studied the solid shadow before him.

"Are you carrying pistols?"

"It's all the same whether I or, indeed, you are. This is a matter for swords."

His voice sounded oddly nasal. He must still be suffering from that headbutt the captain had dealt him. It was only logical, thought Alatriste, that Saldaña should take his escape and the deaths of those catchpoles as a personal affront, and it was only fitting that his comrade from Flanders should want to resolve it man to man.

"This isn't the moment," he said.

Saldaña replied in a slow, calm, reproachful voice:

"You seem to be forgetting who you're talking to, Diego."

The steel blade still glinted before him. The captain raised his sword a little, hesitated, then lowered it again.

"I don't want to fight you. Your constable's staff of office isn't worth it."

"I'm not carrying it with me tonight."

Alatriste bit his lip, his fears confirmed. Saldaña was clearly not prepared to let him leave without a fight.

"Listen," he said, making one last effort. "I'm very close to sorting everything out. There's someone I have to meet . . ."

"I don't care a fig who you have to meet. You and I never finished our last meeting."

"Just forget about it for this one night. I promise I'll come back and explain."

"Who's asking you to explain?"

Alatriste sighed and ran two fingers over his mustache. They knew each other too well. There was nothing to be done. He adopted the en garde position, and Saldaña took a step back, readying himself. There was very little light, but enough for them to be able to see the blades of their swords. It was, thought the captain sadly, almost as dark as it had been on that morning when Martín Saldaña, Sebastián Copons, Lope Balboa, himself, and another five hundred Spanish soldiers cried out "Forward, Spain!," made the sign of the cross, and then swarmed out of the trenches to climb the embankment in their assault on the del Caballo redoubt, in Ostend, an assault from which only half returned.

"Come on," he said.

There was an initial clash of steel, and Saldaña immediately made a circling movement with his sword and stepped away from the wall so as to have more freedom of movement. Alatriste knew who he was dealing with; they had been comrades-in-arms and had often practiced fencing together using buttoned fleurets. His opponent was a cool and skillful swordsman. The captain lunged forward, hoping to wound quickly and unceremoniously.

Saldaña, however, drawing back to gain space, parried the thrust, then sprang forward. Alatriste had to move away from the wall—which had gone from being refuge to obstacle—and as he did so, momentarily lost sight of his opponent's sword. He whirled around, lashing out violently, searching for the other blade in the darkness. Suddenly he saw it coming straight at him. He parried with a back-edged cut and retreated, cursing to himself. Although the darkness made them equal, leaving a great deal to luck, he was nevertheless the better swordsman, and it should simply be a matter of wearing Saldaña out. The only problem with that strategy was that there was no knowing how long it would be before, despite Saldaña's intention to act alone, a patrol of catchpoles heard the sound of fighting and rushed to the aid of their leader.

"I wonder who your widow will hand the constable's staff of office to next?"

He asked this as he was taking two steps back to recover his advantage and his breath. He knew that Saldaña was as placid as an ox in all matters but those concerning his wife. Then passion blinded him. Any jokes about how she had got him the post in exchange for favors granted to third parties—as malicious tongues would have it—quickened his pulse and clouded his reason. "With any luck," thought Alatriste, "this will help me resolve the matter quickly." He adjusted his grip, parried a thrust, withdrew a little to draw his opponent in, and, when their blades clashed again, he noticed that Saldaña already seemed less confident. He decided to return to the attack.

"I imagine she'll be inconsolable," he said, striking again, every sense alert. "She'll doubtless wear deepest mourning."

Saldaña did not reply, but he was breathing hard and muttered a curse when the furious barrage he had just unleashed slashed only thin air, sliding off the captain's blade.

"Cuckold," said Alatriste calmly, then waited.

Now he had him. He sensed him coming toward him in the dark, or rather he knew it from the gleam of steel from his sword, the sound of frantic footsteps, and the rancorous roar Saldaña let out as he attacked blindly. Alatriste parried the blow, allowed Saldaña to attempt a furious reverse cut, then, halfway through that maneuver—when he judged that the constable would still have his weight on the wrong foot—turned his wrist, and with a forward thrust, cleanly skewered his opponent's chest.

He withdrew the blade and, while he was cleaning it on his cloak, stood looking down at Saldaña's body—a vague shape on the ground. Then he sheathed his sword and knelt beside the man who had been his friend. For some strange reason, he felt neither remorse nor sorrow, only a profound weariness and a desire to blaspheme loudly. He moved closer, listening. He could hear the other man's weak, irregular breathing, as well as another far more worrying sound: a bubbling of blood and the whistle of air entering and leaving the wounded man's lung. He was in a bad way, that foolish, stubborn man.

"Damn you," Alatriste said and, tearing a clean piece of cloth from the sleeve of his doublet, he felt for the wound in Saldaña's chest. It was about two fingers wide. He stuffed as much as he could of the handkerchief into the wound to staunch the bleeding. Then he rolled Saldaña onto his side and, ignoring his groans, felt his back; he found no exit wound, however, nor any blood other than that flowing from his chest.

"Can you hear me, Martín?"

Martín replied in a feeble voice that he could.

"Try not to cough or to move."

He lifted Saldaña's head and placed beneath it the wounded man's own cloak, folded up by way of a pillow, to prevent the blood rising up from his lungs to his throat and choking him. "How am I?" he heard Martín say. The last word was drowned in a thick, liquid cough.

"Not too good. If you cough, you'll bleed to death."

Saldaña nodded weakly and lay still, his face in shadow, his pierced lung making an ominous noise each time he breathed. He nodded again a moment later, when Alatriste glanced impatiently from side to side and announced that he had to go.

"I'll see if I can find someone to help you," he said. "Do you want a priest as well?"

"Don't talk such . . . nonsense."

Alatriste stood up.

"You might pull through."

"I might."

The captain moved off, but heard the wounded man calling him. He went back and knelt down again.

"What is it, Martín?"

"You didn't mean . . . what you said . . . did you?"

Alatriste found it hard to open his mouth to speak. His lips felt dry, as if stuck together, and when he spoke, his lips hurt him, as if the skin on them were tearing.

"No, of course I didn't."

"Bastard."

"You know me. I took the easy path."

Saldaña was gripping his arm now, as if all the strength of his battered body were concentrated in his fingers.

"You just wanted to make me angry, didn't you?"

"Yes."

"It was just . . . just a trick."

"Of course. A trick."

"Swear that it was."

"I swear."

Saldaña's wounded chest was racked by a painful cough, or perhaps laughter.

"I knew it . . . you bastard . . . I knew it."

Alatriste stood up and wrapped his own cloak around

him. Now that his blood had cooled and after the physical exertion of the fight, he was conscious of the chill night air, or perhaps it wasn't just the night air.

"Good luck, Martín."

"The same to you. . . Captain . . . Alatriste."

Dogs were barking in the distance, along the San Isidro road. The rest of the nighttime landscape lay in silence, and not even a breath of wind stirred the leaves on the trees. Diego Alatriste crossed the last stretch of the Segovia bridge and stopped for a moment by the washerwomen's sheds. The waters of the Manzanares, swollen by the recent rains, lapped against the shore. Madrid was just a dark shape behind him. On the heights above the river, the dark outline of its belfries and the tower of the Alcázar Real stood silhouetted between sky and earth, and everywhere else was utter blackness apart from a few stars above and a few faint lights below, behind the city walls.

Having checked that all was well, he set off toward the Ermita del Ángel just as the damp was starting to penetrate his cloak. He encountered no further problems, although, making sure to keep his face covered, he did first call at a house near the Rastro, hold out four doubloons, and ask them to find a surgeon to tend to a man lying wounded near the abattoir. He was very close to the hermitage now and determined to take no more risks. He therefore took out one of his pistols, cocked it, and pointed it at the shadow of the man waiting there. The horse neighed anxiously at the noise, and Bartolo Cagafuego's voice asked: "Is that you, Captain?"

"It is," he said.

With a sigh of relief, Cagafuego sheathed his sword. He was glad, he said, that everything had gone well, and that the captain had arrived safe and sound. He handed him the reins of the horse: it was a bay, he added, good-tempered and soft-mouthed, albeit with a slight tendency to pull to the right. Otherwise, he was fit for a marquis or a Chinese emperor or any other lofty personage.

"He can keep going for miles, this one. He's got no scabs on his flanks and no spur marks, either. I've checked his shoes, and there's not a nail missing. I had a look at the saddle, and the girth, too . . . I think you'll find him very much to your likin', sir."

Alatriste was patting the horse's neck: warm, firm, and strong. He felt the horse toss its head contentedly at the touch of his hand. The warm breath of the horse's nostrils dampened his palm.

"He can travel eight or even ten leagues, no problem, as long as you don't push him too hard. I spent some time with the gypsies in Andalusia, so I knows a bit about horses and the like. Men can sometimes spring nasty surprises on you, but not these poor beasts. If you're in a hurry, though, you can always change horses at the relay in Galapagar and get yourself a fresh mount to climb the hill."

"Any food?"

"I took that liberty, yes, sir. One saddlebag containing bread, cheese, and cured meat and a skin containing a liter or so of red wine to wash it down with."

"It's good wine, I hope," joked Alatriste.

"I bought it in Lepre's tavern. Need I say more? Suleiman himself couldn't ask for better."

Alatriste checked headstall, bridle, saddle, girth, and stirrups. The saddlebag with the food and wine in it was hooked over the saddle-tree. He put his hand in his purse and handed Cagafuego two gold coins.

"You've behaved as the man you are, my friend: the cream of the ruffian classes."

Cagafuego's harsh laugh rang out in the darkness.

"On my grandfather's soul, Captain, I didn't do nothing, it wasn't no bother at all. I didn't even have to use my sword to kill anyone, like I did in Sanlúcar. And I'm sorry for it, too. A tiger of a man like me doesn't want his sword to go rusty. Life can't just be about pocketing the money your whore brings in for you."

"Give her my best regards. And I hope she doesn't catch the French disease like poor Blasa Pizorra, may she rest in peace."

Alatriste saw Cagafuego silently cross himself.

"God forbid, sir."

"And as for that brave blade of yours," added Alatriste, "I'm sure you'll have some occasion to use it. Life is short and art is long."

"I don't know much about art, Captain, but life, now, that's a different matter. Anyway, what's family for if not for times like these, eh? I'll always be there when you need me: as dutiful as a pure-blood Spaniard and more reliable than quartan fever. And I can't say fairer than that."

Alatriste had knelt down to put on his spurs.

"Needless to say, we've never seen each other and we don't know each other," he said, buckling on his spurs. "And whatever happens to me, you need have no worries on that score."

Cagafuego gave another laugh.

"That's part of the job. Everyone knows that, however hard-pressed, you wouldn't spill the beans, not even if they stretched you on the rack like Córdoban leather."

"Who knows?"

"Don't be so modest, Captain. I wish I could trust my doxy as I trust your tongue. All of Madrid knows you to be the kind of gentleman as would go to the gallows rather than say a word."

"You'll at least allow me the odd yelp, won't you?"

"Well, seeing as it's you, sir, yes, but nothing more, mind."

They shook hands and said good-bye. Then Alatriste drew on his gloves, mounted, and rode the horse upriver— along the path that ran alongside the wall of the Casa de

Campo—leaving the reins loose, so that the horse could find its own way in the dark. Once they had crossed the little bridge over the Meaque stream, where his horse's hooves made rather too much noise for his liking, he plunged into the trees growing along the banks to avoid the guards at Puerta Real; and after a while spent slouching down in the saddle with one hand on his hat while he ducked the lower branches, he emerged, at last, at the foot of Aravaca hill, beneath the stars, leaving the murmur of the river behind him, amongst the shadowy woods that grew so thickly on its shore. The pale earth made it easier to make out the road, and so he put one of the pistols he was carrying at his waist in the holster on the front of the saddle-tree, wrapped his cloak more tightly about him, dug in his spurs, and set the horse going at a fast trot, so as to get away from there as quickly as possible.

Bartolo Cagafuego was right: the bay did pull a little more to the right than to the left, which meant that he had to rein him in a little, but he was a good mount and fairly soft-mouthed. This was fortunate, because Alatriste was not a particularly good horseman; that is, he knew as much about horses as most people, sat well in the saddle, and was comfortable at a gallop; he was equally at home on a horse or a mule, and even knew certain maneuvers proper to combat and war. However, there is a vast difference between that and being a skilled equestrian. He had spent his whole life trudging Europe with the Spanish infantry or sailing the Mediterranean in the king's galleys, and was more accustomed to seeing horses charging toward him over Flemish plains or Barbary beaches, accompanied by enemy bugles, beating drums, and bloodied pikes. The truth is, he knew more about disemboweling horses than he did about riding them.

Once past the old Cerero inn, which was closed and in darkness, he trotted up the Aravaca hill and then slowed down, allowing the horse to proceed at a walking pace along the flat, almost treeless track that ran between the dark stains formed by the fields of wheat and barley, like large expanses of water. As was to be expected, the cold intensified just before the sky began to lighten, and the captain was glad he was wearing his buffcoat beneath his cloak. When horse and rider passed by Las Rozas, the first light was beginning to appear along the horizon, turning the shadows gray. Alatriste had decided not to take the broader, busier carriage road to Ávila, and so when he reached the crossroads, he turned right, onto the bridle path. From that point on, there were some gentle ups and downs, and the fields gave way to pine woods and scrub. He dismounted and stopped for a while to devour some of the food with which Cagafuego had filled the saddlebag. The dawn found him lost in thought, sitting on his cloak, eating a little cheese and drinking a little wine while his horse rested. Then he remounted, settled back in the saddle, and found himself pursuing the long shadow of horse and rider cast in the first reddish rays of sunlight on the path ahead. Farther on, about three leagues from Madrid and with the sun now warming the captain's back, the path grew steeper and more rugged, and the pine forest became a leafy oak wood amongst which he occasionally caught sight of rabbits scampering away and startled deer. These woods were uninhabited, uncultivated places, the king's hunting preserve. Anyone caught poaching was flogged and sent to the galleys.

Farther on, he began to encounter other travelers—a few muleteers on their way to Madrid—and near the Guadarrama River he overtook another mule-train transporting wineskins. At midday he crossed the Retamar bridge, where the bored guard simply pocketed the toll money without asking any questions or even demanding to see his face. From then on, the going was rougher and craggier, with the path snaking through clumps of white broom, past ravines and rocks on which his horse's hooves rang out as the path twisted and turned through a landscape which, thought Alatriste, studying it with a professional eye, would have been perfect for those gentlemen of the road, the highwaymen. However, one paid with one's life for any crimes committed on the king's lands, and such thieves preferred to carry out their trade a few leagues from there, robbing unwary travelers on the king's highway that passed through Torre Lodones and past the Guadarrama River and into Old Castile. Reminding himself that highwaymen were not exactly his main concern, he checked that the primer was still dry in the pistol he had hung on the saddle-tree, within easy reach.

9. THE SWORD AND
THE DAGGER

I must confess to feeling terrified, and with good reason.
The Count of Guadalmedina in person had sought me out,
and now we were striding along together beneath the
arches of El Escorial's main courtyard. I had been in don
Francisco de Quevedo's room, engaged in making a fair
copy of some lines from his new play, when Guadalmedina appeared at the door, and Quevedo barely had time to
shoot me a somber, cautionary glance before the count ordered me to follow him. The count's elegant cape, which
he wore draped over his left shoulder, swayed as he strode
angrily ahead of me, his left hand on the hilt of his sword
and his impatient footsteps echoing along that eastern side
of the courtyard. We passed the guard, went up the small
staircase adjoining the royal tennis court, and emerged onto
the upper floor.

"Wait here," he said.

I did as I was told, and he disappeared through a door. I was standing in a dreary hallway of gray granite, no tapestries, paintings, or any other ornament in evidence, and all that cold stone made me shiver. I shivered still more when the count reappeared and ordered me curtly to come in, for I found myself entering a long gallery with a painted ceiling and walls adorned with frescoes depicting scenes of war. The only furniture was a chair and a table containing writing implements. Along one wall there were nine windows that opened onto an inner courtyard, and the light from these windows lit up the fresco on the opposite wall, which showed Christian knights fighting Moors and recorded the battle in all its military detail. This was the first time I had entered the Hall of Battles, and I was far from imagining then that, in time, those paintings commemorating the victory at Higueruela, the battle of San Quintín, and the attack on the Azores would be as familiar to me as the rest of the royal palace when, years later, I was made lieutenant and then captain of King Philip IV's guard. At that moment, however, the Íñigo Balboa walking beside the Count of Guadalmedina was merely a frightened boy, incapable of appreciating the magnificent paintings decorating the gallery. My five senses were all focused on the imposing figure waiting at the far end, next to the last of the nine windows. He was a heavily built man, with a thick, closely trimmed beard and a fearsome mustache that grew bushier at the ends. He was wearing a costume made of brown lamé with the green cross of Alcántara on his breast, and his large, powerful head sat on a thick neck barely contained by a starched ruff. As I approached, he fixed me with his dark, intelligent eyes, as threatening as two harquebuses; and at the time I am describing, those eyes could send a shudder of fear throughout the whole of Europe.

"This is the boy," said Guadalmedina.

The count-duke, His Catholic Majesty's favorite and adviser, nodded almost imperceptibly, without taking his eyes off me. In one hand he was holding a piece of paper, and in the other a cup of thick, hot chocolate.

"When is this Alatriste fellow supposed to arrive?" he asked Guadalmedina.

"At sunset, I believe. He has instructions to present himself here as soon as possible."

Olivares leaned slightly toward me. Hearing him say my master's name had left me speechless.

"Are you Íñigo Balboa?"

I nodded, incapable of uttering a word, while I struggled to put my thoughts in order. In between sips of chocolate, the count-duke was reading aloud from the piece of paper he was holding: ". . . born in Oñate, Guipúzcoa, the son of a soldier who died in Flanders, servant to Diego

Alatriste y Tenorio, better known as Captain Alatriste, et cetera. A soldier's page in the old Cartagena regiment. Present at the taking of Oudkerk, at the battles of Ruyter Mill and Terheyden, the siege of Breda . . ." After each Flemish name, he glanced up as if to compare the fact with my evident youth. "And before that, there had been an auto-da-fé in the Plaza Mayor in Madrid, in sixteen hundred and twenty-three.

"Ah, yes, I remember now," he said, looking at me more attentively now, meanwhile putting his cup down on the table. "Some business with the Holy Office of the Inquisition."

It was not at all reassuring to know that one's biography was so precisely documented, and the memory of my brush with the Inquisition did nothing to calm my spirits. However, the question that followed transformed my bewilderment into panic.

"What happened in Camino de las Minillas?"

I looked at Álvaro de la Marca, who nodded reassuringly.

"You can speak openly to His Excellency," he said. "He is fully informed."

I continued to eye him suspiciously. When we met in Juan Vicuña's gambling den, I had described to him the events of that ill-starred night on condition that he told no one until Captain Alatriste had spoken to him. The captain had not yet arrived; Guadalmedina, who was, after all, a courtier, had not played fair. Or perhaps he was merely covering his back.

"I don't know anything about the captain," I stammered.

"Don't be ridiculous," said Guadalmedina. "You were there with him and with the man who died. Tell His Excellency exactly what happened."

I turned to the count-duke. He was still observing me with alarming fixity. That man bore on his shoulders the most powerful monarchy on earth; he could move whole armies across seas and mountains just by lifting an eyebrow. And there was I, trembling inside like a leaf and about to tell him no.

"No," I said.

The count-duke blinked.

"Have you gone mad?" exclaimed Guadalmedina.

The count-duke still did not take his eyes off me, although his gaze seemed more curious now than angry.

"By my life, I'll . . ." began Guadalmedina threateningly, taking a step toward me.

Olivares stopped him by making the very slightest of movements with his left hand. Then he glanced back at the piece of paper and folded it in four before putting it away.

"Why not?" he asked me.

He did so almost gently. I looked across at the windows and chimneys on the far side of the courtyard, at the blue-gray slate tiles lit by the setting sun. Then I shrugged my shoulders and said nothing.

"Ye gods," said Guadalmedina, "I'll make you loosen that tongue of yours."

The count-duke again brought him up short, with that same slight gesture. He seemed to be able to see into every corner of my mind.

"He is, of course, your friend," he said at last.

I nodded. After a moment, the count-duke nodded too.

"I understand," he said.

He took a few steps about the gallery, stopping by a fresco that showed ranks of Spanish infantry, bristling with pikes, all grouped around the cross of San Andrés, marching toward the enemy. Sword in hand, smeared with gunpowder, hoarse with shouting out the name of Spain, I, too, had once belonged to those ranks, I thought bitterly, as had Captain Alatriste. Despite that, there we were. I noticed that the count-duke saw that I was looking at the scene and read my thoughts. The hint of a smile softened his features.

"I believe your master is innocent," he said. "You have my word."

I studied the imposing figure standing before me. I had no illusions. I had some experience of life, and I knew perfectly well that the kindness being shown to me by the most powerful man in Spain—indeed, in the world—was nothing but a highly intelligent ploy, as one would expect from a man capable of applying all his talents to the vast enterprise that was his one obsession: that of making his nation great, Catholic, and powerful, and defending it on land and sea against English, French, Dutch, Turks, against the world in general, for the Spanish empire was so vast and so feared that other countries could hope to achieve their own ambitions only at the expense of ours. As far as the count-duke was concerned, such an enterprise justified any means. I realized that he would use the same measured, patient tone were he issuing the order to have me quartered alive, and, if it came to that, he would do so with no more qualms than he would have about squashing a fly. I was merely the humblest of pawns on the complex chessboard where Gaspar de Guzmán, Count-Duke of Olivares, was playing the very dangerous game of being the king's favorite. Much later on, when life again placed me in his path, I was able to confirm that while our king's all-powerful favorite never hesitated to sacrifice as many pawns as might prove necessary, he never let go of a piece, however modest, as long as he believed it could be useful to him.

Anyway, that afternoon in the Hall of Battles, I saw that every path was blocked, and so I plucked up my courage. After all, Guadalmedina would only have passed on what I had confided to him, nothing more. There was no harm in repeating that. As for the rest, including Angélica de Alquézar's role in the conspiracy, that was another matter entirely. Guadalmedina could not talk about what he did not know, and I—for in my youthful chivalry I was ingenuous in the extreme—would not be the one to utter the name of my lady in the presence of the count-duke.

"Don Álvaro de la Marca," I said, "has told Your Excellency the truth . . ."

At that point, I suddenly realized what the count-duke's first words meant, and the realization troubled me greatly: Captain Alatriste's journey to El Escorial was not a secret. He and Guadalmedina both knew about it, and I wondered who else might know, and wondered, too, if that information—for bad news travels faster than good—had also reached the ears of our enemies.

Soon after the pass, where the broom and the rocks gave way to oak woods and the path grew flatter and straighter, the horse began to hobble. Diego Alatriste dismounted and looked at the creature's hooves, only to find that one of its left shoes had lost two nails and was coming loose. Caga-fuego had not attached to the saddle a bag containing the requisite tools and so he had to fix the shoe as best he could, hammering the nails back in with a large stone. He had no idea how long this repair would last, but the next staging post was less than a league away. He remounted and, doing his best not to ride the horse too hard, and bending over every now and then to check the loose shoe, he continued on his way. He rode slowly for nearly an hour until—in the distance, to the right and with the still snowy peaks of the Guadarrama in the background—he could make out the granite tower and the roofs of the dozen or so houses that made up the little village of Galapagar. The road did not go into the village, but continued on, and when he reached the crossroads, Alatriste dismounted outside the coaching inn. He entrusted the horse to the farrier, took a quick look at the other horses resting in the stable and noticed in passing that two mounts were tethered outside, ready and saddled up. Then he went and sat down on the vine-covered porch of the village inn. Half a dozen mule drivers were playing cards near the wall; a man dressed in country fashion and with a sword at his belt was standing nearby, watching the game; and a cleric accompanied by a servant and two mules laden down with various bundles and trunks, was seated at another table, eating pigs' trotters and brushing away the flies from his plate. The captain greeted the cleric, lightly touching the brim of his hat.

"The peace of God be with you," said the cleric, his mouth full.

A serving wench brought Alatriste some wine, and he drank thirstily, stretched out his legs, and put his sword down on one side while he watched the farrier work. Then he estimated the height of the sun and made his calculations. It was a further two leagues, more or less, to El Escorial; this meant that, with the horse newly shod and making good speed, and as long as the intervening streams—the Charcón and the Ladrón—were not running too high and could be forded on the road itself, he would be at the palace by midafternoon. Pleased with this thought, he finished off the wine, put a coin down on the table, buckled on his sword, and went over to the farrier, who was finishing his task.

"Oh, forgive me, sir."

Alatriste had not noticed the man coming out of the inn and almost bumped into him. He was a burly, bearded fellow, dressed country style, in gaiters and a huntsman's hat, like the man watching the muleteers' card game. Alatriste did not know him. He judged him to be a poacher or a gamekeeper, for he wore a short sword in a leather baldric and a hunting knife. The stranger accepted his apology with a curt nod of the head, but looked at him long and hard, and while the captain was walking over to the stable, he was aware that the man was still watching him. This, he thought, was odd, and it made him feel uneasy. As he was paying the farrier amid the buzz of horseflies, he glanced back out of the corner of his eye. The man was still watching him from the porch. Alatriste felt even more worried when, as he put his foot in the stirrup and hoisted himself up onto the horse, he saw the man exchange a look with the other fellow standing next to the muleteers. For some reason he aroused the man's curiosity, and he could think of no reason that augured well.

Thus, cautiously looking over his shoulder to see if they were following him, he dug his spurs into his horse's flanks and set off for El Escorial.

"There isn't a stage in the world," said don Francisco de Quevedo, "to compare with this."

They were sitting in a niche in the wall beneath the granite colonnade of the Casa de la Compaña, watching the rehearsals for *The Sword and the Dagger* in the magnificent El Escorial gardens. These were at least a hundred feet wide and planted with lush clumps of flowers as tall as a man and with topiary hedges and mazes, all of which provided a setting for the dozen small fountains in which the waters sang and from which the birds drank. Protected from the north wind by the palace-monastery, whose walls were covered with trellises thick with jasmine and musk roses, the gardens formed a pleasant terrace along the south-facing façade of the building, a broad mirador that gave onto a large pond full of ducks and swans. Not far off, to the south and west, one could see the imposing mountains in tones of blue, gray, and green, and in the distance, to the east, the vast fields and royal forests that extended all the way to Madrid.

"In matters of the heart
When you very least suspect it,
From a bow flies a dart,
With your honor as its target."

We heard the voice of María de Castro rehearsing the opening lines of the second act. Hers was, without a doubt, the sweetest voice in Spain, skillfully trained by her husband, who, in that respect, although not in others, always ruled with a firm hand. The sound of her voice was interrupted occasionally by hammering from the scene-shifters, and Cózar, who was using don Francisco's script as a prompt, would call for silence as majestically as an archbishop from Liège or a grand duke from Moscow, characters whose mannerisms he had honed on the stage. The play was to be performed there, in the open air. To this end, a stage had been set up as well as a large awning to protect the royal personages and the main guests from sun or rain. It was said that the count-duke was spending ten thousand *escudos* on fêting the king and queen and their guests with both play and party.

This is truly not a lie:
When in love, we who die
Live, and in living,
We as yet are dying.

These, by the way, were not lines of which don Francisco was particularly proud, but as he himself remarked to me in private, they were worth exactly what he was being paid for them. Besides, such plays on words, verbal sleights of hand, and paradoxes were very much to the taste of the public who attended the theater, from the king himself down to the most insignificant rogue, including the innkeeper Tabarca's *mosqueteros*. And so, in the opinion of the poet—who was a great admirer of Lope de Vega, but who liked to put everyone in his proper place—if the Phoenix could sometimes allow himself such knowing jokes to round out an act or draw applause in a particular scene, he saw no reason why he should not do the same. What mattered, he said, was not that a man of his talent could produce such lines as easily as a Moor could make fritters, but that they amused the king, the queen, and their guests, and, more especially, the count-duke, who held the purse strings.

"The captain should be here soon," Quevedo said suddenly.

I turned to look at him, grateful that he should still be thinking of my master. I found, however, that he was watching María de Castro as impassively as if he had not spoken a word, and indeed he said nothing more. For my part, I could not stop thinking about Captain Alatriste either, still less after my interview, given most reluctantly, with the king's favorite. I was hoping that once the captain arrived and met with Guadalmedina everything would be resolved and our lives would return to normal. As for his relationship with La Castro—she was asking now for some cooling water to drink, and her husband solicitously had some brought for her—I had no doubt that he would cease to play the gallant to that very dangerous leading lady. As for the lovely actress herself, I was surprised how at ease she seemed to be in El Escorial. I understood then how an arrogant, self-confident woman, raised to such heights, might grow quite puffed up with vanity when she enjoyed the favor of a king or some other powerful man. Needless to say, the actress and the queen never met; the actresses only entered the palace garden for rehearsals and none were actually lodging on the palace grounds. It was also said that the king had already made the occasional night visit to La Castro, this time unmolested by anyone, still less by the husband, for it was well known that Cózar slept very soundly indeed and could snore like a saint even with his eyes wide open. All of this was common knowledge and would soon reach the ears of the queen. However, the daughter of Henri IV had been brought up as a princess and knew that such matters must be accepted as part of her role. Isabel de Borbón was always a model queen and lady, which is why the people loved and respected her until her death; and no one could imagine the tears of humiliation our unhappy queen would shed in the privacy of her rooms over her august husband's licentious behavior, which would, in time, so rumor had it, engender as many as twenty-three royal bastards. In my view, the origin of the queen's invincible loathing for El Escorial—she would only return there to be buried—lay not just in the building's grim atmosphere, which fitted so ill with her own cheerful disposition, but in memories of her husband's dalliance with La Castro, whose moment of triumph, by the way, was short-lived, for she was soon to be replaced in the king's capricious favors by another actress, the sixteen-year-old María Calderón. Philip IV was always more attracted to lowborn women—actresses, kitchen maids, serving wenches, and whores—than to ladies of the court. It must be said, though, that unlike in France, where some royal mistresses ended up having more power than certain queens, in Spain, appearances were always preserved and no courtesan ever held sway at court. Prim old Castile, which had embraced the rigid Burgundy etiquette brought from Ghent by the emperor Charles, insisted that nothing less than an abyss should separate the majesty of its monarchs from the rest of vulgar humanity. This is why, once the affair was over—for no one could ride a horse once ridden by the king nor enjoy a woman whom he had made his mistress—the king's concubines were usually forced to enter a convent, as were any daughters born of such illegitimate loves. This provoked one court wit to pen the following inevitable lines:

> *Traveler, this house, this monument*
> *Is not what it appears:*
> *The king first made it a bawdy house*
> *And then a holy convent.*

Such incidents, plus the money squandered on parties, masked balls, and festive lights, on corruption, wars, and bad governance, all contribute to painting a moral portrait of the Spain of that time, which, though still a powerful and much-feared nation, was unstoppably going to the devil. Our lethargic king was full of good intentions, but incapable of doing his duty; during his long forty-four-year reign, he placed all responsibility in the hands of others and devoted himself to fornicating, hunting, indulging his every pleasure, and plundering the nation's coffers. Meanwhile, we lost Rosellón and Portugal; Catalonia, Sicily, and Naples rose up in revolt; Andalusian and Aragonese nobles conspired against us; and our regiments, unpaid and therefore hungry and indisciplined, could only stand by, impassive and silent, still faithful to their glorious legend, and allow themselves to be destroyed. To quote the admirable last line—with all due respect to Señor de Quevedo—of don Luis de Góngora's sonnet "On the Fleeting Nature of

Beauty and Life," Spain was reduced to "earth, smoke, dust, and shadow—naught."

As Captain Alatriste said to me once during a mutiny near Breda: "Your king is your king." Philip IV was the monarch Fate gave me, and I had no other; he was the only king that men of my class and my century knew. No one offered us a choice. And that is why I continued to fight for him and was loyal to him until his death, both as an innocent youth and as a scornful, clear-sighted, battle-worn man, and much later, too, in my more charitable maturity, when, as captain of his guard, I saw him transformed into a prematurely old man, bent beneath the burden of defeat, disappointment, and regret, broken by the ruin of his nation and by the blows of life itself. I used to accompany him alone to El Escorial, where he would spend long hours in silence in the solitude of that ghostly pantheon containing the illustrious remains of his ancestors, the kings whose mighty inheritance he had so wretchedly squandered. The Spain that came to rest on his shoulders was very great indeed, and he, alas for us, was not a man to bear such a weight.

He had allowed himself to be ambushed in the most ridiculous fashion, but there was no time now for lamentations. Resigned to the inevitable, Diego Alatriste dug his spurs in hard and forced his horse to ford the stream, splashing noisily through the water. The two horsemen were closing on him, but the people he was really worried about were two new arrivals, who had emerged out of the trees on the opposite bank and were riding toward him with what were clearly evil intentions.

He looked about him to see what possibilities lay open to him. He had sensed danger ever since he left the inn at Galapagar; then, as he was riding down the hill toward the stream and could just make out the gray mass of El Escorial in the distance, he realized that the men he had seen at the inn were following him. His professional instincts told him at once who they were. He had immediately spurred the bay on, hoping to force the horse across the stream and up the hill as quickly as possible with the intention of reaching the nearby woods, where he would at least have the advantage of surprise. However, the appearance of two more horsemen made the situation clear. They were obviously what, in the army, he would have called "beaters"—a patrol sent out to look for someone—and given the way things stood, the captain had few doubts about who that "someone" was.

His horse almost slipped on the pebbles in the streambed but managed to make it to the other side without falling, about twenty paces ahead of the men galloping toward him along the bank. The captain observed them with a practiced eye: they both had bushy mustaches, were dressed as hunters or gamekeepers, armed with pistols and swords, and one of them had a harquebus resting crosswise on his saddle. They were obviously professionals. The captain glanced behind him and saw the two men from the inn urging on their mounts and racing down the hill from Galapagar. It was all as clear as day. He pulled up his horse and, gripping the reins between his teeth, quietly drew his pistol and cocked it. Then he cocked the other pistol which he had ready in the holster on the saddle-tree. He was not expert in such fighting methods, but dismounting in order to face four mounted men would have been madness. The wryly consoling thought occurred to him that whether on foot, on horseback, or accompanied by a chaconne, there was nothing for it but to fight. When the two men on the bank were about four feet away, he stood up in the stirrups, took careful aim, arm outstretched, and had time enough, as he squeezed the trigger and unleashed a bullet, to see the look on the face of the man he had singled out. He would have killed him, too, if his own horse hadn't started and caused his aim to suffer. The noise and the flash caused the rider with the harquebus to pull his horse up short to avoid the shot. His companion did the same, tugging on the reins. This gave Alatriste time to wheel his horse around, put the discharged pistol away, and take out the other. With this in his hand, he intended to drive his horse forward and get closer, so as not to miss the second time. His mount, however, was no war horse and, terrified by the noise of the pistol shot, set off at a gallop downstream. Cursing, Alatriste found himself with his back to the men and unable to take proper aim. He yanked so hard at the reins that the horse reared up, almost unseating him. When he finally managed to regain control, he had a man on either side of him, each with a pistol in his hand, and the men from the inn were now splashing their way toward him across the stream. They had their swords unsheathed, but the captain was more concerned about the pistols threatening him on either flank. And so he commended himself to the devil, raised his pistol and shot the nearer man at point-blank range. This time, he saw the man slump back onto his horse's rump, one leg sticking up and the other caught in the stirrup. Then, throwing down the pistol and grabbing his sword, Alatriste watched as the other man raised his pistol and aimed it in his direction. Behind the pistol, Alatriste could see the man's fierce eyes, as fixed and black as the mouth of the barrel pointing straight at him. "This is where it all ends," he thought, "and there's nothing to be done about it." He brandished his sword anyway, in an attempt at least, with that one last impulse, to cut down the bastard who was about to kill him. And then, to his surprise, he saw that the black hole of the barrel was aimed instead at his horse's head, and found himself splattered by the creature's blood and brains. He fell forward onto the dead beast and was thrown off onto the stony bank. Dazed, he tried to get up, but his strength failed him and he lay motionless, his face pressed into the mud. Shit. His back hurt as badly as if he had broken his spine. He glanced wildly around for his sword, but saw only a pair of boots and spurs in front of him. One of the boots kicked him in the face, and he lost consciousness.

My anxiety began to grow at the hour of the angelus, when don Francisco de Quevedo, looking very somber, came to tell me that my master had still not presented himself to the Count of Guadalmedina, and that the latter was growing impatient. Gripped by dark thoughts, I went outside and sat on the parapet along the east-facing esplanade, known as La Lonja, from where I could see the road from Madrid. I remained there until the sun, veiled at the last moment by ugly gray clouds, finally sank behind the mountains. Then, feeling uneasy, I went in search of don Francisco but failed to find him. I wanted to go into the main courtyard, but the archers on guard barred my way, saying that the king and queen and their guests were attending a musical evening in the little temple. I asked them to tell don Álvaro de la Marca that I wished to speak to

him, but the sergeant told me that this was not an oppor-
tune moment and that I should wait until the gathering
was over or else go and bother someone else. Finally, an
acquaintance of don Francisco's whom I met at the foot of
the main staircase told me that don Francisco had gone to
dine at the Cañada Real, through the archway opposite the
palace, which was where he usually ate. And so I set off
again, once more crossing the esplanade and going up the
slight hill to the archway, where I turned left and made my
way to the inn.

It was a small, pleasant place, lit by tallow candles set
in lanterns. The walls, made of the same granite as the
palace, were adorned with hams, sausages, and strings of
garlic. There was a large stove tended by the mistress of the
house, and the innkeeper himself waited at table. I found
don Francisco de Quevedo, María de Castro, and her husband all seated there. The poet shot me a questioning
glance, frowned when I shook my head, then invited me to
join them.

"I believe you know my young friend," he said.

They did indeed know me, especially La Castro. The
lovely actress welcomed me with a smile, and her husband
with an ironic and exaggeratedly friendly gesture, for he
knew who my master was. They had just finished eating a
dish of braised trout, it being Friday, and offered me what
was left. My stomach, alas, was too troubled, and I dined

instead on a little bread dipped in wine. It was no ordinary
wine, either, and that night Rafael de Cózar had clearly
drunk his fair share, for he had the red eyes and thick
tongue of someone who has paid generous tribute to the
jug. The innkeeper brought more wine, this time a sweet
Pedro Ximénez. María de Castro—whose outfit, a close-
fitting bodice and long riding skirt, was adorned with at
least fifty *escudos'* worth of Flemish lace at neck, wrist,
and hem—was drinking prettily and only a little at a time;
don Francisco was drinking equally moderately, while
Cózar drank on like a man dying of thirst. Between sips of
wine, the three continued discussing things theatrical—
what gestures to make at a particular moment, or how to
say this or that line—while I awaited the right moment to
speak to don Francisco alone. Despite my great unease, I
was nonetheless able to admire once more the beauty of
the woman for whose sake the captain had set himself
against the king's will. What shook me was the noncha-
lance with which María de Castro threw back her head to
laugh, sipped her wine, played with the round coral earrings that hung from her lovely ears, or looked at her husband, at don Francisco, and at me in the particular way she
had of looking at men, making each of us feel that she had
singled us out as the only man on earth. I could not help
thinking of Angélica de Alquézar, and that made me
wonder if La Castro cared a jot about what happened to the

captain, or even to the king himself, or if, on the contrary, in the game of chess played by women like her—and perhaps by all women—kings and pawns were all the same: temporary and dispensable. And I found myself toying with the idea that María de Castro, Angélica, and other such women were like soldiers in hostile territory, who saw themselves as foragers prowling a world of men and forced to use their beauty as ammunition and the vices and passions of the enemy as their weapons. It was a war in which only the bravest and cruelest could survive and one in which, almost always, the passage of time would finally vanquish them. Seeing María de Castro in all the perfect beauty of her youth, no one would have thought that, a few years later, for reasons that have no bearing on this story, my master would visit her for the last time in the hostel for sick women opposite Atocha Hospital, and find her aged and disfigured by syphilis, covering her face with her cloak, ashamed to be seen in that state. Or that I, standing unseen by the door, would see Captain Alatriste, when the time came to say good-bye, lean toward her and, despite her resistance, draw aside the cloak and place a final kiss on her withered lips.

Just then, the innkeeper came over and whispered something to María de Castro. She nodded, stroked her husband's hand, and stood up with a rustle of skirts.

"Good night," she said.

"Shall I come with you?" asked Cózar distractedly.

"There's no need. Some friends are expecting me, the queen's ladies."

She was looking at herself in a small mirror and touching up her rouge. At that hour, I thought, the only ladies who weren't safe in bed were whores and the queens in a deck of cards. Don Francisco and I exchanged a meaningful glance, which Cózar caught. His face was an impassive mask.

"I'll have them bring the coach around for you," he said to his wife.

"There's no need," she said confidently. "My friends have sent theirs."

Her husband nodded indifferently, as if he didn't care one way or the other. He was bent over his wine and seemed entirely unmoved.

"May I know where you'll be?"

She gave a charming smile and put away the mirror in her little silver mesh bag.

"Oh, somewhere or other. In La Fresneda, I think. But don't sit up for me."

With another smile and with great aplomb, she said good-bye, arranged her cloak to cover head and shoulders, gathered up her skirt, and departed, gently shaking her head at don Francisco, who had gallantly stood up in order to accompany her to the door. I noticed that her husband did not stir from his seat, but sat with doublet unfastened and mug in hand, staring into his wine with an absorbed expression on his face and a strange grimace of distaste beneath that long mustache of his. If that remarkable woman is leaving alone, I thought, while her drunkard husband stays here with don Pedro Ximénez and with that look on his face, she's clearly not simply going off to say her prayers before bed. Don Francisco shot me a grave glance, eyebrows raised, which only confirmed me in my view. La Fresneda was a hunting lodge on the royal estate, just over half a league from El Escorial, at the far end of a long avenue of poplars. Neither the queen nor her ladies had ever been known to set foot there.

"It's time we all went to bed," said don Francisco.

Cózar still did not move, his eyes fixed on his mug of wine. The ironic, scoundrelly smirk had grown more marked.

"Why the rush?" he murmured.

He seemed quite different from the man whom I had previously only seen from afar; it was as if the wine were revealing shadowy corners that normally went unperceived in the glare of the stage lights. Then, abruptly raising his glass, he said:

"Let's drink to young Philip's health!"

I eyed him uneasily. Even famous actors had to watch what they said. In truth he was not the sparkling, witty character we had seen on stage, always with a sharp riposte on his lips and always in a buoyant mood, with that peculiarly mocking air about him, as if he were saying: "I'm enjoying myself, the worms can wait." Don Francisco again looked at me, then poured himself some more wine and raised it to his lips. I was fidgeting in my seat, shooting him impatient glances. He, however, shrugged his shoulders, as if to say: "There's not much we can do. Your master holds all the cards, but where is he? As for this other man, sometimes a few glasses of wine reveal things that sobriety keeps at bay."

"How does that wonderful sonnet of yours go, Señor de Quevedo?" Cózar had placed one hand on don Francisco's arm. "Something about a ruddy-faced silversmith pursuing the nymph Diana . . . Do you know the one I mean?"

Don Francisco observed him intently, as if trying to see what was going on behind the other man's eyes. The light from the candles was reflected in the lenses of his spectacles.

"I can't remember," he said at last.

He was anxiously twirling his mustache. I concluded that he had not liked what he saw inside Cózar. Even I sensed in the actor's tone of voice something I would never have imagined—a vague rancour, contained and dark—entirely opposed to the person Cózar was, or usually seemed to be.

"You don't? Well, I do," Cózar raised a finger. "Wait."

And albeit rather hesitantly, he proceeded to recite with actorly skill, for he was a magnificent player possessed of an excellent voice:

> *"Grave Jupiter, or so we're told,*
> *Once lifted up a maiden's skirts*
> *And had her in a shower of gold."*

One didn't have to be a literary expert to be able to decipher the symbols, and the poet and I exchanged another uncomfortable look. Cózar, on the other hand, seemed entirely unperturbed. He had once more raised his mug of wine to his lips and appeared to be chuckling to himself.

"And what about that other poem of yours?" he said, having taken two long gulps of wine. "Don't you remember that one, either? Of course you do. 'A cuckold, you are, sir, up to your brows.'"

Don Francisco was shifting uneasily in his seat, looking around like someone seeking an escape route.

"I have no idea what you're talking about."

"Really? Well, you wrote it, and it's famous. In the gossip-shops they say it may be a reference to me."

"Ridiculous. You've had too much to drink."

"Of course, but I have a superb memory for poetry. Listen:

"My Queen, what I order is just,
  If not, what's the point of being king
  If one cannot make a law of lust
  When one's own lust doth sing.

"Not for nothing am I Spain's finest actor. But wait, Señor Poet, for another particularly apt sonnet springs to mind. I refer to the one that begins: 'The voice of the eye that we call a fart.'"

"That, as far as I know, is anonymous."

"Yes, but everyone attributes it to your illustrious pen."

Don Francisco was beginning to get really angry now, although he still kept glancing to left and right. The relieved expression on his face was saying, "At least we're alone and the innkeeper's nowhere to be seen." For Cózar, with no prompting, was declaiming:

"To hell with vaunting, boastful kings
  Who, puffed up by toadying courtiers,
  Think life and death their own playthings."

These lines had, in fact, been written by don Francisco, although he swore blind that they hadn't. Written at a time when the poet was rather less popular at court, manuscript copies were still making the rounds in Spain, and he would have given his right arm to have them withdrawn. On this occasion, they proved to be the final straw. Don Francisco summoned the innkeeper, paid for the meal, and got angrily to his feet, leaving Cózar sitting there. I followed behind.

"In a couple of days, he's going to perform before the king," I said uneasily, once we were out in the hallway. "And in *your* play, too."

Still frowning, don Francisco glanced back.

"Oh, there's no need to worry," he said at last in a wry, mocking tone. "It's just a temporary lapse. Tomorrow morning, once he's slept off the wine, everything will be as normal."

He threw his short black cape over his shoulders and fastened it.

"By my life, though," he added after a moment's thought, "I never suspected that such a tame beast would have had qualms about his honor."

I cast a last astonished glance at the small figure of the actor, whom I, like don Francisco, had always taken to be a jolly man of great good humor and few morals. All of which goes to show—and he was to surprise me still further in the hours that followed—one can never fathom the hearts of men.

"Have you ever considered that he might love her?" I asked.

I blushed as soon as these unconsidered words had left

my mouth. Don Francisco, who was tucking his sword into his leather belt, paused in what he was doing and regarded me with interest. Then he smiled and slowly finished buckling on his belt and sword, as though my remark had given him food for thought, yet he said nothing. He put on his hat and we walked silently out into the street. Only after we had gone a few steps did I see him nod as if after long reflection.

"You never can tell, my lad," he murmured, "you never can tell."

It had grown cooler and there were no stars to be seen. As we crossed the esplanade, gusts of wind were whirling up leaves torn from the tops of the trees. When we reached the palace, where we had to give the password because it was after ten o'clock, there was still no news of the captain. According to what don Francisco told me after he had exchanged a few words with the Count of Guadalmedina, the latter wished him in hell. "I hope for Alatriste's sake," he had said, "that he doesn't create problems for me with the count-duke." As you can imagine, that thought tormented me, and I wanted to stay there at the door, in case my master should arrive. Don Francisco tried to reassure me by giving me various sensible explanations. It was seven long leagues from Madrid to El Escorial. The captain might have been delayed by some minor accident, or perhaps preferred to arrive at night for greater safety. Whatever the case, he knew how to take care of himself. In the end, more resigned than convinced, I agreed that he was right, aware that he was not entirely persuaded by his own eloquence. The truth is that we could do nothing but wait. Don Francisco went about his business, and I again walked over to the great palace gate, where I decided I would remain all night, awaiting news. I was walking between the columns of the courtyard where the kitchens were located when, by a narrow staircase, ill lit and half hidden behind the thick walls, I heard the rustle of silk, and my heart stopped as if I had been shot. Even before I heard her whisper my name, even before I turned toward the shape crouched in the shadows, I knew that it was Angélica de Alquézar, and that she was waiting for me. Thus began the happiest and most terrible night of my life.

10. THE BAIT AND THE TRAP

Despite having his hands tied behind him, Diego Alatriste managed, with some difficulty, to raise himself up so that he was sitting with his back against the wall. He could remember falling off his horse and being kicked in the face, and his head hurt so much that, at first, he thought that either the fall or the kick must be the cause of the surrounding darkness. With a shudder, he said to himself: "I must have gone blind." Then, after turning anxiously this way and that, he saw a line of reddish light under the door and gave a sigh of relief. It was perhaps simply that it was night or that he was being held in a cellar. He moved his numb fingers and had to bite his lip so as not to groan out loud; his veins felt as if they were full of a thousand pricking needles. Later, when the pain had eased slightly, he tried to piece together out of the confusion in his head exactly what had happened. The journey. The staging post. The ambush. He recalled, with bewilderment, the pistol-shot which, instead of killing him, had felled his horse. The man firing had not, he concluded, simply missed or made a mistake. They were clearly men who knew what they were about and were rigorously carrying out orders. So disciplined were they, in fact, that, even though he had shot one of their comrades at point-blank range, they had not given in to the natural desire for revenge. He could understand this because he worked in the same trade. The really weighty questions were these: Who held the purse strings? Who was paying the piper? Who wanted him alive, and why?

As if in answer to these questions, the door was suddenly flung open and a bright light dazzled his eyes. A black figure stood on the threshold, with a lantern in one hand and a wineskin in the other.

"Good evening, Captain," said Gualterio Malatesta.

It seemed to Alatriste that, lately, he always seemed to be seeing the Italian framed in doorways, either entering or leaving. This time, however, he was the one who was tied up like a sausage and Malatesta was seemingly in no hurry at all. He came over to him, crouched down beside him, and took a close look at him.

"I'm afraid you're not your usual handsome self," he commented drily.

The light hurt Alatriste's eyes, and when he blinked, he

realized that his left eye was so badly swollen he could barely open it. Nevertheless, he could still see his enemy's pockmarked face and the scar above his right eyelid, a souvenir of their fight on board the *Niklaasbergen.*

"I could say the same of you," he said.

Malatesta's mouth twisted into an almost conspiratorial smile.

"I'm sorry about this," he said, looking at Alatriste's bound hands. "Is the rope very tight?"

"Pretty tight, yes."

"I thought so. Your hands are about the size and color of aubergines."

He turned toward the door and called out. A man appeared. Alatriste recognized him as the man he had almost bumped into in Galapagar. Malatesta ordered him to slacken the rope binding Alatriste's hands. While the man was doing this, Malatesta took out his dagger and held it to Alatriste's throat, just to make sure that the captain didn't take advantage of the situation. Then the man left, and they were alone again.

"Are you thirsty?"

"What do you think?"

Malatesta sheathed his dagger and held the wineskin to the captain's lips, letting him drink as much as he wanted. He was observing him intently. By the light of the lantern, Alatriste could, in turn, study the Italian's hard, dark eyes.

"Now, tell me what this is all about," he said.

Malatesta's smile broadened. It was, thought the captain, a smile that seemed to counsel Christian resignation, which, given the circumstances, was hardly encouraging. Malatesta thoughtfully probed one ear with his finger, as if carefully considering which word or words to use.

"Basically, you're done for," he said at last.

"And are you the one who's going to kill me?"

Malatesta shrugged, as if to say: "What does it matter who kills you?"

"Yes, I suppose I will be," he said.

"On whose behalf?"

Malatesta slowly shook his head, still not taking his eyes off the captain, but did not reply. Then he got to his feet and picked up the lantern.

"You have some old enemies," he said, going over to the door.

"Aside from you, you mean?"

The Italian gave a harsh laugh.

"I'm not your enemy, Captain Alatriste, I'm your adversary. Do you not know the difference? An adversary respects you even if he stabs you in the back. Enemies are something else entirely. An enemy loathes you, even though he may praise and embrace you."

"Cut the philosophy, please. You're going to slit my throat and leave me to die like a dog."

Malatesta, who was about to close the door, stopped for

a moment, his head slightly bowed. He seemed to be hesitating over whether to add anything further or not.

"Well, 'dog' is perhaps a trifle strong," he said at last, "but it will do."

"Bastard."

"Don't be too upset about it. Remember the other day . . . in my house. And, by way of consolation, I will just say that you'll be in illustrious company."

"What do you mean, 'illustrious'?"

"Guess."

Alatriste put two and two together. The Italian was waiting at the door, circumspect and patient.

"You can't be serious," blurted out the captain.

"In the words of my compatriot Dante," replied Malatesta, *'Poca favilla gran fiamma seconda.'* From a little spark may burst a mighty flame."

"The king again?"

This time Malatesta did not reply. He merely smiled more broadly at Alatriste's look of stupefaction.

"Well, that doesn't console me in the least," replied Alatriste, once he had recovered his composure.

"It could be worse. For you, I mean. You're about to make history."

Alatriste ignored the comment. He was still considering the really important question.

"According to you, then, someone still has one too many

kings in the pack, and I've been chosen as the one to discard that king."

As Malatesta was closing the door, Alatriste heard him laugh again.

"I said no such thing, Captain. But at least I'll know that when I do kill you, no one will be able to say that I'm dispatching an innocent or an imbecile."

"I love you," Angélica said again.

I couldn't see her face in the darkness. I was gradually coming to, waking from a delicious dream during which I had not, for one moment, lost consciousness. She still had her arms about me, and I could feel my heart beating against her satiny, half-naked flesh. I opened my mouth to utter those identical words, but all that emerged was a startled, exhausted, happy moan. After this, I thought confusedly, no one will ever be able to part us.

"My boy," she said.

I buried my face in her disheveled hair, and then, after running my fingers over the soft curve of her hips, kissed the hollow above her shoulder blade, where the ribbons of her half-open chemise hung loose. The night wind was whistling in the roofs and chimneys of the palace. The room and the rumpled bed were a haven of calm. Everything else was excluded, suspended, apart from our two young bodies embracing in the darkness and the now slowing beat of my heart. And I suddenly realized, as if it were a revelation, that I had made that whole long journey—my childhood in Oñate, the time I had spent in Madrid, in the dungeons of the Inquisition, and in Flanders, Seville, and Sanlúcar—that I had survived all those hazards and dangers in order to become a man and to be there that night, in the arms of Angélica de Alquézar, that girl who, although only about the same age as me, was calling me "her boy," and whose warm, mysterious flesh seemed to hold the key to my destiny.

"Now you'll have to marry me," she murmured, "one day . . ."

She said this in a tone that was both serious and ironic, in a voice that trembled strangely in a way that reminded me of the leaves on a tree. I nodded sleepily, and she kissed my lips. This kept at bay a thought that was trying to make its way through my consciousness, like a distant noise, rather like the wind blowing in the night. I tried to focus on that noise, but Angélica's mouth and her embrace were stopping me. I stirred uneasily. There was something wrong. A memory of foraging in enemy territory near Breda surfaced in my mind. I recalled how that apparently tranquil green landscape of windmills, canals, woods, and undulating fields could unexpectedly unleash on you a detachment of Dutch cavalry. The thought returned, more intense this time. An echo, an image. Suddenly the wind howled more loudly outside the shutter, and I remembered. The captain's face. A lightning flash, an explosion of panic. The captain's face. Of course. Christ's blood!

I sat up, detaching myself from Angélica's arms. The captain had not kept his appointment, and there I was in bed, indifferent to his fate, plunged in the most absolute of oblivions.

"What's wrong?" she asked.

I did not reply. I placed my feet on the cold floor and began groping in the darkness for my clothes. I was completely naked.

"Where are you going?"

I found my shirt and picked up my breeches and my doublet. Angélica had left the bed too, but was no longer asking questions. She tried to grab me from behind, but I pushed her roughly away. We struggled in the dark. Eventually I heard her fall back on the bed with a moan of pain or perhaps anger. I didn't care. At that moment, all I cared about was the anger I felt against myself, the anguish of my desertion.

"You wretch," she said.

I crouched down again, feeling about on the floor. My shoes must be there somewhere. I found my leather belt and was going to put it on when I noticed that it was not as heavy as it should be. The sheath for my dagger was empty. "Where the hell is it?" I thought. I was about to ask that question out loud, a question that already sounded foolish before it had even reached my lips, when I felt a sharp, very cold pain in my back, and the surrounding blackness filled up with luminous dots, like tiny stars. I uttered one loud, brief scream. Then I tried to turn and strike my attacker, but my strength failed me and I dropped to my knees. Angélica was holding on to my hair, forcing my head back. I was aware of blood running down the back of my thighs and then felt the blade of the dagger at my throat. With a strange lucidity I thought: "She's going to slit my throat as if I were a calf or a pig." I had read once about a witch, a woman who, in antiquity, used to change men into pigs.

She dragged me back onto the bed, tugging at my hair, keeping the dagger pressed to my throat, forcing me to lie down again, this time on my stomach. Then she sat astride me, half naked as she was, her thighs gripping my waist. She still had a firm hold on my hair. Then she removed the dagger from my throat, and I felt her lips on my still bleeding wound, felt her licking the edges, kissing it just as she had kissed my mouth.

"I'm so glad," she whispered, "that I haven't killed you just yet."

The light was paining Diego Alatriste's eyes, or, rather, his right eye, because his left was still swollen, and both eyelids felt as heavy as loaded dice. This time, he saw two shadows moving about near the door of his cell. He sat looking at them from his position on the floor, his back against the wall, having failed to free his bound hands, despite almost rubbing the skin raw in his efforts.

"Do you recognize me?" asked a dour voice.

The man was lit now by the lantern. Alatriste recognized him at once, with a shiver of fear and surprise that must, he thought, have been evident on his face. Who could forget that vast tonsure, that gaunt, ascetic face, those fanatical eyes, the stark black-and-white Dominican habit? Fray Emilio Bocanegra, president of the Court of the Inquisition, was the last man he would have expected to meet there.

"Now," said the captain, "I really am done for."

Behind the lantern, Gualterio Malatesta gave a harsh, appreciative laugh. The Inquisitor, however, lacked any sense of humor. His piercing, deep-set eyes fixed on the captain.

"I have come to confess you," he said.

Alatriste shot an astonished look in the direction of Malatesta's dark silhouette, but this time the Italian neither laughed nor commented. This offer of confession was clearly intended seriously, too seriously.

"You are a mercenary and a murderer," the Inquisitor went on. "During your unfortunate life, you have broken each and every one of God's commandments, and now you are about to be called to account."

The captain finally recovered the use of his tongue, which had stuck to the roof of his mouth when he heard the word "confession." Surprising even himself, he managed to keep his composure.

"My accounts," he retorted, "are my own affair."

Fray Emilio Bocanegra regarded him impassively, as if he had not heard that last remark.

"Divine Providence," he went on, "is offering you the chance to reconcile yourself with God, to save your soul, even if you must then spend hundreds of years in Purgatory. In a few hours' time, the holy swords of the archangel and of Joshua will fall and you will have been transformed into an instrument of God. You can decide whether to go to your death with your heart closed to God's grace or to accept it with goodwill and a clear conscience. Do you understand?"

The captain shrugged. It was one thing for them to kill him and quite another to come bothering his head with such stuff. He could still not fathom what Bocanegra was doing there.

"One thing I do understand is that today is not a Sunday, so please spare me the sermon and tell me what is going on."

Fray Emilio Bocanegra fell silent for a moment, but his eyes remained fixed on the prisoner. Then he raised one bony, admonitory finger.

"Very shortly, the world will know that a hired killer named Diego Alatriste, acting out of jealousy for some vile imitator of Jezebel, liberated Spain of a king unworthy to wear the crown. A base instrument wielded by God for a just cause."

The friar's eyes were flashing now, aflame with divine wrath. And Alatriste's suspicions were finally confirmed. He, Alatriste, was to be the holy sword of Joshua, or would, at least, pass into the history books as such.

"The ways of the Lord are unknowable," commented Malatesta, who was standing behind the friar and saw that the captain had finally understood.

He sounded almost encouraging, persuasive, respectful. Too respectful, thought Alatriste, knowing as he did the depths of Malatesta's cynicism. Malatesta must have been enjoying this absurd little interlude immensely. Grave-faced, the Dominican half turned toward the Italian, and the latter's derisive comment died on his lips. In the presence of the Inquisitor, even Gualterio Malatesta did not dare overstep.

"Just what I needed," said the captain with a sigh. "To fall into the hands of a mad friar."

The slap was as loud as a whiplash and flung his face to one side.

"Hold your tongue, wretch." The Dominican still held his hand high, threatening to slap him again. "This is your last chance before you face eternal damnation."

The captain looked again at Fray Emilio Bocanegra. His cheek smarted from the blow, and he was not the kind of man to turn the other cheek. Despair formed a knot in the pit of his stomach. "By Lucifer's balls," he said to himself, repressing his anger. Up until that night, no one had ever slapped him in the face—ever. By Christ and the father who engendered him, he would gladly have sold his soul, always assuming he had one, just to have his hands free for a moment to strangle this friar. He glanced over at the black shape that was Malatesta, still concealed behind the lantern. No laughter and no jocular remarks emerged from him now. That slap had not pleased him one iota. Among their kind, killing was one thing—part of the job—but humiliation was another matter entirely.

"Who else is involved in this?" Alatriste asked, pulling himself together. "Besides Luis de Alquézar, of course. One doesn't just kill a king like that. An heir is needed, and our king has not yet had a son."

"The natural order will be followed," the Dominican said coolly.

So that was it, thought Alatriste, biting his lip. The natural order of succession would fall on the Infante don

Carlos, the eldest of the king's two brothers. It was said that he was the least gifted of the family, and that given his weak will and lack of intelligence, he could easily fall under the influence of the right confessor for the purpose. Despite his youthful licentiousness, Philip IV was nevertheless a devout man; however, unlike his father, Philip III, who spent all his life beset by priests, he never gave the clergy a free hand. On the advice of the Count-Duke of Olivares, the Spanish king always maintained a certain distance from Rome, whose pontiffs knew, much to their regret, that the Hapsburg army was the main Catholic bulwark against the Protestant heretics. Like Olivares, the young king showed some sympathy for the Jesuits, but in a land where one hundred thousand priests and friars and monks were ever battling it out amongst themselves for control of men's souls and of ecclesiastical privileges, it was neither easy nor advisable to come down in favor of any one group. The Jesuits were hated by the Dominicans, who ran the Holy Office of the Inquisition and were the implacable enemies of the Franciscans and Augustinians, yet they all joined forces when it came to eluding royal authority and justice. In that struggle for power, driven by fanaticism, pride, and ambition, it was hardly surprising that the Dominican order, and, of course, the Inquisition, enjoyed an excellent relationship with the Infante don Carlos. And it was no secret that he, in turn, favored them to the extent of having chosen a Dominican as his confessor. If it was red and served in a jug, Alatriste decided, it must be wine. Or blood.

"If the infante involves himself in this," he said, "he's an utter rogue."

Making a gesture as if brushing away a fly, Fray Emilio Bocanegra resorted to professional rhetoric:

"The right hand does not always know what the left hand is doing. What matters is that we serve the Almighty, and that is our sole aim."

"It will cost you your heads—you, that Italian over there, Alquézar, and the infante himself."

"Worry about your own head," remarked Malatesta phlegmatically.

"Rather," added the Inquisitor, "worry about the health of your soul." Again his terrible eyes fixed on Alatriste. "Will you make your confession to me?"

The captain leaned back against the wall. It would have to have happened some time, but it was grotesque that it had to be like this. Diego Alatriste, regicide. That isn't how he wanted to be remembered by the few friends who would be likely to remember him in a tavern or a trench. It would be worse, though, he concluded, to end up ill and dying in a hospital for veterans, or else crippled and begging for alms at the door of a church. At least in his case, Malatesta would act cleanly and quickly. They couldn't risk him blabbing on the rack.

"I'd rather confess to the devil. I know him better."

He heard the Italian spluttering in the background in spontaneous laughter, which was interrupted by a fierce look from Fray Emilio Bocanegra. Then the Inquisitor studied Alatriste's face long and hard, finally shaking his head, as if handing down a sentence against which there could be no appeal. He got to his feet, smoothing his robes.

"So be it. The devil and you, face-to-face."

He left, followed by Malatesta bearing the lantern. The door closed behind them like a tombstone closing over a tomb.

We rehearse our death in sleep, which serves us as both rest and warning. I was never more aware of the truth of these words than when I emerged, bathed in an unwholesome sweat, from a strange half-sleep, a state of unconsciousness filled with images, like some kind of slow nightmare. I was lying facedown and naked on the bed, and my back hurt me terribly. It was still night. Always assuming, I thought with some alarm, that it was the same night. When I felt for my wound, I found my torso swathed in a bandage. I moved cautiously, making sure that I was alone.

The memory of what had happened rose up inside me—beautiful and terrible. Then I remembered Captain Alatriste and wondered what fate he might have met.

This thought decided me. I stumbled to my feet, looking for my clothes, and clenching my teeth so as not to cry out in pain. Each time I bent down in search of some item of clothing, I felt dizzy and feared I might faint again. I was almost fully dressed when I noticed a light underneath the door and the sound of voices. As I moved toward that sound, I accidentally kicked my dagger where it lay on the floor. I froze, but no one came. I carefully slipped the dagger into its sheath, then finished tying the laces on my shoes.

The noise outside stopped, and I heard footsteps moving off. The line of light on the floor trembled and grew brighter. I moved back and hid behind the door as Angélica de Alquézar, holding a lighted candle, came into the room. She was wearing a woolen shawl over her chemise and had her hair caught back. She stood very still, staring at the empty bed, but uttered no exclamation of surprise, not a word. Then she spun around, sensing me behind her. The reddish light of the candle lit up her blue eyes, as intense as two points of frozen steel, almost hypnotic. At the same time, she opened her mouth to say something or to cry out, but I was ready and prepared and could not allow her such a luxury. This was no time for reproaches or conversation. The blow I struck hit her on one side of the face, erasing that hypnotic look and causing her to drop the candle. She stumbled backward. The candle was still rolling about on the floor, not quite extinguished, when I clenched my fist again—I swear to you I felt no remorse—and punched her, this time on the temple, and she fell back unconscious onto the bed. I felt my way toward her—for the candle had burned out now—to make sure she was still breathing. I placed one hand on her lips—after that punch my knuckles hurt me almost as much as the wound in my back—and felt her breath on my fingers. That calmed me a little. Then I got down to practical matters. Postponing until later any consideration of my emotions, I first made my way over to the window and opened it, but it was too big a drop for me to consider jumping. I returned to the door, cautiously pushed it open, and found myself on the landing. I groped my way downstairs to a narrow passageway, lit by an oil lamp hanging from the wall. There was a rug at the far end, a door, and another flight of steps. I tiptoed past the door. I had one foot on the second step when I became aware of people talking. Had I not heard Captain Alatriste's name, I would have simply continued on down.

Sometimes God, or the devil, guides your feet in the right direction. I turned back and pressed my ear to the door. There were at least two men on the other side, and

they were talking about a hunt: deer, rabbits, beaters. I
wondered what the captain had to do with all that. Then
they said another name: Philip. He'll be there at such and
such a hour, they were saying. In such and such a place.
They only mentioned his name, but I had a sudden pre-
sentiment that sent a shudder through me. The nearness
of Angélica's room made it easy enough to make the logical connection. I must be standing outside the room of Luis
de Alquézar, Angélica's uncle, the royal secretary. Then a
word and another name reached me through the door:
"dawn" and "La Fresneda." My knees almost buckled beneath me, whether this was because I was still weak from
my wound or because I was so shaken by the idea that had
suddenly installed itself inside my head, I don't know. The
memory of the cavalier in the yellow doublet resurfaced
and threaded together all those disparate fragments. María
de Castro had gone to spend the night at La Fresneda. The
person she had gone to meet was planning to go hunting
at dawn, with just two beaters as escort. The Philip they
had mentioned was none other than Philip IV. They were
talking about the king!

I leaned against the wall, trying to order my thoughts.
Then I took a deep breath and gathered all my strength—
for I was going to need it, just as long, that is, as the wound
in my back didn't open. My first thought was to go to see
don Francisco de Quevedo. So I went down the stairs as

quietly as I could. Don Francisco, however, was not in his room. I went in and lit a candle. The table was full of books and papers and the bed undisturbed. Then I remembered the Count of Guadalmedina and walked across the large courtyard to the rooms occupied by members of the royal entourage. As I feared, I was not allowed through. One of the guards, who knew me, said that they wouldn't wake up His Excellency at that hour for all the wine in Spain. "No matter what," he added. I did not tell them just how urgent this particular matter was. I knew what catchpoles, soldiers, and guards were like, and knew that telling my story to such lumps of flesh was tantamount to talking to a wall. They were typical big-bellied, mustachioed veterans who simply wanted a quiet life. Getting involved wasn't part of the job, which was to make sure that no one got past them—and no one did. Talking to them about conspiracies and regicides would be like talking to them about the man in the moon, and I risked, in the process, getting thrown in a dungeon. I asked them if they had paper I could write on and they said no. I went back to don Francisco's room, where, making use of his pen, inkwell, and sandbox, I composed, as best I could, a note for him and another for Álvaro de la Marca. I sealed both letters with wax, scrawled their respective names on them, left the poet's note on his bed, and returned to the guards.

"This is for the count as soon as he wakes up. It's a matter of life and death."

They seemed unconvinced, but they kept the note. The guard who knew me promised that he would give it to the count's servants if one of them happened to pass or, at the very latest, when he came off duty. I had to be content with that.

The Cañada Real was my last faint hope. Don Francisco might have gone back for more wine and might still be there, drinking and writing; or, having bent his elbow one too many times, he might have decided to sleep there rather than wend his unsteady way back to the palace. I went over to one of the servants' doors and walked across the esplanade beneath a black, starless sky that was just beginning to grow light in the east. I was shivering in the cold wind blowing down from the mountains in brief rainy gusts. While this helped to clear my head, it gave me no new ideas. I walked quickly, anxiously. The image of Angélica came into my mind. I sniffed my hands, which still smelled of her. Then I shivered to remember the touch of her delicious skin and cursed my bad luck. The wound to my back hurt more than I can say.

The inn was closed, with only a dim lamp hanging above the lintel. I knocked several times at the door and then stood there, deliberating, uncertain what to do. All paths were blocked to me, and time was passing implacably.

"It's too late to be drinking," said a voice nearby, "or too early."

Startled, I turned round. In my anxiety, I had failed to notice the man sitting on the stone bench beneath the chestnut tree. He had no hat on and was wrapped in his cloak, with his sword and a demijohn of wine beside him. I realized it was Rafael de Cózar.

"I'm looking for Señor de Quevedo."

He shrugged and looked distractedly about him.

"He left with you. I don't know where he is."

His words were somewhat slurred. If he had been drinking all night, I thought, he must be as drunk as a lord.

"What are you doing here?" I asked.

"Drinking and thinking."

I went over to him and sat down beside him, pushing his sword out of the way. I must have looked the very picture of despair.

"In this cold?" I said. "It's hardly the weather for sitting outside."

"I carry my own heat inside me," he said and gave a strange laugh. "It's good, that, isn't it? Heat inside and horns outside. How does that verse go?"

And, taking two more drafts from the demijohn, he recited mockingly:

> *"Yes, business is good, no need to skimp,*
> *But tell me, please, where did you learn*
> *To be your mistress's husband*
> *And your own wife's pimp?"*

I fidgeted uneasily on the bench, and not just because of the cold.

"I think you've had too much to drink."

"And how much is 'too much'?"

I didn't know what to say, and so we sat for a while in silence. Cózar's hair and face were spattered with drops of rain that glittered like frost in the light of the lamp. He was studying me hard.

"You seem to have your own problems," he said at last.

When I did not reply, he offered me some wine.

"No," I said glumly, "that isn't the kind of help I need."

He nodded gravely, almost philosophically, stroking his long side whiskers. Then he raised the demijohn, and the wine gurgled down his throat.

"Any news of your wife?"

He gave me a vague, sullen, sideways look, the demijohn still held high. Then he put it slowly down on the bench.

"My wife leads her own life," he said, wiping his mustache with the back of his hand. "And that has its advantages and its disadvantages."

He opened his mouth and raised one finger, ready to recite something else. But I was in no mood for more poetry.

"They're going to use her against the king," I said.

He was staring at me hard, mouth open and finger raised.

"I don't understand."

This sounded almost like a plea to be allowed to continue in that state of incomprehension. I, however, had had enough of him and his bottle of wine, of the cold and the pain in my back.

"There's a plot against the king," I finally said in exasperation. "That's why I'm looking for don Francisco."

He blinked. His eyes were no longer vague, there was a frightened look in them.

"And what has that got to do with María?"

I pulled a scornful face. I couldn't help it.

"She's the bait. The trap is set for dawn. The king is going hunting with only two men as escort. Someone wants to kill him."

There was the sound of broken glass at our feet. The demijohn had just fallen to the ground, shattering inside its wicker covering.

"Od's blood," he murmured. "I thought I was the one who was drunk."

"It's the truth."

Cózar was staring thoughtfully at the mess on the ground.

"Even if it is," he said, "what do I care whether it's the king or his knave?"

"As I said, they're trying to implicate your wife—and Captain Alatriste."

When he heard my master's name, he gave a quiet, incredulous chuckle. I seized his hand and made him place it on my back.

"Touch it."

I felt his fingers on the bandage and saw the look on his face change.

"You're bleeding!"

"Of course I'm bleeding. Less than three hours ago, someone stuck a knife in me."

He jumped to his feet as if he'd felt a snake brush past him. I stayed where I was, watching him pace up and down, taking short strides.

"Come the Day of Judgment," he said as if to himself, "all will be revealed."

Then he stopped. The gusts of rain-filled wind were growing stronger, snatching at his cloak.

"They want to kill young Philip, you say?"

I nodded.

"To kill a king . . ." he went on, getting used to the idea now. "It has its comic side, you know. Yes, it's like a scene from a comedy."

"A tragicomedy," I said.

"That, my boy, depends on your point of view."

Suddenly my brain woke up.

"Have you still got your carriage?"

He seemed confused. He stood, looking at me, swaying slightly.

"Of course I have," he said at last. "It's in the square. The driver's asleep inside; that's what I pay him for. Mind you, he's had his fair share of wine too. I had them take him over a few bottles."

"Your wife has gone to La Fresneda."

His confusion changed to distrust.

"So?" he asked warily.

"That's almost a league away, and I can't make it on foot. In a carriage, I could be there in an instant."

"To do what?"

"To save the king's life and possibly hers as well."

He started laughing mirthlessly, but stopped almost at once. Then he stood thoughtfully shaking his head. Finally, he wrapped his cloak about him and intoned theatrically:

> *"In leaving Fate to go its own sweet way,*
> *I've been unfortunately fortunate,*

For my revenge comes early in the day
Before offense has even had its say.

"My wife can take care of herself," he said, grave-faced. "You should know that."

And with the same grave expression, he struck a fencing pose, albeit without his sword, which still lay on the bench beside me. En garde, attack, and parry. "What a strange man this Cózar fellow is," I thought. Then he suddenly looked at me again and smiled, and neither smile nor look were those of a cuckolded man about whom everyone gossips behind his back. But there was no time to ponder such things.

"Think of the king, then," I said.

"Young Philip?" He made the gesture of elegantly sheathing his imaginary blade. "By my grandfather's beard, I wouldn't mind someone showing him that only in plays do kings have blue blood."

"He's the king of Spain, our king."

The actor seemed unaffected by that "our." He arranged his cloak about his shoulders, shaking off the drops of rain.

"Look, my boy, I deal with kings every day on stage, be they emperors or the Great Turk or Tamburlaine. Sometimes I even play them myself. On stage, I've done the most extraordinary things. Kings, be they alive or dead, don't impress me very much."

"But your wife . . ."

"Enough! Forget about my wife."

He looked again at the broken demijohn and stood for a moment, motionless and frowning. Then he made a tutting noise with his tongue and regarded me with some curiosity.

"Are you going to La Fresneda on your own? And what about the royal guard, and the army, and the galleons from the Indies, and all the other sons of whores?"

"At La Fresneda there must be guards and people from the king's household. If I get there, I'll give the alarm."

"Why go so far? The palace is right here. Why not tell someone there."

"That's not so easy. At this hour, no one will listen to me."

"And what if you're met with knife-thrusts? The conspirators might be there already."

This caused me to hesitate. Cózar was pensively scratching his side whiskers.

"I played Beltrán Ramírez in *The Weaver of Segovia*," he said suddenly. "I saved the king's life.

> "*Follow them and find out who they are,*
> *These men who dare to place a filthy hand*

Upon the sovereign's pure and sacred breast
And to wield that impious, treach'rous, steely wand."

He again stood looking at me, awaiting my reaction to his artistry. I gave a short nod. It was hardly the moment for applause.

"Is that by Lope?" I asked, just to say something and to humor him.

"No. It's by the Mexican, Alarcón. It's a famous play, you know. It was a great success. María played Doña Ana and was applauded to the echo. And I, well, what can I say?"

He fell silent for a moment, thinking about the applause, and about his wife.

"Yes," he went on, "in the play, the king owed his life to me. Act one, scene one. I fought off two Moors. I'm quite good at that, you know, at least with stage swords, pretend swords. As an actor, you have to know how to do everything, even fencing."

He shook his head, amused, absorbed in his own thoughts. Then he winked at me.

"It would be amusing, wouldn't it, if young Philip were to owe his life to Spain's finest actor, and if María . . ."

He stopped. His gaze grew distant, fixed on scenes only he could see.

"The sovereign's pure and sacred breast," he murmured, almost to himself.

He continued shaking his head and muttering words I could not hear now. More lines from a play perhaps. Then his face lit up with a splendid, heroic smile. He gave me a friendly pat on the shoulder.

"After all," he said, "it's simply another role to play."

11. THE HUNTING PARTY

When the rain-soaked blindfold was finally removed, Alatriste found the dawn shrouded in a grim, gray light and low dark clouds. He raised his hands—which were bound in front now—to rub his eyes; his left eye still bothered him, but he found at least that he had no problem now in opening it. He looked about him. They had brought him there mounted on a mule at first—and he had been aware of the sound of horses' hooves beside him—then on foot across some rough ground. That short walk had warmed him up a little, although with no cloak or hat on he still had to clench his teeth to keep them from chattering. He was in a wood of oaks and elms. The shadows of night still clung to the horizon in the west, which he could just glimpse through the trees; and the drizzle drenching him and the other men—a fine rain of the kind that lingers— only accentuated the melancholy of the landscape.

Ti-ri-tu ta-ta. The sound of that whistle made him turn his head. Gualterio Malatesta, swathed in his black cape and with his hat down over his eyes, stopped whistling and made a face that could as easily have been a sneer as a greeting.

"Are you cold, Captain?"

"A little."

"And hungry?"

"More hungry than cold."

"Well, console yourself with the thought that your life ends here. We, on the other hand, have to go back."

He made a gesture indicating the men around him, the same men—less the one who had been killed—who had ambushed the captain at the stream. They were still dressed as beaters, and, even more alarming than their rough-and-ready appearance and their bristling mustaches and beards was the array of weapons they had about their persons: hunting knives, daggers, swords, pistols.

"Only the very best," said the Italian, sensing what Alatriste must be thinking.

A hunting horn sounded in the distance, and Malatesta and the three hired killers looked up and exchanged meaningful glances.

"You're going to stay here for a while," said Malatesta, turning to the prisoner.

One of the other men was heading off into the bushes

where the sound of the horn had come from. The other two stood at either side of Alatriste, forcing him to sit on the damp ground, and one of them started tying a piece of rope around his ankles.

"An elementary precaution," explained the Italian. "A compliment to your courage."

The eye with the scar above it seemed to water a little whenever it fixed on anything for any length of time, as it was at that moment.

"I always thought our final meeting would be face-to-face," said the captain, "and alone."

"When we met in my house, you didn't seem prepared to show me such mercy."

"At least I left your hands free."

"That's true, but I can't, I'm afraid, do the same for you today. There's too much at stake."

Alatriste nodded, indicating that he understood. The man tying his ankles made a couple of very tight knots.

"Do these animals know what they're involved in?"

The dull-witted animals did not even blink. The one tying the knots was standing up and brushing the mud from his breeches. The other was making sure the rain did not soak the gunpowder in the pistol he was carrying at his waist.

"Of course they do. They're old acquaintances of yours. They were with me in Camino de las Minillas."

"I assume they've been well paid."

"What do *you* think?"

Alatriste tried to move, but to no avail. His hands and feet were bound fast, although at least now his hands were tied in front of him, a precaution his captors had taken before setting out, so that he could hold himself upright on the mule.

"How do you intend carrying out your orders?"

Malatesta had taken from his leather belt a pair of black gloves, which he was now carefully drawing on. Alatriste noticed that, as well as sword, dagger, and pistol, he also had a knife in the leg of his boot.

"As I'm sure you know, the man in question has a taste for going out hunting early with just two beaters as escort. There are plenty of deer and rabbit here, and he's an experienced, intrepid hunter, a great marksman. All of Spain knows his liking for plunging into the undergrowth alone when he's hot on the trail of something. It's odd, isn't it, that someone so self-possessed, a man who never even blinks in public or looks at anyone directly, should be so utterly transformed when in pursuit of his prey."

He flexed his fingers to make sure his gloves fitted properly, then unsheathed his sword a few inches and put it back again.

"Hunting and women," he added with a sigh.

He remained like this for a moment, apparently absorbed

in thought. Finally, he beckoned to the two ruffians, who hoisted the captain—one holding him by the legs and the other under the armpits—and carried him over to an oak tree, where they leaned him against the trunk. He was hidden there by the bushes.

"It wasn't easy, but we managed," the Italian went on. "We were told that he would be here tonight, taking his ease with . . . well, you know with who. Certain people arranged for him to be accompanied this morning by two trusted beaters. Trusted by us, that is. They have just informed us, by sounding the hunting horn, that everything is going to plan and that the prey is near at hand."

"A difficult task very delicately handled," remarked the captain.

Malatesta thanked him for the compliment by touching the dripping brim of his hat.

"I hope that after such a wanton night, the illustrious personage made his confession before setting out," said Malatesta, and his pockmarked face again twisted into a grimace. "Not that I care, but they do say he is a pious man. I doubt very much he would want to die in mortal sin."

He seemed to find this thought vastly amusing. He gazed off into the distance, as if trying to spot his prey amongst the trees, then burst out laughing, his hand still resting on the hilt of his sword. In a tone that was at once jocular and sinister, he said:

"I like the idea that today we'll be providing two new recruits for hell."

He continued to smile, savoring the thought. Then he again looked at the captain.

"By the way," he added courteously, "I think you were quite right last night to refuse the sacrament of penitence. If either you or I ever recounted our lives to a priest, he'd immediately hang up his habit, write a highly unexemplary novel, and make more money than Lope does each time he puts on a new play."

Despite the situation, Alatriste could not help but agree.

"Fray Emilio Bocanegra," he said, "isn't much of an incentive to unburden one's conscience."

The Italian gave another brief laugh.

"Oh, I'm with you there. If I had to choose between two devils, I'd prefer the one with the tail and the horns to the one with the tonsure and the crucifix."

"You haven't yet told me what my part is in all this?"

"Your part?" Malatesta looked at him for a moment, uncertain how to reply, then he understood. "Oh, of course. The hunter and the prey. I thought you would have guessed what would happen next: a rabbit, say, or a deer rushes into the woods with the royal personage after him. The beaters hang back, and the spurned lover, namely you, appears out of nowhere and promptly runs him through. A simple case of jealousy avenged."

"Will you run him through yourself?"

"Of course. Both him and you. A double pleasure. Then we'll untie you, leaving your sword, dagger, and everything else nearby. Those faithful beaters, arriving at the tragic scene too late, will at least have the official honor of avenging the king."

"I see." Alatriste was studying his own bound hands and feet. "A shut mouth catches no flies."

"You have a reputation, Captain, as a brave man. No one would be surprised to learn that you fought like a tiger to the death, and many would be disappointed if they thought you had surrendered your life without a struggle."

"And what about you?"

"Oh, I know that isn't how it was. You can depart this life with an easy mind. After all, you killed one of my men yesterday and another in Camino de las Minillas."

"No, I meant what will you do afterward?"

Malatesta smugly stroked his mustache.

"Ah, that's the best part. I will disappear for a while. I'd like to go back to Italy with some ballast in my purse. I left there with far too little."

"It's a shame they don't ballast your balls with an ounce of lead."

"Patience, Captain," said the Italian, smiling encouragingly. "All in good time."

Alatriste leaned his head against the tree trunk. The rain

was running down his back, soaking the shirt underneath his buffcoat. His breeches were already sodden with mud.

"I'd like to ask you a favor," he said.

"Ye gods," said Malatesta, eyeing him with genuine surprise. "*You* asking a favor, Captain? I hope the prospect of meeting the Grim Reaper isn't turning you soft. I would prefer to remember you as you were."

"Is there some way in which Íñigo could be left out of this?"

Malatesta continued to study him impassively. Then a flicker of understanding seemed to cross his face.

"As far as I know, he's not involved," he said. "But that doesn't depend on me, so I can't promise you anything."

The man who had made off into the bushes returned and gestured to Malatesta, pointing in a particular direction. Malatesta gave the two men some orders in a low voice. One stationed himself next to the captain, his sword and pistol at his belt, and one hand resting on the hilt of his knife. The other went over to join the third man, who was waiting farther off.

"He's a very brave lad, Captain. You should be proud of him, and I can assure you that I, too, hope he gets out of this all right."

"So do I. Then, one day, he can kill you."

Malatesta was about to go over and join his men, leaving one to guard Alatriste.

"Yes, perhaps," he said. Then he turned around and once more fixed Alatriste with his dark eyes. "As with you, someone will have to kill me sometime."

It was drizzling harder now, drenching our faces. With the two mules almost at a gallop, the carriage was clattering along toward La Fresneda beneath the gray sky and past the dark poplars flanking the road. We had found the driver lying on one of the seats inside the carriage, sleeping off the effects of the wine he had drunk, which was why Rafael de Cózar, his sword tucked in his belt, was the one now holding the reins and urging on the mules. Cózar was not entirely sober himself, but the activity, the cooling rain, and a kind of obscure determination that seemed lately to have taken hold of him, were all helping to dissipate the vinous vapors. He was racing along in the carriage, urging the mules on with shouts and lashes of the whip, and I could not help but ask myself uneasily if this speed was a tribute to his skill as a driver or merely the irresponsible behavior of a drunkard. Whatever the truth of the matter, the carriage seemed positively to fly. I was sitting beside Cózar, wrapped in the coachman's cloak, hanging on as best I could, ready to throw myself off if we overturned. I closed my eyes each time the actor took a bend in the road, or when the mules or the lurchings of the carriage spattered us with mud.

I was just pondering what I was going to say or do in La Fresneda, when we left behind us the lead-gray smudge of the lake—glimpsed through the branches of the trees—and I saw, still far off, the stepped Flemish roof of the royal hunting lodge. At that point, the road forked, and the left fork led into the leafy wood; when I looked down that path, I saw a mule and four horses half hidden round a bend. I pointed this out to Cózar, who pulled so violently on the reins that one of the mules almost bolted and the carriage nearly overturned. I jumped down from the seat, cautiously looking all around. The dawn was far advanced now, although, beneath the rain-laden sky, the countryside still looked dark. Perhaps, I thought fearfully, there was nothing to be done and going to the hunting lodge itself would be a waste of time. I was still hesitating when Cózar took the decision for us both: he, too, jumped from the driver's seat, but fell face first into an enormous puddle, got up, shook himself, then, tripping over his own sword, fell in again. He got to his feet, cursing angrily. His face was covered in mud, filthy water was dripping from his side whiskers and mustache, and yet his eyes were shining. For some strange reason, for all his cursing, he seemed to be enjoying himself hugely.

"Have at 'em," he said, "whoever they are."

I took my borrowed cloak and picked up the coachman's sword, for the coachman had, during that rackety journey, slid to the floor of the carriage and lay there, snoring like a baby. The sword was of very poor quality, but that and my dagger were better than nothing, and there was no time to lose. Utter confidence, Captain Bragado used to say in Flanders, was dangerous when discussing any preliminary plan of attack, but vital at the moment of execution. And that moment had arrived. I indicated the horses tethered to the trees.

"I'm going to take a look. You go to the lodge and ask for help."

"Certainly not, my boy. I wouldn't miss this for anything in the world. We're in it together."

Cózar seemed a different man, and he probably was. Even his tone of voice was not the same. I wondered what role he was playing. He suddenly went over to the coachman, who was still asleep in the carriage, and started slapping him so hard that the noise startled the mules.

"Wake up, you fool!" he demanded with all the authority of a duke. "Spain needs you."

A moment later, the coachman—still dazed and, I imagine, suspecting that his master was not quite right in the head—was cracking the whip and driving on to La Fresneda to give the alarm. He seemed a rather dim-witted fellow, and so Cózar, in order not to complicate matters further, had given him some very elementary instructions: "Go to the hunting lodge, kick up a fuss, and bring as many people back here with you as you can. Explanations will follow.

"If, of course, we live to provide them," he added dramatically, for my benefit.

Then he solemnly folded back his cloak, adjusted his sword, and set off into the woods, a small, determined figure. A few paces later, he tripped over his sword again and fell face forward into the mud.

"God save me," he said from where he lay on the ground, "I'll pickle the next man who pushes me."

I helped him up, and he once again brushed down his clothes. "I just hope the coachman can convince the people at La Fresneda," I thought despairingly. "Or that the captain, wherever he is, can sort things out alone. Because if everything depends on Cózar and me, Spain will be left without a king just as sure as I was left without a father."

The hunting horn sounded again. Still sitting with his back to the tree trunk, Diego Alatriste noticed the man guarding him turn in the direction from which the sound had come. He was the same short, bearded, broad-shouldered fellow he had seen at the staging post at Galapagar before the ambush. He was also, it seemed, a man of few words and had not moved since Malatesta left, standing motionless beneath the increasingly heavy rain, with only a short waxed cape as protection. As Alatriste could appreciate better than anyone, the fellow was clearly accustomed to this life, the kind of man to whom you say: stay there, kill, die, and who will carry out those orders without a murmur; the kind of man who could be a hero when it came to attacking a Flemish bastion or a Turkish galley, or a murderer when it came to private matters. There was no easy way of drawing a line between the two. It all depended on how the dice fell—the dice of life—or on whether you were dealt the seven of clubs or the whore of hearts.

When the sound of the horn had died away, the ruffian rubbed the back of his neck and glanced at his prisoner. Then he came over to him and looked at him dully for a moment before unsheathing his knife. With his bound hands in his lap, Alatriste rested his head back against the trunk of the tree, keeping his eyes fixed on the blade. He felt an unpleasant tingling in his groin. Perhaps, he thought, Malatesta had changed his mind and was delegating the task to his subordinate. What a grubby way to die, sitting in the mud, tied hand and foot, his throat slit like a pig's, and with a long future ahead of him in the history books as an exemplary regicide. Shit.

"If you try to escape," warned the man dispassionately, "I'll pin you to that tree."

Alatriste blinked away the rain running down his face. Apparently the fellow had other plans. Instead of slitting his throat, the man was cutting the ropes binding his ankles.

"Get up," the man said, giving him a shove.

The captain got to his feet, the other man never once taking his eyes off him and keeping the blade only an inch from his throat. He gave the captain another shove.

"Come on."

Alatriste finally understood. They were not going to kill him now only to have to drag his corpse over to the king's body, leaving tracks in the mud and the scrub. He would simply have to walk to the site of that double execution, measuring out, step by step, what was left of his time and his life. It occurred to him, on the other hand, that this was also an opportunity, his very last. After all, as things stood, he might as well consider himself dead and buried, so anything else was a bonus.

"Mercy!" he cried, sinking down with one knee on the ground, the other slightly flexed.

The ruffian, who was following behind, was taken by surprise.

"Mercy!" the captain cried again.

Turning around, he just had time to catch the look of scorn in the other man's eyes. "I thought you had more balls," that look was saying.

"You mis—" he began.

Even as he was saying this, the man realized he had

been tricked; but, momentarily distracted, he was no longer pointing his knife directly at his prisoner, and Alatriste, springing up from his half-kneeling position, was already hurling himself, shoulder first, at the man's belly. The blow almost dislocated the captain's shoulder, but he managed to knock the man off his feet. The unfinished word became a roar, and there was a great splashing of mud as the captain, making one fist of his two bound hands, gathered all his strength together to deliver one devastating blow to the man's face, while the man, in turn, was trying to knife him. Luckily for Alatriste, the knife was quite long; had it been shorter, the man could have knifed him in the ribs there and then. At such close quarters, however, the knife-thrust wasn't forceful enough to penetrate the captain's rain-sodden buffcoat and merely slithered off. With one knee the captain pinioned the arm carrying the knife. Despite being bound, he had enough freedom of movement in his hands to grab the man's jaw and press a thumb into each eye. This was no time for fancy footwork or flourishes or fencing protocol, and so he pressed as hard as he could, mentally counting five, ten, fifteen, until he got to eighteen, and the man let out a yell and stopped struggling. The rain diluted the blood pouring down the face of the fallen man and over the captain's hands, and the captain, unopposed now, grabbed the knife, placed it point down on the man's throat and drove it in hard through his neck and into the mud. He held it there, bearing down with the whole weight of his body, trying to restrain the man's flailing legs, until the man, with a weary sigh that emerged not from his mouth but from the blade stuck in his throat, ceased all movement. Alatriste rolled off and lay on his back in the mud to recover his breath. Then, wrenching the knife from the dead man's throat, he wedged the handle of the knife between knee and tree trunk and managed to cut the rope binding his hands without severing a vein. While he was doing this, he watched as one of the dead man's feet began to tremble. "How odd," he thought, even though he had seen the phenomenon before. Even when a man was dead, it was as if something inside him refused to die.

He pillaged the corpse for anything useful. Sword, knife, pistol. The sword was a good one, from Sahagún, although somewhat shorter than what he was used to. He hurriedly strapped on the leather belt. The hunting knife had a horn handle and was two spans in length; he would have preferred a dagger, but it would do. The pistol probably wouldn't be much use after the struggle in the mud, but he stuck it in his belt anyway, his hands trembling as the cold took hold of him after all that activity. He gave one last glance at the body: the foot had stopped moving now, and beneath the drumming rain, the blood, like watered-down wine, was spreading all around. The dead man's clothes were soaked and dirty; they would afford the captain little protection from the cold and so he took only the waxed cape and put it on.

He heard a noise to one side, among the bushes, and unsheathed his sword. The weight of it in his hand was soothing and familiar. "You won't find it so easy to kill me now," he said to himself.

I froze. Captain Alatriste was standing before me, with sword in hand, a corpse at his feet, and mud caking his face like a mask. He looked as if he had just emerged from a Flemish marsh, or like a ghost returned from the beyond. He cut short my exclamations of delight and stared at Rafael de Cózar, who had just appeared behind me, splashing through puddles and stepping on branches that snapped as loudly as pistol-shots.

"Good God," he said, sheathing his sword. "What's he doing here?"

I explained as briefly as I could, but before I had even finished, the captain had turned and set off, as if he had suddenly lost all interest in my answer.

"Have you given the alarm?" he asked.

"I think so," I replied, remembering uneasily the coachman's drunken, bloated face.

"You *think* so?"

He was striding away into the bushes, and I was follow-

ing. Behind me I could hear Cózar muttering unintelligibly;
sometimes he seemed to be reciting poetry and at others
mumbling curses. "Have at 'em," he would say now and
then. "Snip 'em off like a bunch of grapes. Have at 'em!
Give them no quarter! Forward for Santiago and Spain!"
When we occasionally stopped for the captain to get his
bearings, my master would look around, shooting the actor
an ill-humored glance before continuing on his way.

From somewhere nearby came the sound of a hunting
horn—I thought I had heard it in the distance before we
found the captain—and we stood quite still in the rain.
The captain raised one finger to his lips, looking first at
Cózar and then at me. Then he held out one hand to me,
palm down—the silent gesture we used in Flanders to
indicate that we should wait while someone else went forward as a scout—and he moved cautiously off into the
bushes. I positioned myself very close to the trunk of a
tree and made Cózar join me; we stayed there, waiting.
Clearly surprised by all these gestures and by the almost
military understanding that existed between my master
and myself, the actor was about to say something, but I
covered his mouth. He nodded sagely, regarding me with
a new respect, and I was sure that he would never call me
"boy" again. I smiled at him, and he returned my smile.
His eyes were bright with excitement. I studied this
small, grubby man, dripping water, with his extravagant

mustache and his hand ready on his sword. He looked alarmingly fierce, like one of those short, apparently peace-loving men who might suddenly jump up and bite your ear off. Maybe it was just the wine, but Cózar seemed to feel no fear at all. This, I realized, was his finest role. The adventure of a lifetime.

At last the captain returned, as silently as he had left. He looked at me and raised his hand, this time with the palm turned toward me and with his five fingers extended. Five men, I translated mentally. He turned his thumb down: enemies. He then made another gesture, moving his hand from his shoulder to his opposite hip, as if describing a sash, and immediately raised his forefinger. An official, I translated. One. Thumb turned up. A friend. Then I understood who he meant. The red sash was a sign of rank in the army. In that wood, there could be only one high-ranking official.

From the safety of a tree trunk, Diego Alatriste again peered out into the clearing. Twenty paces away, at the foot of a huge oak, was a rock surrounded by a thicket of broom, and next to it stood a young man carrying a gun. He was tall and fair and was wearing a tabard, green breeches, and a peaked hat. His high gaiters were spattered with mud, and he wore no sword at his belt, only a folded pair of gloves and a hunting knife. He was standing very erect and still, with his back to the rock, his head high and one foot slightly in front of the other, as if hoping that such a pose would keep at bay the five men forming a tight semi-circle around him.

Alatriste could not hear what the men were saying, only the occasional isolated word, their voices drowned out by the sound of the rain. The man dressed as a huntsman said nothing, and it was Gualterio Malatesta, his black cloak and hat wet and shiny, who did most of the talking. He was the only one who had not yet unsheathed his sword; the others, two of whom were dressed as royal beaters, were standing, swords in hand, on either side of him.

Alatriste removed his cape. Then, ignoring the pistol he had at his waist because he could not be sure that it would fire in all that rain, he rested one hand on his sword and the other on his knife, while he studied the terrain with an expert eye, calculating the distance and how long it would take to cross it. The fair-haired man, he thought grimly, did not look as if he would be much help. He stood there, mo-tionless and aloof, his gun in his hand, regarding the mur-derers surrounding him as indifferently as if the whole affair had nothing whatever to do with him. Alatriste no-ticed that, like any wise hunter, the young man kept one tail of his tabard over the hammer of his gun to protect it from the rain. Were it not for the rain, the mud, and the five threatening men, he might have been posing for a court portrait by Diego Velázquez. A smile appeared on the captain's face, half admiring, half scornful. Was it courage, he wondered, or was it, above all, stupidity and an absurd example of the Burgundian sangfroid that Charles V had introduced into the Hapsburg court a century before? At least he had one bitter consolation: the king for whom he was risking his life would not lose his composure even when under threat of death. And that was good. Although perhaps that palace peacock simply could not comprehend what was happening, or was about to happen.

More to the point, thought Alatriste, what was *he* doing involved in all this? Why was *he* risking his life for a man who could not even be bothered to lift a finger in his own defense, as if he were expecting the angels to descend from the heavens, or for his own archers to emerge from the undergrowth, invoking God and Spain? A palace upbringing created bad habits. Absurdly, the only "palace guards" here were himself, Íñigo, and Cózar—with the shade of María de Castro hanging in the rain. There was always some idiot willing to get himself killed. The memory of what had happened in Camino de las Minillas made him tremble with rage. By Christ and his father, it would serve that fair-haired fool right—accustomed as he was to risk-free adventures with the wives of other men—if just this once he saw the boar's tusks close-up. There was no Guadalmedina to get him out of trouble. Damn it, let him pay the price that all men pay sooner or later; and with Gualterio Malatesta on hand, he would have to pay it in cash.

"Hand over the gun, Your Majesty."

Alatriste heard the Italian's words quite clearly from his position behind the tree, where he was watching the scene with a kind of morbid curiosity. The king had little opportunity to defend himself: the hunting knife did not count, and he had no sword; at best, he might manage one shot with his gun, assuming it was loaded and the powder dry.

"Hand it over," said one of the ruffians impatiently, walking up to the king, sword at the ready.

Philip IV did something very strange then. His face remained utterly impassive, but he inclined his head a little to look at his gun, as if, up until then, he had quite forgotten about it. He did this with the indifference of a man observing an object of no importance to him. After that brief moment of immobility, he cocked the hammer and raised the gun to eye level. Then, coolly taking aim at the ruffian, he felled him with a shot to the head.

That explosion was like a signal. I was with Cózar on the opposite side of the clearing, in accordance with the captain's latest instructions to position ourselves so that we could attack Malatesta and his men from there. When I saw

my master leave his hiding place and run toward them,
sword in one hand and knife in the other, I immediately
unsheathed my sword and went ahead too, not bothering
to see whether Cózar would follow me.

"God save the king!" I heard Cózar bawl out behind me.
"Stop at once, I order you."

Holy Mother of God, I thought, that's all we need.
When the Italian and the ruffians heard these shouts and
the sound of our footsteps splashing through the mud and
puddles, they spun round, surprised. That is my last clear
memory: Malatesta wheeling about to face us, then furiously barking out orders, meanwhile whipping out his
sword with lightning speed, while, in the pouring rain,
his men stood, with raised swords, ready to fight us. And,
behind them, motionless, his gun still smoking, stood the
king, watching us.

"God save the king!" Cózar kept shouting, fierce as a
tiger now.

There were two of us against four, for I assumed the
actor would be of little, or negligible, help. We had to
be quick and careful. As soon as I found myself face-to-face
with one of the beaters, I delivered such a hard thrust that
I made him drop his sword. Then, slipping past, nimble as
a squirrel, I confronted the man behind him. He attacked,
blade foremost. I steadied myself as best I could and took
my dagger in my left hand, praying to God that I did not

slip in the mud. I parried well with my dagger, changed position, and then, crouching down, drove my sword upward, sticking at least three spans of steel into the soft part of his belly. When I drew back my elbow to remove the blade, he fell forward, a look of astonishment on his face, as if to say, "How could such a thing happen to this mother's son?" However, I was no longer concerned with him, but with the first man, who now had no sword, only a dagger. I whirled around, expecting to find him already on top of me, but then I saw that he was embroiled with Cózar, defending himself as best he could, with one arm injured and his dagger in his left hand, from the fearsome, double-handed blows the actor was dealing out.

Things were not turning out so badly after all. As for me, the wound Angélica had inflicted on me hurt abominably, and I just prayed that with all this activity it did not open up again, leaving me to bleed to death like a stuck pig. I turned to help the captain, and at that instant, as my master was withdrawing his sword from the entrails of a ruffian—who was bent double, blood gushing from his mouth like a bull in a bullring—I noticed that Gualterio Malatesta, a large black figure in the rain, had shifted his sword to his left hand, taken his pistol from his belt, and, after looking first at my master and then at the king, was now pointing it at the latter from a distance of only a few paces. I was too far away to do anything and had to watch, helpless, as the captain, having recovered his sword, rushed to interpose himself between the bullet and its target. Malatesta straightened his arm and took careful aim. I saw how the king, looking his killer in the face, threw down his own gun, stood very erect, and folded his arms, determined that the pistol shot would find him suitably composed.

"Turn your fire on me!" cried the captain.

The Italian took no notice. He held his aim on the king. He squeezed the trigger and flint struck steel.

Nothing happened.

The powder was wet.

Sword in hand, Diego Alatriste placed himself between Malatesta and the king. I had never seen such an expression on Malatesta's face. He was almost beside himself. He kept shaking his head incredulously and staring at the pistol that lay useless in his hand.

"So close," he said.

Then he seemed to recover himself. He looked at the captain as if seeing him for the first time, or as if he had forgotten he was there, and then, from beneath the dripping brim of his hat, he gave a faint, sinister smile.

"I was so close," he repeated bitterly.

Then he shrugged and threw down the weapon, taking his sword in his right hand.

"You've ruined everything."

He took off his cloak, which was hampering his movements. He indicated the king with a lift of his chin, but continued staring at Alatriste.

"Do you really think such a master is worth it?"

"Come on," said the captain coldly, meaning, "We have business of our own to settle." He used his sword to point to the one Malatesta was holding. The Italian looked first at the two blades and then at the king, wondering if there was some way he might still finish the job. Then he shrugged again while carefully folding up his rain-sodden cloak as if to wrap it around his left arm.

From Rafael de Cózar, still embattled with his opponent, there came repeated cries of: "God save the king!"

Malatesta glanced over at him with a look that was part amused and part resigned. Then came that smile. The captain noticed the dangerous white slit in that pockmarked face, the cruel glint in those dark eyes. And he said to himself: "The snake isn't beaten yet." This certainty came to him suddenly, forcing him to react and put himself on guard just moments before the Italian threw his cloak over the captain's sword, rendering it useless. Alatriste lost valuable seconds disentangling his blade from the wet cloth, and while he was doing so, Malatesta's blade glittered before him as if seeking somewhere to bury itself, then shifted from him to the king.

This time, the Monarch of Two Worlds stepped back. Alatriste caught the startled look in his blue eyes, and this time, the august, prominent Hapsburg lower lip quivered in expectation of what would follow. That deadly thrust came far too close for him to remain entirely unmoved, thought the captain, given that he was obliged to gaze into Malatesta's dark eyes, which was like gazing into the eyes of Death itself. However, the brief moment gained in divining his enemy's intention proved long enough for the captain to act. His sword clashed with Malatesta's, averting what, it had seemed, would be an inevitable blow. Malatesta's blade slid along his, missing the royal throat by inches.

"Porca miseria!" cursed the Italian.

And that was that. He turned tail and ran like a deer into the woods.

I had watched the scene from a distance, unable to help in any way, for it all happened in less time than it would take to say "Ave Maria." When I saw Malatesta fleeing, and while the captain was making sure that the king had not been wounded, I, without thinking, raced after Malatesta, through the puddles, sword in hand. I ran with my arm held high to protect me from the branches showering me with raindrops. Malatesta had little advantage over me; I was young and had strong legs, and so I soon caught up with him. He suddenly turned, saw that I was alone, and stopped to recover his breath. It was raining so hard now that the mud beneath my feet seemed to be seething.

"Stay where you are," he said, pointing his sword at me.

I stopped where I was, uncertain what to do. The captain was perhaps not far behind, but for the moment Malatesta and I were alone.

"That's enough for today," he added.

He started walking again, backward this time, without taking his eyes off me. Then I noticed that he was limping. Each time he put his weight on his right foot, he grimaced with pain. He had probably been wounded in the skirmish or hurt himself running. In the rain, drenched and dirty, he looked very tired. His hat had fallen off as he ran, and his long, wet hair clung to his face. Injury and fatigue, I thought, might make us more equal and give me a chance.

"It's not worth it," he said, guessing what was in my mind.

I kept walking. The wound in my back was intensely painful, but I was still full of energy. I advanced farther. Malatesta shook his head as if in disbelief at my folly. Then he gave a faint smile, retreated another step, repressing a grimace of pain, and readied himself. Very cautiously I tested him out, the ends of our blades touching, while I sought some way of getting under his guard. He, the more experienced, merely waited. He may have been injured, but, as we both knew, he was by far the more skillful swordsman. I, however, felt almost intoxicated, enclosed in a kind of gray bubble that fogged my judgment. Here he was, and I had my sword in my hand.

He dropped his guard for a moment, as if carelessly, but I could see it was a trick, and so remained where I was, not attacking, elbow bent and the hilt of my sword on a level with my eyes, watching for a genuine opening. The rain continued to fall, and I was taking care not to slip in the mud, for I would not survive long if I did.

"You've grown prudent, boy."

He was smiling, and I knew his intent was to draw me in. I resisted. Now and then, I wiped the rain from my eyes with the back of my knife hand, but always kept my eyes trained on him.

Behind me, amongst the trees and the scrub, I could hear someone calling my name. The captain was looking for us. I called out to him so that he could find us. Meanwhile, from beneath the hair clinging to his face in the rain, the Italian's eyes darted to and fro, looking for some way out. In a flash, I lunged forward.

The whoreson was good, though, very good, and very skilled. He effortlessly parried a thrust that would have run a lesser man through, and when he counterattacked, he dealt me a back-edged cut so close to my eyes that had his injured leg not held him back, I would have taken a five-inch wound to my face. He managed to disarm me, however, sending my sword flying several feet. I didn't even think to cover myself with my dagger, but stood there frozen like a startled hare, waiting for the coup de grâce. Then I saw Malatesta's face contract in pain; he suppressed a howl of rage, involuntarily retreated two steps, only to have his bad leg fail him again.

He fell backward and sat down in the mud, his sword in his hand and a curse on his lips. For a moment, we looked at each other, me stunned and him shaken. It was an absurd situation. Finally, I managed to get a grip on myself and ran over to fetch my sword, which lay at the foot of a tree. When I stood up, Malatesta, still sitting on the ground, made a rapid movement; something whisked past me like a metallic flash of lightning, and a dagger fixed itself, quivering, in the trunk, only a few inches from my face.

"Something to remember me by, boy."

I went over to him, determined now to run him through, and he saw this in my eyes. Then he threw his sword into the bushes and leaned back a little, resting on his elbows.

"I'm having a very bad day today," he said.

I approached cautiously, and with the point of my sword checked his clothes, looking for concealed weapons. Then

I placed the point on his chest, just above his heart. His wet hair, the rain dripping down his face, and the dark rings under his eyes made him look suddenly very weary and much older.

"Don't do it," he murmured softly. "Best leave it to him."

He was looking at the bushes behind me. I heard footsteps splashing through the mud, and Captain Alatriste appeared at my side, breathing hard. Fast as a bullet and without a word, he hurled himself on the Italian. He grabbed him by the hair, set aside his sword, took out his huge hunting knife, and held it to Malatesta's throat.

A rapid thought went through my mind—or, rather, I saw the captain and me in the woods, and remembered the count-duke's stern countenance, the Count of Guadalmedina's hostility toward us, and the august personage we had left behind us with only Rafael de Cózar as escort. Without Malatesta as witness, there would be a lot of explaining to do, and we might not have answers to all the questions. This realization filled me with sudden panic. I grabbed my master's arm.

"He's my prisoner, Captain."

He appeared not to hear me. His stubborn face was hard, resolute, deadly. His eyes, which appeared gray in the rain, seemed to be made of the same steel as the knife he was holding. I saw the muscles, veins, and tendons in his hand tense, ready to plunge the knife in.

"Captain!"

I almost flung myself on top of Malatesta. My master pushed me roughly away, his free hand raised to strike me. His eyes pierced me as if I were the one he was about to stab. Again I cried out:

"He surrendered to *me*! He's my prisoner!"

It was like a nightmare: the wet and the dirt, the soaking rain, the mud, the struggle, the captain's agitated breathing, Malatesta's breath only inches from my face. The captain again made as if to lunge forward, and only by dint of brute strength did I stop the knife following its inevitable path.

"Someone," I said, "will have to explain to the powers that be exactly what happened."

My master still did not take his eyes off Malatesta, who had his head thrown right back as he awaited the final blow, teeth gritted.

"I don't want you and me to be tortured like pigs," I said.

This was true. The mere idea terrified me. Finally, I felt the captain untense, although his hand still gripped the knife. It was as if the meaning of my words were gradually seeping into him. Malatesta had already understood. "Damn it, boy," he exclaimed. "Let him kill me!"

EPILOGUE

Álvaro de la Marca, Count of Guadalmedina, held out a
mug of wine to Captain Alatriste.

"You must have a devil of a thirst on you," he said.

The captain took the mug from him. We were sheltering on the porch steps of the hunting lodge, surrounded by
royal guards armed to the teeth. The rain was beating down
on the blankets covering the bodies of the four ruffians who
had died in the forest. The fifth, after his battering by
Rafael de Cózar, had sustained a gash to the head and a
couple of minor stab wounds and been carried away, more
dead than alive, on an improvised litter. Gualterio Malatesta
received special treatment. The captain and I watched as he
departed, in shackles, on a miserable mule, guarded on all
sides. He rode past, dirty and defeated, and looked at us
with inexpressive eyes as if he had never seen us before in

his life. I remembered his last words to us in the woods, the captain's knife pressed to his throat. And he was right. When I imagined what awaited him—the interrogation and the torture to make him reveal all that he knew about the conspiracy—he would, I thought, have been better off dead.

"I believe," added Guadalmedina, lowering his voice a little, "that I owe you an apology."

He had just emerged from the hunting lodge after a long conversation with the king. My master took a sip of wine and did not respond. He seemed very tired, his hair disheveled, his face muddy and worn, his clothes torn and sodden after the fighting. He turned his cold, green eyes first on me and then on Cózar, who was sitting a little farther off, on a bench on the porch; he had a blanket draped over his shoulders and was smiling beatifically. His face was crisscrossed with scratches, he had a gash on his forehead, and a large black eye. He, too, had been given wine to drink, which he dispatched with alacrity; indeed, he already had three mugfuls under his belt. He was clearly very happy, bursting with pride and wine in his ripped doublet. He occasionally hiccupped, cried "Long live the king!," roared like a lion, or else misquoted to himself fragments from Lope's *Peribañez and the Comendador of Ocaña*:

> "*I am the vassal, she is his mistress,*
> *I defend him with sword and knife,*

Prepared he may be to besmirch my honor,
But I am here and will save his dear life."

The archers of the royal guard gazed at him in disbelief, unable to tell whether he was drunk or raving mad.

The captain passed me the mug, and I took a long drink
from it before handing it back. The wine warmed me a
little and stopped me shivering. I glanced at Guadalmedina,
who was standing next to us, cool and elegant, hand
nonchalantly on hip. He had arrived just in time to receive
his laurels, having read my note when he got out of bed and
galloped straight there with twenty archers in tow, only to
find that everything had been resolved: the king, unharmed,
sitting on a rock underneath a greak oak in a clearing in the
forest; Malatesta, lying facedown in the mud with his hands
tied behind his back; and us, trying to revive Cózar after he
had passed out while grappling with his enemy, who lay
pinned beneath him, even more battered and bruised than
he was. The archers, however, with no clear idea of what
had happened, immediately seized us and held their swords
to our throats, and it was only when they were close to
killing us—during which time Guadalmedina said not a
word in our favor—that the king himself explained. These
three gentlemen—those were the king's exact words—had,
very bravely and at great risk to themselves, saved his life.
With such a royal commendation, no one troubled us any

further, and even Guadalmedina changed his tune. So there we were, encircled by guards and with a mug of wine between us, while His Catholic Majesty was attended to within, and things—whether for better or worse, I cannot say—returned to normal.

Álvaro de la Marca, with a click of his fingers, ordered another mug of wine to be brought, and when the servant placed it in his hands, he raised it in a toast to the captain.

"Here's to your exploits today, Alatriste," he said, smiling. "To the king and to you."

He drank and then held out his gloved hand to shake my master's hand, either that or to help him to his feet in the hope that he would join him in the toast. The captain, however, remained sitting where he was, not moving, his own mug in his lap, ignoring the proffered hand. He was watching the rain falling on the corpses that lay in a row in the mud.

"Perhaps . . ." Guadalmedina began, then fell silent, and I saw his smile fade on his lips. He glanced at me, and I looked away. He stood for a while, observing us, then, very slowly, he put his mug down on the ground and walked off.

I still said nothing, but sat next to my master, listening to the sound of the rain on the slate roof.

"Captain," I said at last.

That was all. I knew it was enough. I felt his rough hand on my shoulder, felt him pat me gently on the back of the neck.

"We're still alive," he said at last.

I shivered from the cold, and from my own thoughts. I wasn't thinking only about what had taken place that morning in the woods.

"What will happen to her now?" I asked quietly.

He didn't look at me.

"Her?"

"To Angélica."

He said nothing for a while. He was gazing pensively at the path along which Gualterio Malatesta had been carried off on his way to meet his torturer. Then he shook his head and said:

"One can't always win."

There came the sound of voices and martial footsteps, the clatter of weapons. The archers, their cuirasses beaded with rain, were mounting their horses as a coach drawn by four grays approached the door. Guadalmedina reappeared, donning an elegant jeweled hat and accompanied by various gentlemen of the royal household. He shot us a perfunctory look and issued orders. More commands were given, horses neighed, and the archers, looking very gallant on their mounts, formed into disciplined ranks. Then the king came out of the lodge. He had exchanged his huntsman's outfit for a costume of blue brocade and was wearing boots, hat, and carrying a sword. Everyone removed his hat, apart from Guadalmedina, who, as a grandee of Spain, was entitled to keep his on. The king gazed impassively into the distance, looking as remote and aloof as he had during the skirmish in the forest. Head erect, he walked along the porch toward the carriages, passed us without even a glance, and got into the coach that was waiting by the steps. Guadalmedina was about to step in behind him when the king said something in a low voice. We saw Guadalmedina lean toward the king to hear what he was saying, despite the drenching rain. Then he frowned and nodded.

"Alatriste," he called.

I turned to the captain, who was staring in some confusion at both Guadalmedina and the king. Finally, he went over to them, leaving the shelter of the porch. The king's blue eyes fixed on him, as cold and watery as the eyes of a fish.

"Give him back his sword," ordered Guadalmedina, and a sergeant approached with the captain's sword and belt. It did not, in fact, belong to the captain but to the first ruffian from whom he had plundered it after cutting his throat. My master, apparently more bewildered than ever, stood there, holding the sword. Then he slowly buckled on the belt. When he looked up again, his aquiline profile and bushy mustache—from which the rain was now dripping—gave him the appearance of a wary falcon.

"Turn your fire on me," said Philip, as if thinking out loud.

I was confused at first, then I remembered that these

had been the captain's words when Malatesta was aiming his pistol at the king. My master was now looking at the king coolly and inquisitively, as if wondering where this would all end.

"Your hat, Guadalmedina," said His Catholic Majesty.

There was a long silence. At last, Álvaro de la Marca obeyed and rather grumpily did as he was asked—he was getting thoroughly soaked—and handed the captain that lovely hat adorned with a pheasant's feather and a band sewn with diamonds.

"Put it on, Captain Alatriste," ordered the king.

For the first time since I had known my master, I saw him utterly dumbfounded. And he remained so for a moment, fidgeting with the hat, uncertain what to do.

"Put it on," repeated the king.

The captain nodded, as if he had only then understood. He looked at the king, and at Guadalmedina. Then he thoughtfully studied the hat and put it on very slowly, as if giving everyone time to change their mind.

"You will never be able to speak of this in public," warned the king.

"No, I imagine not," replied my master.

For a long moment, that obscure swordsman and the Lord of Two Worlds stood eye to eye, and on the latter's impassive Hapsburg face there appeared just the flicker of a smile.

"I wish you luck, Captain. And if you're ever condemned to be hanged or garrotted, appeal to the king. From today on, you have the right to be beheaded like an hidalgo and a gentleman."

Thus spoke Philip II's grandson on that rainy morning at La Fresneda. Then he gave an order; Guadalmedina got into the coach, raised the footboard, and closed the door. The coachman cracked the whip and the carriage set off, ploughing through the mud, followed by the archers on horseback and Cózar's cries of "Long live the king!," for, drunk again, or perhaps pretending to be, the actor kept roaring: "Long live the Catholic king," "Long live the House of Hapsburg," "God bless Spain, guardian of the true faith, Spain, and the whore who bore her."

I went over to the captain, quite overcome. My master was watching as the royal carriage disappeared. Guadalmedina's elegant hat was in marked contrast to the rest of him, for, like me, he was cut, bruised, beaten, and mudsplattered. When I reached his side, I saw that he was laughing softly to himself. When he saw me, he turned and winked, taking off the hat to show me.

"With a bit of luck," I sighed, "we can get something for those diamonds."

The captain was studying them. Then he shook his head and put the hat on again.

"They're fake," he said.

EXTRACTS FROM

POETRY

WRITTEN BY VARIOUS WITS

OF THIS COURT

Published in the XVIIth century with no imprint
and preserved in "The Counts of Guadalmedina"
section in the Archive and Library of
the Duques de Nuevo Extremo (Seville).

O petty lawyer, plumping out your purse
With other people's cash and gold doubloons,
The cream of rascals, no one could be worse,
Brother superior, sucking blood from other's
    wounds,
The pen that you wield—a wild and coarsening
    quill—
Can only spit the vilest blots on earth.
"A professor of vile verses" fits the bill,
Arselicker extraordinary, malformed from birth,
A stinking heap, a dunghill of a man,
Of pride and lechery a steaming cesspit,
The greatest farter of lies since the world began
And miner of the muses' dregs—no respite.
Never your lyre, always a purse you follow,
You offspring of Cacus, you bastard of Apollo!

BY DON LUIS DE GÓNGORA

ON THE FLEETING NATURE OF BEAUTY AND OF LIFE

Whilst gold—sun-burnished—tries to catch
The glitter and the brightness of thy hair;
Whilst the lily-of-the-field can never match
The whiteness of thy brow—beyond compare;
Whilst more eyes yearn to pluck thy ruby lips
Than gaze upon the first carnation of the year;
And whilst thy lovely, glowing neck outstrips
The shiniest crystal—for you have no peer—
Take now enjoyment in thy neck and brow,
Thy lips and hair, before this—thy prime
Of lily, gold, carnation, crystal—now
Is changed to silver or dead violas by time,
And you and they together soon be wrought
To earth, smoke, dust, and shadow—naught!

BY FÉLIX LOPE DE VEGA CARPIO

ON THE DELIGHTS AND CONTRADICTIONS OF LOVE

Fainting, daring, full of rages,
Tender, rough, expansive, shy,
Treacherous, loyal, cowardly, courageous,
Hoping, despairing to live or to die;

Away from one's love—no center or repose,
Furious, brave, yet ready for flight,
Humble, haughty, all joy, then all woes,
Offended, wary, then dizzy with delight;
Averting one's gaze from evident deceit,
When poison foul gives off a honey'd smell
And pain is loved and pleasures all retreat,
Then, one believes that heaven's found in hell
And body and soul are at illusion's behest,
Such is love—as he who tastes it can attest.

STATEMENT OF APPROVAL

I have read the book entitled *The Cavalier in the Yellow Doublet*, the fifth volume of the so-called *Adventures of Captain Alatriste*, for which don Arturo Pérez-Reverte asks to be granted a license to publish. As with the previous volumes, I found in it nothing repugnant to our Holy Faith or to good customs; rather, as child of the wit and qualities of its author, it contains much salutary advice, which, in the guise of an amusing story or fable, embodies all that is most grave and serious in human philosophy. While it does not abound in Christian or pious reflections, I believe that it will prove edifying to the young reader, for the rhetorically minded will find much to admire in the language, the curious will be entertained by the events described, and, by the ideas, the learned will approve of its rigor, the prudent will take due warning from it, and there is much wholesome wisdom to be gleaned from its somewhat harsh examples and teachings. In short, it offers as much profit as delight.

For all these reasons, it is my view that the author should be granted license to publish.

Dated in Madrid, on the tenth day of the month of October, in the year 2003.

Luis Alberto de Prado y Cuenca,
Secretary of the Council of Castile

ABOUT THE AUTHOR

Arturo Pérez-Reverte lives near Madrid. Originally a
war journalist, he now writes fiction full-time. His novels
The Flanders Panel, *The Club Dumas*, *The Fencing
Master*, *The Seville Communion*, *The Nautical Chart*, and
The Queen of the South have been translated into twenty-
nine languages and published in more than fifty countries.
In 2003, he was elected to the Spanish Royal Academy. Visit
his website at: www.perez-reverte.com.